Land, Lore, Legacies and Livelihoods
Further Tales of Axholme

by Robert E. Fish

Published jointly by Haywood Books Ltd and JJMoffs Independent Book Publisher Ltd 2020

Copyright ©Robert E. Fish 2020

All rights reserved.
No part of this publication may be reproduced, stored in a retrieval system or transmitted in any form or by any means, without the prior permission in writing of the publisher. Neither may it be otherwise circulated in any form of binding or cover other than that in which it is published and without a similar condition including this condition being imposed on the subsequent purchaser.

Robert E. Fish has asserted his right under The Copyright, Designs and Patents Act, 1988 to be identified as the author of this work.

Haywood Books Ltd, 7 Burnham Road, Epworth, North Lincolnshire and
JJMoffs Independent Book Publisher Ltd, Grove House Farm,
Grovewood Road, Misterton, Nottinghamshire, DN10 4EF.

Typeset and cover design by Anna Richards

Contents

1	Prologue
3	The Isle of Axholme – forgotten land to cherished jewel
6	From a Grandmother's Knee
13	A Bit of History
41	Death by Misadventure
50	Bringing the News to Axholme
70	Some People
85	Axholme at Play
98	Going to the Cinema
104	Crashes and Explosions
110	An Axholme School - 1880
124	Working the Land
138	More People
151	The First World War
167	Letters from the Front
176	The Second World War
200	An Axholme Miscellany

Also by Robert. E. Fish

*Misadventure, Mayhem, Myth and Murder –
The Dark Side of Axholme's Past*

PROLOGUE

Working back through two generations of my maternal ancestors takes my traceable Axholme roots back to William Pettinger, born in 1543. Given that it was unlikely for families to move away from their localities in early mediaeval times it is within the bounds of conjecture that the rest of my family line in Axholme could extend back to the time of the Conquest. Whether this holds true or not, I will settle for a connection to the lands of Axholme that spans almost 500 years.

William Pettinger was a yeoman farmer – a commoner who cultivated his own land throughout the reign of Queen Elizabeth I. From that date on, his descendants worked the soil, through times of discord, disturbance, famine and plenty. In my more fanciful moments, I imagine his grandson, John Pettinger, joining those pitted against Vermuyden's drainage scheme and his great-great-grandson, another John, standing in Epworth Churchyard to listen to John Wesley preach from his father's tombstone.

As a young boy, my mother would take me to Epworth Churchyard and show me the gravestones of my ancestors. The place is littered with them; grandfathers, great-grandfathers, uncles, aunts, great uncles and great aunts. She spoke of them in terms that 'brought them to life,' and through them and thanks to her, I became a committed Islonian. Knowing them, I created faces, forms and characters – they had been real people, and they were again to me. I learned of a relation who went out into his fields during a Second World War blackout and couldn't find his way home. I often stand in front of my great-grandfather's grave and see him for the alderman he was in the late 1800s or stand and look down on a piece of Lake District rock that signifies the place where the ashes of a much beloved cousin lie.

Many of the articles in this book, I wrote and published through 'Facebook' during the period of quarantine in the spring and summer of 2020. Several people suggested I should turn these into a book, and one suggested it could be entitled 'Lockdown Tales.' It was a reasonable suggestion but didn't account for the other 'tales' I eventually included. I wanted a reference to the land of my ancestors and their influence over it. The title I came up with was 'Land, Lore, Legacies and Livelihoods – Further Tales of Axholme.' Unless otherwise stated these stories come from researching back issues of the Epworth Bells; family accounts and anecdotes told me by the people of the Isle, both past and present. It is not comprehensive by any means but reflects much of what may be termed 'my Axholme.'

CHAPTER ONE

The Isle of Axholme – forgotten land to cherished jewel

Eleven thousand years ago, when the great sheets of ice ceased their grinding march southwards and began to retreat, they left behind a vast expanse of water bounded today by Scunthorpe and Gainsborough to the east, Gringley to the south and Doncaster to the west. Named Lake Humber, in places the water reached a depth of thirty metres. Having silted up after some 4,000 years, Lake Humber left behind a broad plain, crossed by slow, meandering rivers interspersed by higher land and low 'islands' of glacial sand and gravel. In the low-lying areas, the flood created extensive pools of water; the largest being Messic (Messy) Mere, an area that covered some hundred acres, about two-and-a-half miles almost due west of Epworth. In places where the rivers Idle, Torn and Don flowed into each other it was impossible to ascertain which river was which. The complex evolution of the area is best left to geographers; suffice it to say that over subsequent millennia the area underwent natural and artificial drainage leading to its prominence today as one of the country's most fertile and productive regions.

Geographically distinct from the rest of its mother county of Lincolnshire and its topographical home of Yorkshire, the area developed a spirit of robust independence, driven by man's forays into this inhospitable and challenging environment. Today the main settlements sit astride a ridge of high ground running north-to-south along the spine of Axholme or at natural ferry points on its eastern boundary – the River Trent. Working in tandem with the River Ouse to the north, these two major watercourses channel one-fifth of the country's rainwater into the North Sea. The high ground is made up of Red Sandstone, a lime-rich marl of clays and silt. In places, these thick, cloying beds have been excavated; the clay being worked for brick and, to a lesser extent, roof tiles, clay pipes and decorative pottery. In the mid-19th century, Crowle became the centre for a major brick manufacturer, with the brickworks located close to the railway and canal for easy transport. Within the clay beds run ribbons of gypsum, known locally as 'chicken chalk.' Although of relatively poor quality, when ground to powder, this provided a fertiliser and soil sweetener, and in 1842 led to Reverend Thomas Skipworth of Belton opening a quarry for the extraction of this calcium-rich mineral.

Standing on the Isle's highest point at High Burnham gives one a 360-degree panorama encompassing open farmland and sylvan turbaries, that stretch out to a seemingly unattainable horizon. On a clear day, those of moderate vision can spot Emley Moor with ease, but it takes a keen eye to spot Lincoln Cathedral (had you been around in the 15th century when the spires on the cathedral made it the tallest building in the world it would have been a much easier task). Taken as a whole that's a 180-degree distance of over 70 miles. High Burnham also offers views into eight counties (or county regions), North Lincolnshire (of course), Nottinghamshire to the south, the hills of Derbyshire to the far west, South Yorkshire, the moors of West Yorkshire, Drax Power Station in North Yorkshire, the cranes of Goole in East Yorkshire, and across the Trent into Lincolnshire.

Twenty years ago, one would have also seen eight major power stations - Ferrybridge, Eggborough, Thorpe Marsh, Drax, Keadby, West Burton, High Marnham and Cottam. Today, (admittedly with a telescope) one can see the towers and spires of scores of churches.

Beneath the dome of a spacious, over-arching sky one can

An artist's impression of the proposed power station at Keadby

easily feel inconsequential, a tiny figure on what is little more than an insignificant blemish on the skin of the earth. And yet ... here, where the wind blows harder from the Axholme lowlands, it elevates the soul, filling the body with a power close to eternity. It's a place to cleanse the spirit; a place of inspiration and rejuvenation. I have gazed at Kangchenjunga and Mount Kenya and travelled through the Rockies and the Andes, but nothing surpasses the view over the land my Axholme forebears helped create and nurture.

CHAPTER TWO

From a Grandmother's Knee

Born in 1880, my grandmother grew up a farmer's daughter. Married in her early twenties to a hard-working 'son of the soil' her life was governed not by the hands of the clock or the dates on a calendar but by the rhythm of the seasons and through a keen observation of the vagaries of the Axholme weather. In my previous book of Axholme tales, 'Misadventure, Mayhem, Myth and Murder', I touched on her 'special talents' stemming from being 'born under the veil' a piece of the amniotic sack that covered her face known as a caul. Tradition has it that 'caul bearers' have the gift of second sight. I can't swear to that, but I know my grandma had a fund of stories that kept me entertained as we sat through the dark days of winter. She would take me on her lap, close her eyes and regale me with long-forgotten tales of Axholme's past. I can still recall the sound of her soft, yet sincere voice, and the slightly musty, yet comforting smell, of the Victorian materials in her dress and coat. On one of our garden walls, I have several horseshoes that we have picked up on our walks in the countryside. Obviously, they hang the right side up so as to catch the good luck. When walking as a child with my grandmother, she told me to throw a found horseshoe over my left shoulder and see if it caught good luck. She then told me to retrieve it and take the good luck home – hence the shoes on my wall.

When lightning appeared in the vicinity, the old lady would rush to cover all the mirrors in the house with tablecloths and towels. She reasoned the mirror could attract lightning, and the reflection could kill her. On New Year's Day, she would not open the door until a dark-haired male carrying a piece of coal stepped over the threshold. To admit someone else first would bring bad luck into the house (a custom known as 'First Footing'). Old Epworth residents may recall a gentleman called Tommy Dawson, who would go around the village early on 1st January and on payment of a tanner would become the 'first foot', thereby bringing good luck to all who accepted his invitation. In his later years he was not quite dark-headed but ….

If a lone dog howled after 11pm, my grandma would expect to hear of a death in the village the next day. She would never cross a fork with a knife, and if a bird got into the house, she would usher it out as fast as she could – another sign of bad luck, more so if it was a robin!

If a visitor left their gloves behind on departure, grandma would not touch them until the visitor returned. She always bought a sprig of 'lucky heather' from a house-to-house hawker whether the seller was of Romany descent or not. She was not so accepting of clothes pegs made from carved wood and held together by a strip of metal cut from a 'National Dried Milk' tin.

Each Christmas Day she would make one extra dinner and take it out to the barn. At five pm she would bring back an empty plate; the dinner having been eaten by a wandering tramp she called 'Billy', who turned up at her farm each year over the festive period. He never spoke to or frightened anyone; he just came and went unobtrusively. Imagine her sadness when one year she brought back an untouched meal!

Her favourite sayings were – 'Strip before you sweat, dress before you're cold if you want to live to be old!' and; 'A famine in the stall means famine in the hall'. She called a fine day in winter a 'borrowed' day, but one that would have to be paid back with interest later on.

There was one story she told me that I never grew tired of

hearing; one that has bounced its way down the decades of my life. It's one that I have written about before, but I trust, you may accord me the same indulgence my grandma did when I pestered her to tell me, again and again, the story of Tiddy Mun.

She would begin in her time-honoured fashion; 'Long before there were trains, cars and aeroplanes, a tiny creature lived in the watery land of Axholme. Smaller than a human baby, he had no name, so the people of this remote and mysterious land called him Tiddy Mun. Those who claimed to have seen Tiddy Mun told of his straggly hair that touched his drooping shoulders, his long beard that reached beyond his waist and his skin, wrinkled and dark like the shell of a walnut. They said he came with the sound of trickling water and moved over the land like the sighing wind. He was old, they said, older than the stones in the ground that made him hop and hobble as he walked barefoot across the waterlogged land. Old age may have bent his back and turned his beard grey, but deep in his rumpled face, his eyes sparkled and danced like sunlit jewels on an Axholme mere. And there was something else that marked him out as 'special' to the people of Axholme; even on the sunniest of days, his body never cast a shadow!

Tiddy Mun lived in the fenny holes, where he cloaked himself in the matted, green water. It was not an attractive place for a home, but Tiddy Mun loved living in Axholme; in truth, he could not remember living anywhere else. He loved the way the rivers twisted and crawled across the countryside and how the shimmering meres seemed to stretch to the distant horizon. He would spend hours watching the saw-bladed reeds and the thick clusters of sedge grass wave in the gentle breeze as though bending to the caress of a huge invisible hand. Above all, he liked to watch the brown head of the bulrush rise up from its water-bound roots until with a 'pop' it cast its downy seeds into the golden sunlight. He was a friend to all. He helped the herons find the best place to catch their fish; he found the best places for ducks and geese to build their nests away from the skulking grass snakes and the night-hunting weasels; he cared for the baby otters while their parents went out to hunt.

For the people who lived in this watery land, however, life was hard. There were no roads, just a few winding footpaths that often disappeared beneath the peaty water. The only safe way to travel was by boat, but even then, the cruel winter winds that churned the water of the lakes into angry waves could tip over the best-made boat and leave it plunging into the watery depths. In autumn, when the land outside Axholme was bathed in golden light, thick grey mists sucked the colour out of flowers and trees and made the secret places even more secretive and the dangerous places even more dangerous. The people of Axholme called it their autumn blanket, for the mist wrapped itself around them as they toiled in the fields and gleaned the hedgerows for fruits and berries. It drenched their faces and hands, leaving their hair damp and their clothes wet and clammy. The cloying mist brought shivers and chills to the adults who worked outdoors and coughs and colds to tiny babies disturbing their sleep throughout the night in their rough-hewn cots.

In this murky, sodden land, however, there were dry, clay-clagged patches where the people of Axholme built their cottages and bent the soil to their will. The 'strangers' who visited Axholme, thought it an impossible place to live and work. Those who lived there, however, knew differently. They knew the best places to spread their fishing nets over the meres and lakes; how to weave reeds and stems into baskets and bags, and they knew if they cut the peaty soil and allowed it to dry, it would burn in their hearths to give warmth when the cold, dark fingers of winter clawed their way into the furthest corners of their mud-daubed cottages.

Whatever hardships came their way, the people of Axholme

sought refuge in their land. It was not an enemy to be beaten into submission but a comrade that ensured they could carry on living the way they had always done. There was one thing the people of Axholme feared above all else, something over which they had no control. In the spring and autumn, when the rains came, the level of water rose around their homes. At times like this they would stand on their doorstep and shout, 'Tiddy Mun, Tiddy Mun, help us. The floods are coming, the water's rising'. And they would stay there and listen until they heard Tiddy Mun's answer, a sound like the cry of a lapwing, that echoed from the desolate wilderness beyond. On hearing the call, they returned to their hearths safe in the knowledge that Tiddy Mun's special powers would control the rising tide and keep the water from their thresholds. To thank him for keeping them safe they would leave him gifts of bread and oatcake on their doorsteps little realising they were inadvertently feeding other creatures of the night.

Tiddy Mun was, indeed, a special friend. He did not annoy the people of Axholme like the Todlowries who danced throughout the night on the grassy humps around the Islonians cottages giggling and banging stones together. He was not mischievous like the boggarts who lived in the woodpiles, stables and sheds, causing sparks to fly from the burning wood, horses to go lame and milk to turn sour. Above all, he was not cruel like Will o' the Wisp, whose flickering light led folk along the watery pathways only to leave them stranded and alone.

One day, strangers wearing dark clothes and tall hats arrived in Axholme. They brought plans and maps, laid them on the ground and gazed across the wastes beyond. From his hiding place close by, Tiddy Mun watched as the men disagreed and bickered, then drew straight lines on sheets of paper with their long rulers and charcoal pencils.

'Who were these strangers?' 'Why had they come to Axholme?'

'What did the straight lines mean?' The questions filled Tiddy Mun's head as he watched and listened. Something strange was going on and although Tiddy Mun did not understand what the men were saying he knew their actions would not bring good news.

The next day, Tiddy Mun and the people of Axholme were shocked to see men with wheelbarrows, carts and spades tramping across their land and digging up the peaty ground. With their machines and tools, they piled earth up by the rivers. It took a while, but eventually, the people of Axholme asked these strangers what they were doing.

'We are working for the King,' the men said, 'he wants this land to grow crops and raise cattle.'

'But it's our land,' they replied, 'the King has no right to take it from us.'

'He has every right,' said one of the men, and taking a piece of paper from his pocket, he showed it to the people of Axholme.

'See that!' he said, pointing to a red, waxy blob on the bottom of the paper; 'That is the King's seal. It means we have permission to do whatever it takes to drain the water from this land!'

'Drain the water from the land!' The words shocked the people of Axholme. Draining the water would take away their source of food, their work and leave them to starve. It could not be true! Surely the King would not do such a thing! But he could, and he had sent these men into Axholme to carry out his wishes.

In desperation, the people of Axholme wrote letters to the ministers of the King and travelled all the way to the great capital to meet them, but it was hopeless, nothing they said or did could change the King's mind! They returned to Axholme to find the strangers had delved further into their precious land, making their drains and dykes longer and deeper, and drawing off the water to leave the soil muddy. They knew then they had to do something to stop these people changing their watery homeland. They met together in their homes and secret places and came up with a daring plan – they would sneak out on nights when clouds hid the light of the moon, knock down the river banks to let the floods come back, break the strangers' shovels, and set fire to their wooden wheelbarrows. And that is what they did. Things became so bad that the King had to send some of his soldiers into Axholme to protect the men draining the land from these angry crowds.

After many years the people of Axholme realised that their land would be changed forever, they would have to alter the way they lived. Some bought more cows, others tried growing different crops, some even packed up their few possessions and moved away. And what, you must be thinking, happened to Tiddy Mun? Well … some people say that when the land became dry, he too left his beloved Axholme for good and went in search of another place to live. But … others believed differently. They say he never went away and that he is hiding in the drains and dykes waiting … waiting for the floodwaters to return to Axholme. And, although it may take hundreds of years when the people once again call out for help, he will be ready, and his cry will once more echo over the dark Axholme skies.'

And there she ended her tale.

CHAPTER THREE

A Bit of History

The Celtic tribe most closely associated with Axholme is the Corieltauvi who appear to have offered only scant resistance to the invading Romans unlike the warmongering Brigantes to the north and the rebellious Iceni to the south and east, both of whom clashed violently with the occupying Roman legions. Today some of the earliest Romano-British objects found in Axholme include simple, early bow and fantail brooches made by the Corieltauvi and trumpet brooches from the Brigantes. A small hoard of late 2nd century Roman coins was found near Owston Ferry in the early 1950s. However, there is little more archaeological evidence to suggest the presence of systematic colonisation of the area by the Romans. With Roman Doncaster (Danum) to the west and Ermine Street to the east, however, it seems some form of contact between the two could have included Axholme, but there appears to be no evidence of a permanent land crossing over the Isle.

On 4th March 1986, the BBC began a series of five television programmes entitled 'The Grain Run'. The programmes charted the journey taken by the one hundred foot, Roman barges as they transported grain from the River Witham at Boston, through the Fosse Dyke and along the River Trent to their garrisons on the River Ouse in York. The route was one of Britain's most popular, ancient water-highways. Of particular note to the folk of Axholme was the section from Gainsborough to the Humber. The presenter, Pete Morgan, sailed this section on the Amy Howson, a Humber sloop that worked in the first half of the 20th century delivering grain from Sheffield to Hull and returning with coal.

It is a boat well-known to the residents of Owston Ferry; at the time the chief port for Axholme. Owned today by the Humber Keel and Sloop Preservation Society, the boat's base is at South Ferriby. During the summer months, she carries 12 passengers on her regular sailings on the Humber as well as attending rallies and festivals up and down Britain's canals and rivers. Below deck, there are historical exhibits, ship's tools and ropes, and a display of old photographs and newspaper cuttings that inform visitors about a once traditional way of life.

Unlike Pete Morgan's somewhat sedate passage through Axholme, it was, for those 1st century Roman sailors, a journey not without its perils. Showing a healthy disapproval of those invading their land – something Islonians would carry forward in succeeding centuries, the inhabitants delighted in taunting and tormenting their Roman masters. Following the removal of Roman troops from Britain, tribes from the near continent filled the void bringing the Angles and Saxons to the Isle.

Late in the 8th century Scandinavian raiders or Northmen, began to attack the coastal and riverside settlements of Anglo-Saxon 'England'. In their shallow draughted long-ships, they sailed up the Humber and the rivers of Axholme. The first documented attack on Lincolnshire by these, so-called, Vikings was in the year 841, and very soon the inhabitants of Axholme were calling upon God to deliver them 'from the fury of the Norsemen'. In particular, one of these heathen leaders, Ivar 'the Boneless', a shrewd and fearless warrior, brought consternation to the area when, in 866, he and his army rode north along the Ermine Street pillaging the area as he passed. This army had already spent several years raiding large parts of northern and eastern England, and its location on the banks of the River Trent would have provided an easy supply of necessities to advance an extensive trading network.

By the end of the 9th century thousands of Vikings had come

over the sea to settle. Unlike the Anglo-Saxons before them, they were not daunted by the marsh and swamp of Axholme. Evidence of Viking settlements locally can be seen in the place names of Swinefleet, Ousefleet, Scunthorpe, Gunthorpe and Garthorpe, (the 'thorpe' referring to a farm). Archaeological finds from the area include dress fittings, horse gear, household equipment and pottery. Though not plentiful, they do represent the type of activities one associates with small residential settlements. Finds containing accessories from swords and other such material, around Haxey confirm a powerful Viking presence in the area.

The developing situation that pitted invader against resident called for a political settlement, and it fell to Alfred 'the Great' to define the boundaries between the lands of the Saxons and Vikings. As such, Axholme came under the control of Guthrum, Cnut and Harald Harefoot, Danish kings charged with establishing civilian peace between the two cultures. The system of governance, known as Danelaw, generated legal areas compatible with many of Saxon origin; for example, the Viking 'wapentake', a standard for land division, was little different to the previously existing 'hundred'.

An archaeological find of great significance from this pre-Norman period in the Epworth area is a Saxon Sceatta coin from the reign of Eadberht, King of Northumbria, dated to the late 8th century. It is worthy of note that King Alfred's wife, Lady Ealhswith of the Gaini, spent her youth in the Axholme area but, following 9th century West Saxon custom, she was not given the title of queen. Further disruption came to the region in 1013 when Sweyn Forkbeard, together with his son Canute, arrived at Gainsborough with an army of conquest and established a fortified base on Axholme. Sweyn, described as a 'murderous character' who deposed his father Harold Bluetooth, led a brutal regime that saw women roasted alive, children impaled on lances and men suspended by their private parts. Declared King of England on

Christmas Day, he took up high office at Gainsborough Castle (on the site of the present-day Old Hall). For five weeks, until Sweyn's death, (the result of a fall from his horse) Gainsborough was the erstwhile capital of England. Some historians believe that it may have been here that his son and successor, Canute, demonstrated to his ingratiating followers that he had no control over the incoming tide and that his earthly power was nothing compared to the pre-eminence of God. He would have been aware that Gainsborough was the furthest reach of the Aegir, the River Trent's tidal bore.

The time before 'The Drainage'
Look closely at a map of Axholme before the arrival of Vermuyden, and you are immediately struck by large areas labelled 'fenny' and 'morische soyle'. To the north of Crowle, right up to the banks of the River Ouse there is hardly any evidence of what one could term 'a road'. For further proof of this watery landscape, one has only to look to Garthorpe, where we find Island Road, Shore Lane and Ness Lane. Today, the course of Old River Don has all but disappeared, but its presence can be seen in some of the parishes on the North Isle, most notably at Eastoft. Here the river 'split' the village into two civil parishes, known as Eastoft, Yorkshire and Eastoft, Lincolnshire. At the time, the church, the school and the vicarage were all located in Yorkshire. Today, although in Lincolnshire they still come under the Diocese of Sheffield. Those driving through the village on the A161 can see the course of the Old River from the main road through the village (aptly called Yorkshireside) as a long stretch of grass separating the parallel road High Street.

The Old Don passed through the ribbon development of Luddington before separating Fockerby in Yorkshire from its neighbour Garthorpe on the Lincolnshire side of the river. Today it is hard to distinguish between the two villages. The

Course of the River Don, Eastoft.

river entered the Trent at Adlingfleet which at that time was one of the wealthiest parishes in England.

Mere journeys by carr

Pre-drainage there were few roads and paths linking village to village and hamlet, this was a land of carrs, turbaries and moors. Along the western edge of Axholme, the waterlogged carrs separate the reed-covered marshland from tree supporting soils. Their main characteristics are shrub and scrub where reeds decay, allowing vegetation such as sedge, alder and willow to grow, creating a wooded fen in a waterlogged terrain. The word is Old Norse in origin where 'Kjarr' meant a 'brushwood marsh'.

Starting just to the south of Axholme we find Gringley Carr and Misterton Carr. Between Misterton and West Stockwith is North Carr while further west is Star Carr (from the Old Norse 'storr' meaning sedge grass), Haxey Carr, Roe Carr, West Carr, Carrside (Epworth) and Carrhouse (Belton). It was from these carrs that ferrymen operated connecting the Isle to Yorkshire which, although not without hazard, proved a safer way than trying to pick one's way through a confusing jumble of 'dry ways'.

The carrs gave way to meres, a dialect word from Old English, meaning a sheet of standing water. These tracts of water that varied in size covered the Isle. The first one encountered when travelling from the south was in the flat land between Misterton and Haxey. By far the largest, however, was the previously mentioned Messic Mere, where the River Torne joined the River Idle in the area of Scawcett and Ninevah Farm between Wroot and Sandtoft. Another significant area of water was that between Epworth Turbary and Haxey Turbary, known as the Skiers. It was the only area of water retained by John de Mowbray when he ceded his rights to the commoners of Axholme in his deed of 1360.

The Turbaries

On the western edge of Axholme lie the turbaries of Haxey, Epworth and Belton. These areas of scrub and heath had some of the poorest land around, and were only good for digging peat, rough sods and turf (hence the name turbary - turfery). Having served their communities for centuries - people from the parish were allowed three free cartloads of peat annually (though more could be taken for a fee). From the mid-1800s, the poor were allowed to 'take on' about an acre of this meagre land. The rent was cheap, and those taking up the offer saved themselves the indignity of being placed in the parish poorhouse. It was left to them to build a cottage, farm the land and keep stock and fowl. The two-room cottages they built were mainly of 'mud and stud' though some used brick and tile. They had no foundations and had floors made from paddled clay covered in heather. On the moors of Crowle, mainly along Ribbon Row, small areas were also set aside, allowing settlers to move in to cut the peat.

Life for the families on the turbary was hard but amazingly many prospered. On Epworth Turbary, Mark Pilsworth and his

Turbary Cottage, Haxey. Photo courtesy of Mary Fish.

wife Anne found themselves supporting 18 children. By the time of his death, Mark was the head of a family of 136 children and grandchildren. The Fox brothers, John and Septimus, right up to their eighties, walked their cows to Doncaster market, leaving home in the early hours and arriving back late at night. Not afraid of hard work, in their younger years, they worked twelve-hour days helping to construct the Axholme Joint Railway. Today, nearly all of the original turbary cottages have been knocked down and rebuilt as larger houses or extended beyond their 19th century construction.

Crowle Moors

This area of moorland is little more than an extension of Thorne Moor. In 1630 inhabitants and tenants of Crowle gained the right of turbary but the land granted was in the neighbouring county of Yorkshire. It was an anomaly corrected in 1888 when a commission for local government moved the county boundary west, thereby bringing Crowle Turbary into Lincolnshire. For many years a number of small peat moss mills operated just off Moor Middle

Road along a stretch of land known today as 'Ribbon Row'. Here, horses pulled wagons loaded with hand-cut turves along a single tramway track to a mill. Later on, the British Moss Litter Company extracted peat from Crowle Moors and using narrow gauge locomotives transported it to Medge Hall and Swinefleet Works. Taken from the top layer of the peat, the light brown litter is only slightly decomposed but can hold up to eight times its own weight of water.

Following the closure of peat extraction on Crowle and Thorne Moors the original tramway tracks used for transporting the peat were removed. These areas now form part of the Humberhead National Nature Reserve with Crowle Moors a designated Site of Special Scientific Interest (SSSI). Today the Crowle Peat Railway Society, with significant grants from North Lincolnshire Council, the Isle of Axholme and Hatfield Chase Landscape Partnership and the Heritage Lottery Fund, has set about renovating the old locomotives and part of the track. The hope is the railway project will help visitors appreciate and enjoy the moors heritage and history.

Vinegarth

In the mid-1800s, there was excitement in Epworth when several 'superior' bricks and floor tiles were found in the Vinegarth area south of the church. One was found when digging the foundations for a shed on the premises of the Epworth Free School. Another with a broken corner was in the possession of watch and clockmaker Thomas Clark having been found by his father when planting trees in Church Walk. A third, found by Mr. Jenkinson was the best preserved and clearly showed the arms of the Mowbray family – a Lion Rampant within a Shield, said to represent magnanimity or courage. The finds reawakened interest in the Vinegarth site.

It led to one noted historian of the times advancing the theory that some of the stonework from the manor house forms the outer rubble walls of the North and South Aisles and porches of St. Andrew's Church. His belief was that it would have been 'easier formerly than now to fetch away portions of the ruins' and that many form the foundations of several buildings in Epworth.

In the 1960s, Reverend W.B. Harvey, the rector at Epworth, and his sexton came across some brick foundations extending into the graveyard east of the church. They followed these south and revealed the stone foundations of what they believed to be the manor house of the Mowbray family. They removed several patterned floor tiles from this area. The red clay tiles had a lion motif on them, which they took to represent the arms of the Mowbray family. Of significance, however, is the anomaly that the lion faces the opposite direction to that of the Mowbrays.

In 1975-76 rushed excavations in the area of Vinegarth took place before a small housing estate covered much of the ground. They revealed what appeared to be the south wall of a mediaeval hall. In the south-west corner were the remains of a kitchen, the floor of which was covered in diagonal tiles bearing the 'Mowbray shield'. Further south was what appeared to be a cloistral walk. Immediately south of the church there seems to have been service buildings. Archaeologists concluded that the hall fell into disrepair in the 16th century.

Life on the manor

In mediaeval Axholme, the villeins worked Mowbray's fields for three days each week and in return received justice and protection from theft and marauding robbers. A farmer's ploughing duties began at daybreak and lasted from Candlemas (2nd February) to Easter. Depending on the weather, the workers could take between twenty and thirty days to plough their ten acres with a team of oxen. The wheeled ploughs required a large team of oxen to pull them — as many as eight on 'strong' soils — and were awkward to turn around. This meant the long-furrowed strips or selions, each approximately 220 yards were ideal (naming that distance one 'furrow long' or furlong). The team driver controlled his team with an iron rod, occasionally pricking the oxen to hasten their pace.

The length for this 'goad' was 6 feet, which became the standard length of the rod, pole, or perch measurement. The driver would lay this goad at right angles to his first furrow to measure the breadth of the land he had to till, thereby creating strips. In many of the open fields of England, these often curving strips were marked by green baulks or large stones, but in Axholme, they were often delineated by no more than a deeper furrow. These open fields of the Isle remain the largest and most varied to survive in the country and, consequently are of national importance.

The first day of August, known as Lammas Day (loaf-mass day), usually signalled the beginning of the wheat harvest and the end of the hay harvest that usually began at Midsummer. Harvest time placed huge demands on the whole family. As the men swung their sickles, the women picked up the sheaves to stook and the children gleaned. Their harvests consisted mainly of rye, wheat, oats, barley, peas and beans with farmers storing the best grain as seed for the following year. Yeoman farmers, with a holding of ten acres or more, could feed their family, pay rent to the Mowbrays, taxes to the King, one-tenth (tithe) of all produce to the rector and still earn a little extra by selling any excess.

By modern standards, however, 14th century arable farming was painfully slow, and life was hard, especially when the harvests were poor. Starvation was an ever-present threat, and under such circumstances, the families of Axholme relied on the structure of the manor and judgements made by the manor court. Here the Lord of the manor, or those appointed to represent him, dealt with civil wrongs and disputes between villagers, arranged local contracts and land tenure and ruled over more mundane issues such as straying pigs and trespass.

Strips of land

Some of the best examples of ancient open fields in the country as a whole are found around Belton, Epworth and Haxey. To the discerning eye, these open fields still reflect a system of farming in use since early mediaeval times. Based on a system of equivalence, the allocation of strips ensured farmers received fair access to good quality soil. The strips were not separated by hard boundaries, such as hedges or ditches, and, when adjacent strips were owned by different farmers, the overall effect was one of ribbons of crops that created a linear patchwork. Local topography also played its part in determining the morphology of individual components in the open fields.

Those with responsibility for the open fields in Axholme took the title of Field Reeve. It was their job to 'lay down in a husband-like manner the baulks by boundary stones or other such marker to distinguish the lands to be ploughed'. Their job also involved keeping the fences and ditches in good order and regulating the times during which animals were permitted to pasture. Through careful planning, the reeves ensured the crops were varied, well-maintained and managed subject to the instructions of the owner

Strip Farming

(usually the Lord of the manor). They resolved any issues or disputes and managed the letting or sale of the individual strips. Their role required them to 'meet and assemble at some convenient place yearly and, on the 21st of May or within three days after, elect or choose one or more proper person or persons to be the Field Reeve(s) for the ensuing year'.

For many years' past, the role of the Field Reeve has fallen to local farmers, landowners and members of the community who were keen to keep alive this traditional way of managing the landscape. Today, there are three surviving members of the Field Reeves of Epworth. With no one likely to take on the role for the future they have sought to pass on their responsibilities to North Lincolnshire Council who already attend to many of their duties such as the maintenance of public rights of way.

Living at 'holme'

Look carefully at a map of Axholme, and you are immediately struck by the number of places ending in 'holme'. The word is Norse in origin and refers to a small island, generally in a lake. So out in the Isle landscape, we have the green island (Greenholme); the thin one (Thinholme); the island of thorns (Thornholme); the island of Linden trees (Lindholme) and long island (Langholme). It was to these holmes that the mediaeval farmers of Axholme took their beast to pasture.

Of course, the most difficult 'holme' to categorise is the word 'Axholme' itself. Etymologists suggest that Axholme means 'island by Haxey', as we find the name Hakirholme in documents from 1196. The suffix 'ey' in 'Haxey' also indicates an island. When taken to its most logical conclusion, that makes the Isle of Axholme, the Isle by the island on the island!

Technically the Isle of Axholme refers to the central archipelago of 'islands' raised above the marsh from Owston Ferry and Haxey/

Westwoodside northwards. Some topographers even claim that the term Isle of Axholme ended at Belton and Crowle was a separate island. Most of the other settlements stand on ground less than 4 metres above the 'inundation'. The area to the east of this spine was categorised as 'Riverside'. To the west, in a land of carrs, turbaries and meres the area since Vermuyden became known as 'The Levels'. Farmers used the most fertile and best-drained soil for their arable crops, the lower land below this for hay meadows ('ings'), and the wettest for pasture, peat cutting, and as supplementary activities during the winter flooding - fishing and fowling. As a final confirmation/reminder – 'old-timers' will talk of living in Axholme but living on the Isle.

Fowlers at work

Often referred to as 'slodgers' the fowlers of Axholme lived in crude huts, constructed from local materials including peat, wood, sedge, reed and clay, much of which would have been harvested or gathered from their surroundings. In this wetland landscape, they lived a life of wild liberty, yet the damp climate offered little in return except for a creeping ague that left their rheumatic bodies twisted and deformed.

They became adept at breeding decoy ducks that given care and attention grew tame enough to attract wild birds to their ponds and meres. Some birds they lured into areas where huge flight nets could be drawn up into a hoop by teams of men working together. If pulled over their heads swiftly, the ducks found themselves trapped as they attempted to fly away. The process involved a good deal of skill and split-second timing. Others were shepherded down channels into the open mouths of nets or scared there by the bark of a dog. Driven into the narrow end of the net, they too found themselves trapped. Fowlers working alone would employ a small version of the hoop net. Having singled out the decoy ducks and calmed them, the fowlers released them to begin the process of entrapment again. The men of Axholme were not particular and took whatever birdlife came within reach – wild geese, herons, cranes, coots and cormorants as well as a whole range of wading birds.

Providing food all year round was not always possible as the fowlers worked to the birds' migration patterns – leaving autumn and winter as the most profitable outside the breeding season. Men would attach stilts to their legs and feet and wade up and down the channels looking for the eggs of waterfowl though many studiously avoided taking the eggs of the bittern. Everyone knew that coming face-to-face with this bird was the portent for an approaching death.

One major fowling location on the Isle was about a mile west of Crowle Church. Relying on the movement of wildfowl moving from the lands of Axholme to the Humber marshes, the site was in use up until the 1830s. Known as Crowle Old Decoy the area held a number of species of ducks including, mallard, scaup, wigeon, pochard, pintail and teal. The fowlers might have fed well on their catch, but they knew the birds were more valuable if sold. In this way, many found their way to the table of the Lord of the Manor.

Fishing

Detailed knowledge of the varying characteristics of the Axholme wastes enabled fishermen to utilise the opportunities for fishing and eel trapping. In the undrained waste, water was their friend and at times their enemy. Serious flooding was a destructive force, but they were adept at adjusting their methods to changing water levels. In Anglo-Saxon Axholme, fishermen used five foot long willow traps made from withies cultivated for at least three years to catch all manner of fish including pike, perch and on occasions salmon. The main advantage of these traps was that smaller fish could be caught, and there was little danger of the fish swimming away from them as was the case with a net. In addition, they were relatively easy to maintain. Eels were particularly welcome at the table of an Axholme home. There were two methods of catching eels; one was with an eel-trap of willow work, but the principal one used on the Axholme fens was a spear. If you knew the best places, several hundred eels might be caught at a time. The spearheads would have two or more prongs and resemble a trident with barbs or serrated edges.

The Domesday Book of 1086 makes numerous references to fisheries in the villages of Axholme. Crowle had 31 fisheries listed, Haxey had nine, while Epworth and Haxey each had eleven. Later, during the reign of Henry VIII, the aforementioned traveller John Leland described the area as 'full of good fish and fowl – soil by the water is fenny, and marshy and full of carres'.

Leland's Axholme in his own words

The principal wood of the Isle is at Bellegreve Park by Hepworth, and at Melwood Park not far from Hepworth.

There is also a praty wood at Croole, a lordship a late longing to Selleby Monasterie.

Hepworth is the best uplandisch toun for building in one streate in the isle.

Axey is a bigge paroche, but the houses be more sparkelid then at Hepoworth.

There was a castelle at the south side of the chirch garth of Oxtun, whereof no peace now standith. The dike and hille wher the arx stoode yet be seene: it was sumtime caullid Kinard, the fery over Trentis a quarter of a mile of.

By Milwood Park side stoode the right fair Carthusianes, wher one of the Mulbrais dukes of Northfolk was buried in a tumbe of alabaster.

There was many years sins an old manor place at Westbutter Wike apon Trent ripe.

The upperpart of the isle hath plentiful quarres of alabaster, communely caullid plaster: but such stones as I saw it were of no great thikness. They ly yn the ground lyke a smothe table: and be beddid one flake under another: and at the bottom of the beddes of them be roughe stones to build withal.

The reed cutters' round

January frosts: A time of hard frosts which often led to an encouraging start to the reed harvest.

February Filldyke: When the rain falls solidly, it holds up the cutting. The Axholme reed cutters need water, but there are occasions when this becomes too much for productive work to continue.

March winds: The time is right to take a break from cutting and catch some eels. When the roach and bream spawn, there's more than enough to go around. Hold them down with a cloth and bang the head violently against the side of the boat. Slit the skin in a circle and pull hard down the body. It takes practice!

April showers: When this year's reeds begin to show green in the ground, it's time to stop the harvest.

May flowers: With the reeds stacked in the water to keep them supple, it's time to look ahead to summer.

Flaming June: Time to move on and harvest the sedge. Coats off and sleeves rolled up, there's more hard work to be done.

July heat: Sedge cutting is going well. The hay in the marshes has grown well so the animals will be well-fed. Got to save some to thatch the corn stacks though.

Mellow August: The dykes are starting to clog up with mud and weed. It'll need clearing out, or even the shallowest of boats won't get through.

September stall: Time to do those jobs around the farm that we've put off.

October mists: Time to clear the bushes from the fenland. If they are left there, they'll strangle the reeds and next year's crop will suffer.

November rain: A few wild ducks bring some extra meat to the table. A couple for the constable and he might ignore a fenman's 'bit of sport.'

December snow: Time to sharpen the scythes and clean out the boats. It'll be time to harvest the reeds again when the old year ends.

During the drainage

Charles I and Cornelius Vermuyden came up with an ingenious plan to carve up the land in Axholme. Charles would reserve one third for himself as 'Lord of the Soil', allow the drainers one third 'for their charges', and gracefully grant 'the remainder to the respective Tenants for their Common'. Many Islonians didn't realise the enormity of the proposal until it was almost too late to challenge the decision. It brought many native Dutch to the Isle. Brought up to be protestant they sought solace from their devoutly Catholic homeland. The opportunity to practice their religious way of life by buying and owning rich agricultural land and securing religious freedom was too good an offer to ignore.

Quoting from a manuscript written in the late 1700s, the Epworth Bells notes; 'These lands were quietly enjoyed at first, [with] great numbers of Dutch and French Protestants being planted there. [A] Church and Minister's House was erected at Sandtoft for their congregation, and a salary of eighty pounds per annum was settled on their Minister, and he preached to them on each Lord's day in both languages.' What they didn't bargain for was the gathering hostility they would encounter from the people

Haxey Church in 1700s

of Axholme. As relationships between natives and the settlers deteriorated, fighting broke out repeatedly, resulting in death on both sides. Forced to build a stockade on the only available solid ground at Sandtoft, itself a natural island, just a few metres above the surrounding level of water, they turned it into their headquarters and from there planned and organised their activities.

The Islonians claim to their land

The Islonians believed their cause was just. They put their trust in John de Mowbray's 'Deed' granted to them in 1360 that gave them unparalleled rights to their Axholme land. Written in French, it was, for its time, a remarkable charter that stripped away complex and sophisticated laws and gave the people of the manor unparalleled privileges. It allowed them the freedom to farm, fish and fowl wherever they pleased, and this had an immediate and positive effect on the occupants of Axholme. It was in John de

The Mowbray window, Haxey church.

Mowbray's power to do so for building on the effectiveness of his forebears his power over the manor was absolute. He could use the land however he wished and under riparian law, he 'owned' the water that ran across his land. He could produce his own currency and administer his own system of justice. Work on the manor was both flexible and self-supporting, and it was perhaps to maintain this that John instigated this legal charter that would bring significant benefit to the occupiers of common land. Stonehouse records that the deed was jealously guarded by the commoners of Axholme in Haxey Church 'in a chest bound with iron, whose key was kept by some of the chiefest freeholders, under a window wherein was a portraiture of Mowbray, set in ancient stained glass, holding in his hand [what was] commonly reported to be an emblem of the deed'.

A meeting place for a mob
The Church of St. Nicholas, Haxey, has rightly been called the 'Cathedral of the Isle'. It is the biggest church with the tallest tower. Impressive both inside and out, the church has many stories to tell. What happened to the Mowbray Deed is a matter for conjecture. Stonehouse implies that it could have been 'spirited away' by a foreign hand during the riots. He is certain the window containing Mowbray's portrait was broken down in these 'rebellious times'.

During the drainage, mobs of Axholme men and women often used Haxey Church as a rallying point before setting off to seek out, harass and, on occasions, submit the Dutch and French settlers to acts of barbarity. The Islonians' hatred of Vermuyden's scheme is well documented, and this only intensified when he received a knighthood and became a British citizen. His actions and those of the King fuelled a century of rioting. It brought (Freeborn) John Lilburne, a political Leveller, to the Isle to help fight the cause of Axholme. A champion for individual rights, Lilburne had been flogged, pilloried and imprisoned for his beliefs. His 'country manners' chimed with the folk of Axholme; he spoke their language, and they looked to him for guidance. At their head, his cry was; 'This be our common, ye shall come here no more less you be stronger than we.'

The Mowbray Deed (See Appendix for the Deed in full)
The document which was as important to Axholme as the Magna Carta was to Britain, rewrote the rules for commoners who previously had been denied access to the manor's hunting grounds on pain of death or lifelong imprisonment. Now they had the

right of mast, a right that allowed them to turn out pigs in wooded areas. They had estovers – the right to cut wood, primarily as a material for building and repair and marl; the right to take sand and gravel; the right of pasture, for commonable animals – ponies, horned cattle and donkeys; the right of piscary – allowing for the taking of fish, and finally, the right of turbary – the permission to cut turf for fuel or building. It was the last three of these that held the greatest significance for the people of Epworth. Their fishing rights allowed them to catch fish on Wednesdays and Fridays as far as the River Idle. Their cattle had greater access to pasture and, in an area where trees were relatively scarce, it was to the turfery, or Turbary, that the inhabitants headed to cut turves to roof and heat their houses. The rough size of each turf had to be about 18 inches by 9 inches, but so as not to exhaust supplies, for every turf cut, a space equivalent to two turves would be left. The charter also allowed access to 'certain waters' for retting hemp (except in the Skiers, which the Lord reserved for his use).

Joining the New Model Army

That the folk of Axholme were firmly on the side of Parliament during the Civil War hardly needs stressing. After the way the King acted (by appointing Vermuyden to drain the area) there was little if any local support for the crown. Hardly surprising then that the Isle of Axholme raised at least two companies of foot soldiers in support of the Parliamentary cause. It seems our Victorian historian, the Venerable Archdeacon Stonehouse had in his possession for a time the muster roll of at least one company. According to him, the document came from an old cottage in Belton. If, as reported, there were 493 names on it, then it would have been quite a sizeable force raised in the locality. As volunteers, these rural men might have enlisted for guaranteed pay, but many would have followed the habits of their civilian life and enlisted because some local landowner told them to do so. A regiment of foot consisted of ten companies that in total came to approximately 1200 soldiers. These would be both pikemen and musketeers; the accepted proportion being two musketeers to one pikeman. The regiments were provided with red coats, that being the least expensive colour of dye and not, as popular myth has it, to conceal the blood from battlefield wounds. It did, of course, make them very visible targets but hey, it was cheap!

The Axholme regiment came under the command of Captain William Manning who supplied £33-16s-8d for the payment of three hundred soldiers and officers. Other senior officers included Lieutenant William Tull, Ensign Thomas Pergint and Sergeant William Stanis.

I have always placed great store by the thought of 'ordinary' men from Axholme going on crusade with the likes of Roger de Mowbray. The idea of them standing on battlefields such as Marston Moor, Edgehill or Naseby under the command of Oliver Cromwell and Sir Thomas Fairfax never entered my head!

After the drainage

The rerouting of the River Don northwards towards the River Aire (it will later join the River Ouse near Goole via The Dutch River), turning the River Idle into the Bykersdyke and the construction of the New Torne bring about an immediate change to the Axholme landscape. Pathways across the fen are reinforced with flagstones and, whilst the ferries still operate in parts their use is on the wane.

Much of the drained land, is divided up into fields surrounded by straight boundaries of ditch and drain - a necessity if the land is to be kept dry. Farmers leave their village bound farmsteads and build granges out in these new enclosures. The drained land may require warping, a deliberate inundation with river water, but this brings rich alluvial mud to help increase yields. For the strip-loving farmers, the fowlers and the fisherman, however, there is little joy in this developing landscape. They much prefer to see their land divided into strips with their long curvilinear forms, the wildness of the open fen and the fish-laden meres.

The enclosures

The common grazing land on the high ground was enclosed in two Acts: Epworth, Haxey, Owston Ferry and Belton in 1795; and Crowle and surroundings in 1822. The fields were to be divided up into individual compounds (better termed closes). In Crowle, the owners of lands and common rights held a meeting concerning enclosures on the manor in the White Hart Inn, at the end of July 1812. According to The Stamford Mercury, they decided to go ahead, and the first meeting with the enclosure commissioners, Anthony Bower (Lincoln), Jonathan Teal (Leeds) and Francis Raynes (Everton, Notts) took place on 13th September 1813. The commissioners each received three guineas a day in fees. The Act specifically named Lord of the Manor Earl Manvers and two other owners of 'great tithes', William Johnson and Robert Popplewell Steer.

Given the importance of hemp and flax, one provision in the Act stated that no pits for steeping hemp, line, or flax were to be dug on Ealand Common, between Ealand village and the Stainforth to Keadby Canal, or nearer to the road from Crowle Wharfe to Crowle than 500 yards. There were none to be dug on Townend Green (Tetley Green).

The Commissioners' Award – a permanent legal record of enclosure – was finally signed on 17th June 1822. The Act compelled that no person 'shall be permitted to overflow their land with water, or use sluices or drains for this purpose, until he or they shall make sufficient interior banks, sluices, tunnels and other works, for preventing any other lands or grounds from receiving any damage as a consequence of letting in such water ... after each season of warping'. To fully warp the land might take three summers but in hot weather when the tides contained more alluvial mud, this could be accomplished after two consecutive dry ones. In this way, land on Crowle Moors became first-rate soil capable of producing abundant crops of wheat, beans, oats and potatoes.

Money from the rents and profits of these enclosures went toward the upkeep of the road. The owners were responsible for fencing and gates at the end of these roads but could not allow their stock to feed on the sides of the highways. The gates prevented cattle straying from one parish to another – hence the names Haxey Gate and Belton Gate (the former name for Belton Road).

In total over 170 enclosures were granted, ranging from 400 acres to the vicar of Crowle (in place of tithes) to the 7 perches (about 210 square yards) given to George Cock. In the 1800s, an Axholme farm of around 300 acres was considered a large farm.

The enclosure of land brought further change to the Isle in the mid-19th century. Four of the eight ecclesiastical parishes were divided further creating four new parishes: West Butterwick formed from Owston Ferry in 1841; Amcotts from Althorpe in 1850; Eastoft from Crowle in 1855, and Garthorpe from Luddington in 1866.

Did the Dutch leave their mark?

Of course, the answer to the above question would be a resounding 'Yes!' After all, one only has to look at the topography of the Isle and the plethora of dykes, drains and ditches to come up with an answer in the positive. However, when looking at the question in its broadest context, there are several other ways in which the 'invaders' of the 1600s left a record. There can be few who do not recognise Epworth Post Office with its Dutch-influenced frontage and the house at Kelfield dated 1689 with its equally impressive gables.

Just off the A18, close to Dirtness are a couple of farms going by the names of Jacques Farm and Smaque Farm. Christian Smaque was one of the original settlers who came at the beginning of the drainage scheme and the area is close to the Sandtoft stronghold set up by Vermuyden and his 'participants'. Another of those first settlers was Matthew Brugne, who through a corruption of the name ended up as Brunyee. The family name is synonymous with Crowle where there is a street called Brunyee St. – the only example of that name in Britain. Other Axholme names such as Sleight, Kelsey, Gilliatt, Burnup (pronounced Bonnet), Ducker, Theaker and Threadgold reveal their Dutch origins.

A less observable feature is the number of local houses and buildings that were built using the Flemish bond system introduced to Britain in 1631. Look around in your locality for the system of laying bricks in a header-stretcher pattern, one brick sideways one brick end on and so on.

Photographs of women workers on the land wearing a hood-type bonnet that tied beneath the chin reveal elements of the Dutch costume still prevalent in the early 20th century.

Finally, and perhaps less credible, Edward Peacock in his Anthropological Review of Axholme (published in 1870) states, 'the strongest evidence we have [of the Dutch influence] is the present appearance of the people. Their build is decidedly larger, their under-jaw massive, hair lighter, feet and hands proportionately larger. There is a greater proportion of blue eyes, and it is said that the teeth have a much slighter tendency to decay.' He also postulates that the Axholme accent and dialect owe much to the Dutch in making it 'distinctive from that of Yorkshire, Nottinghamshire, or other parts of the county of Lincoln[shire]'.

The River Idle - East from Idle Stop.

The Axholme dialect and superstitions

Perhaps it was less to do with the Dutch and more to do with the insular character and inaccessibility of the region that fostered the heavy agricultural dialect of Axholme. In a predominantly farming area with its associated trades (smiths, thatchers, millers, etc), sons inherited their fathers' lands or occupations and people rarely strayed from their own community.

As a youngster I spent my school holidays working for local farmers. The work was backbreaking but hardest of all was trying to understand what they were saying for many spoke in 'owd Axholme'. The greatest exponent of this 'art' I came across, was West End farmer, George Ward. I soon came to realise that to understand his dialect there were a few simple rules that might help.

In ai words such as rain, reverse the 'a' and 'I' to get rian, trian stian.

Put an 'a' after an 'o' as in hoam (home), coam (comb) doam (dome) stoan (stone - but if using it to describe weight then it becomes ston).

Adding sen instead of self – hissen, hersen, thissen, mysen, yoursen.

If a word ends in 'ird', dropping the 'r' and replacing the 'i' with an 'o' give us 'wods', 'thods' and 'bods' for words, thirds and birds.

'Old timers' would even assert that the church bells (particularly those at Haxey) chimed with an Axholme dialect.

When turning to sayings there is only one question worth asking - where does one stop?

There were (maybe still are) people in Axholme who could be described as 'orkad as a fallo' field buzzard' or having a 'hob gob' – a mouth as wide as a chimney back! My grandma would check

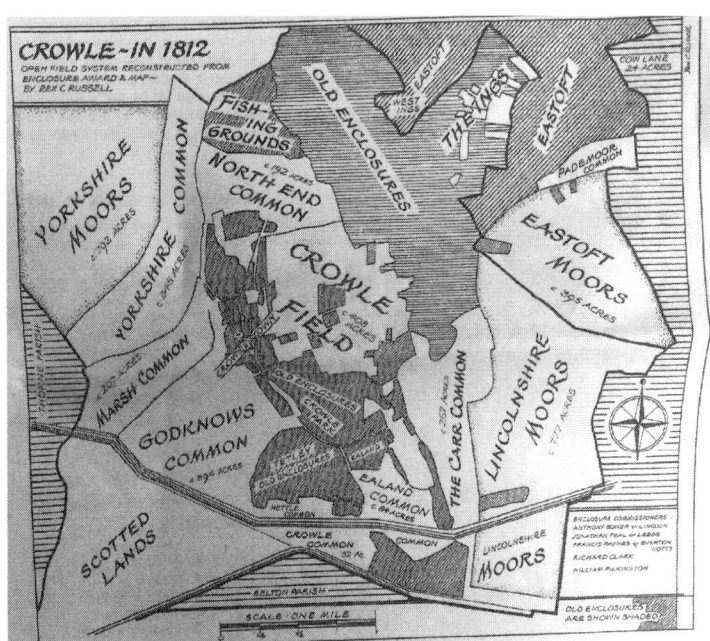

Crowle enclosures.

my ears regularly and on occasions would exclaim, 'Ya cudha set taties in them ear hoals'. She sometimes described a slow moving or slow-witted person, 'as wick as a deead dog!'

Flemish Bond brickwork.

CHAPTER 4

Death by Misadventure

Those who have read my book 'Misadventure, Mayhem, Myth and Murder' may have reflected on many of the Isle's horrific incidents and unexplained deaths. Call it carelessness, ignorance, or just plain stupidity, the late 1800s was a time when misfortune stalked the Isle. The fatal accidents presented here were all reported in the local press. While taking the core of the text from these reports, I have tried to keep the tone ironic but respectful. However, in this modern world where the tentacles of the Health and Safety monster extend into every facet of human endeavour, I'll leave it up to you to see if your judgement confers with that of the coroner.

A loaded gun
In what can only be described as a depressing report, the Epworth Bells ran the story of 18-year-old Mary Ann Cook who worked as a servant at Easingwood House, the home of Frank Glossop, a Crowle farmer. Evidence from the inquest revealed that Thomas Huntington, one of the men employed by Mr. Glossop, had been out shooting on the farm with a double-barrelled shotgun, used to frighten away crows. On his return, he gave the gun to Frank Glossop who placed it behind the kitchen door with the hammer down. At some point, one of the servants while cleaning the kitchen, placed the gun on the dresser neglecting to put it back behind the door. At about eight o'clock that evening, Ann and fourteen-year-old Benjamin Meggitt, a farm boy, saw the gun on the dresser and questioned whether in its current state the gun was loaded. Ann was kneeling in front of the fire, with young

Meggitt about two yards away when he picked up the gun and pointed it towards her. The girl laughed telling Meggitt she did not think the gun would go off. The words had scarcely passed her lips when there was an explosion, and the contents of the cartridge entered her left temple, making a hole larger than the diameter of a half-crown. The poor boy, 'fearfully distracted at the dreadful and unforeseen consequences of his act', rushed off for assistance. Although help arrived quickly, there was nothing anyone could do for poor the girl. Traumatised by his action, the event left Benjamin unable to speak for some considerable time.

At the inquest, those involved in the tragedy gave detailed evidence about why a loaded gun was kept in the house. In returning a verdict of 'accidental death', the coroner condemned the practice of keeping a loaded gun in the house.

Choked by a misguided act of kindness

Another sad report from the time told of the unfortunate death of a three-week-old baby. When the child's father came home from work late one night, he found the family asleep, but the baby unsettled. To quieten the child, he placed a strawberry in its mouth, reasoning that the motion of sucking might settle the infant to sleep. Next morning, when the family woke, they found the baby dead. At first, they were puzzled but eventually concluded that the infant must have choked on the strawberry. At the inquest the coroner confirmed this, having found strands of strawberry flesh wedged in its throat and gums. Although he pointed the finger at the stupidity of the father's action, he declared himself bound to bring in a verdict of 'accidental death through suffocation'.

A watery grave

The dangers of living in an environment crossed by rivers, drains and dykes have been ever-present in Axholme, and two reports in newspaper editions from early in the 20th century only highlight this further. In Beltoft, eleven-year-old Raymond Harrison asked his friend, Joseph Armitage, and two other boys, Horace Elliff and Victor Redfern, if they would like to go and see a water hen's nest. All the boys had been warned to stay well clear of the pond but, yielding to Raymond's mild persuasion they all set off to a large pond about half a mile from Raymond's house. When they arrived at the pond, Raymond took off his clothes and walked around the outside of the pond until he found a place where he could enter the water. Although he could swim a little, Raymond soon found himself in difficulties and, as he struggled to get back to the edge of the pond, he sank beneath the water. In a statement given later by the other boys, it seems he came up twice before disappearing altogether. Too shocked to react positively, the three boys ran away. Joseph Armitage ran down the hedge side towards his house, only to find his mother out shopping. When she returned and asked him where he had been his instinct was to keep quiet as he knew mum would be cross to know he had been to the pond.

Later that day, when walking home from work, George Harrison, Raymond's father, heard a 'rumour' that Raymond had drowned in the nearby pond. As he rushed to the place, he met young Armitage and asked him if he had seen Raymond at the pond. Armitage said he had not, which made George believe that the rumour was false. With this thought in his mind, George turned around and went home in better spirits. Had he continued to the pond he would have found Thomas Drakes and Mr. Kelsey, dragging the pond. Half-an-hour later they found poor Raymond's body and went to the Harrison house to tell the family of their grisly discovery. The coroner admonished the boys for their stupidity and Armitage's reluctance to tell the truth, but there was no other verdict he could deliver except 'accidental death'.

Some weeks later and further north, six-year-old Jane Fox

and some of her friends were playing a game at Keadby Lock that involved crossing a narrow plank over the sluice with their eyes closed. The girls had watched watermen crossing and recrossing the plank from the lock side on many occasions and hatched a plot to play their 'eyes-shut' game. When it came to her turn, little Jane began nervously and after a few steps, missed her footing and slipped into the black water. Instead of raising the alarm to workmen close by, the girls ran home to tell their mothers. The women rushed to the scene, shouting for help along the way. Several dockers began frantically raking the water with gaffs and boat hooks, and after dragging the watercourse for some minutes, Mr. Tate recovered the girl's lifeless body. At the inquest, the jury returned a verdict of 'Accidentally Drowned', and asked the coroner to approach the Hatfield Chase Corporation with a view to them reducing the danger of such a structure, especially when further evidence revealed that five children had drowned at the same place in recent years.

Taking the bull by the horns
When nine-year-old Samuel Harrison set off to bring back one of the family's cows from a field close to the road to Beltoft with a few of his friends, he took a rope, looped at one end, with the instruction to put it over the cow's head and lead the beast home. Their journey to the field brought much hilarity, and by the time they arrived at the pasture, the boys had hatched what turned out to be a foolish plan. Their idea was for Samuel to attach the rope to one of the cow's horns, instead of putting it over the animal's neck. Setting off home, with Samuel leading the cow, the boys took to fooling around once again, pushing each other and engaging in what could be described (somewhat inaptly) as 'horse-play'.

Not wanting to miss out on the fun, Samuel decided to free his hands by tying the other end of the rope around his midriff. The beast seemed happy to plod along, but, as the boys push and pull games became more animated, the cow took fright. Setting off for Belgarthorne Hill, it reached a speed whereby the hapless boy could no longer keep pace. He tried in vain to release the rope from his waist but, in a riot of flailing arms and legs, he fell to the ground. His petrifying cries, and those of his playmates, brought further panic to the scene. For over half a mile, the cow dragged the poor lad along, over road, field and furrow. Unable to regain his feet, he rolled and skidded along suffering severe abrasions and broken bones. By the time the cow stopped close to Vine Garth, Samuel was unconscious and bleeding severely from multiple puncture wounds. The first person to him was Mr. Archer and, finding him slumped in a crumpled mass, he attempted to revive Samuel by pouring some water into the lad's mouth. Unable to swallow, and after struggling for breath for a few short moments, Samuel died in Mr. Archer's arms. At the inquest, the family refused to hold the boys responsible for the tragedy, thanked Mr. Archer for his efforts and, perhaps, more prosaically 'laid no blame at the feet [or the horns] of the cow'!

Distracted by a fish cart

Nineteen-year-old Percy Parkin of Crowle worked as a flagman. Employed by his father, the driver of a traction engine, his job was to walk in front and warn the public of the approaching machine. Working for Nicholas Ella of Eastoft, the pair were proceeding down Washinghall Lane with Percy 'only a short distance ahead of the engine'. Somewhat distracted by the fish cart coming in the opposite direction, he only partially heard his father's call for him to 'walk on' to avoid being run over. As the lad turned to question his father's instruction, he inadvertently stepped in front of the engine, and the front right wheel caught his heel and threw him down. Try as he might Percy was unable to extricate himself

Reeds threshing engine, Epworth.

before both right-side wheels passed over him. His father heard the lad shout and after stopping the machine, gazed back in horror at his son's mutilated body. Dr. Alexander was quickly in attendance, and found the lad barely clinging to life. He ordered the immediate removal of Percy's body to Goole Cottage Hospital. Father Smith of St. Norbert's Priory, Crowle, passing at the time of the incident, placed his trap at their disposal. Hauling the poor lad into the carriage, they set off for Goole, but as they entered Swinefleet Percy passed away. The Epworth Bells reported that a 'painful sensation was caused in the town some hours later when the trap conveying his body passed to his house in Commonside'. At the inquest, held at Crowle a few days later, the jury brought in a verdict of ..., yes, you guessed correctly – accidental death!

A fatal discussion

A further tale in this chapter of woe involves the touching death of Mildred Elizabeth Sharp, the three-year-old daughter of George

Walter Sharp, platelayer of Eastoft. At 8.25 a.m. Mildred's mother left her playing on the hearthrug while she went to a neighbour's house. Mildred was wearing a flannelette dress, a flannelette nightshirt and a woollen shawl. Her mother left the house almost immediately but spent two or three minutes talking to Samuel Phillipson, next door's gardener. After that, she went into her house, but almost immediately came running out shouting that her child was on fire. Samuel ran into the house and found the room full of smoke. The child was lying near the kitchen table, and though her clothes were not on fire, they were smouldering. Samuel picked her up and rolled her in the hearthrug. He took the poor girl into his own house and after rolling her in one of his wife's shawls, took her to her grandmothers. Dr. Dunlop arrived from Crowle sometime later and found the Mildred covered in oily rags; she was unconscious. The only parts of her body not severely burned were her feet which had been saved by her stockings. The doctor knew from the outset that the case was hopeless and so it proved - Mildred never regained consciousness. It was recorded as an accidental death but nevertheless one that with more care and forethought should have been avoidable!

A shocking discovery

Another grim story from around the time that did not reach the pages of my previous book tells the sad tale of twenty-one-year-old John Thomas Thompson of Wroot. At 4.45 a.m., James Dempster, walking down an occupation lane to his garden came upon a body, the sight of which caused shock and alarm. In his account before the coroner, he described the body as being 'virtually headless' with the 'roof of the head being blown in all directions and brains spread around the lane like cold porridge'. It was 'a ghastly spectacle', but Dempster noticed a pistol in the left hand of the corpse, in what he described as a vice-like grip.

He realised from the outset that he was looking at suicide.

It seems young Thompson, having had an emotional relationship with two girls agonised over which one he loved the most. When the one he finally decided upon 'knocked him back', he turned to the other, a young girl called Ada. Annoyed at being seen as 'second best', when she, too, would not commit to John's advances, he stormed off saying; 'If I don't have you, I won't have anyone else. Goodbye, I shan't see you again. I will put a shot into myself before morning'. Although Ada knew John to be a highly-strung individual, she did not take his threat seriously. At the inquest, appearing as a 'broken individual', she gave evidence 'with tears in her eyes'. The coroner sympathised with her and told her she must not shoulder any of the blame. He brought in a verdict of 'suicide while temporarily insane'.

… and another

A second shocking report from Crowle told of the suicide of Philip Stowe, a farm labourer from Godnow Road. For some time, Stowe complained of people saying 'things' about him, but he did not divulge names. The 'deceased had only been out of work for about a fortnight, but had become depressed, yet he had never threatened to take his life'. At the inquest, his wife, Eliza, confirmed that 'the body the jury had seen was that of her [seventy-year-old] husband'. She testified that while out in the yard, 'she heard a noise that aroused her suspicions. She went back and found that he had left the sofa and was sitting back in his chair, and she noticed a blaze on his shirt front. She quickly got hold of his shirt, and the blood soaked out. A single-barrelled gun was lying on the floor. The wound was in his body over the breastbone in an upward direction. He was quite dead'. Dr. Hamilton, who attended the scene, confirmed the bullet had pierced the deceased heart.

When Inspector Skipworth arrived at the scene, he found the

gun on the hearthrug at Stowe's feet. He searched his pockets and found a letter in his trousers which read; 'This letter leaves to say that I am as innocent of anything they have said about me as a child. If ever I do anything rash it will be [names given] that have done it. I have one of the best wives in the world. God help her.' There was no other verdict that the jury could return apart from 'Suicide whilst of unsound mind.'

CHAPTER 5

Bringing the news to Axholme

The Epworth Bells - early beginnings

Foster Barnes, the founder of The Epworth Bells, was born in Londonderry in 1824. He came to Epworth in the early 1850s, having served an apprenticeship as a printer in Preston, to manage the Epworth branch of the printing business of William Caldicott, proprietor of the Gainsborough and Epworth Press and Lincolnshire and Nottinghamshire Advertiser (the paper would soon take on the new title of The Retford, Worksop, Isle of Axholme and Gainsborough News). Caldicott's publishing business was in Market Street, Gainsborough and the company employed seventeen men. William had firm ideas about how a newspaper operated and insisted his papers were run 'on independent lines, tied to no political party or religious denomination', being 'free to express itself for the good of the community in general while supporting worthwhile organisations and championing good causes'. At the top of each page was an inspirational quote, such as; Time is the best cure of everything, and; A rotten apple injures its companions.

Another newspaper circulating in the locality (and one which seems to have a significant influence on Foster Barnes) was the Epworth Herald and Isle of Axholme Advertiser. First published in December 1853, it came out on the first day of each month - priced 1d (or 2d if the newspaper carried a unique embossed postage stamp to pay the cost of mailing). The newspaper, published by William Read and Co. of Albion House Printing Works, Epworth, (founder of the Epworth Mechanics Institute and author and publisher of Read's, 'History of the Isle of Axholme; its manors and parishes, with biographical notices of eminent men)', carried news from all Isle towns and villages. Read's publication had agents in Bawtry, Burringham, Gainsborough, Doncaster, Messingham, Misterton, Misson, Scotter, Thorne and on the Steam Packets that served the Trentside villages between Hull and Gainsborough. The Herald claimed to be the first newspaper ever solely printed in the Isle of Axholme. It ran to eight pages and reported on local events and 'general intelligence with brevity and without prejudice or party bias'. In the words of the editor, it was a 'welcome messenger at the cottage of the labourer, the residence of the farmer and tradesman as well as the mansion of the more affluent'.

By 1855, the masthead of the newspaper changed to The Epworth Herald and General Advertiser for the Isle of Axholme, Thorne, Goole and Marshland. It would now come out every alternate Thursday, no doubt buoyed by its continuing success and the 'cordial cooperation of warm-hearted friends'. It was, however, a short-lived success as the Epworth Herald ceased publication in 1858.

At some point in the next ten years, Foster Barnes left Caldicott's to start his printing and stationer's business in Epworth's High Street. During this time, he married a Jane Ann Glew from Belton, and the couple had four children. Their first, Arthur, died on 5th February aged two weeks; their daughter, Elizabeth died aged four weeks and two days on 28th February 1860 and another son, also named Arthur, died on 19th December 1865. It must have been a painful time for Foster Barnes as, two months earlier, on 20th September 1865, after a severe illness, Barnes' wife, Jane died at the age of 43 years, leaving one surviving child - Joseph. Foster Barnes never remarried.

Based on his previous experience at Caldicots, his knowledge of other local newspapers, notably the Epworth Herald, and his Methodist faith, he began to consider publishing his own periodical. Described by an Epworth contemporary as a man 'beloved and respected by all who knew him', he committed his time to 'doing those little kindnesses which most of us leave undone or despise'. Another contemporary spoke of him as a man whose 'heart went out to all' someone whose 'heart was too large for his mind to be narrow'. An avowed teetotaller, Barnes was one of the founders of the Epworth Temperance Movement and a member of the Oddfellows Friendly Society, which by this time was the most extensive and affluent friendly society in the world, protecting workers and their families against illness, injury or death.

It was on Saturday 26th October 1872, almost twenty years after coming to live in Epworth, that Foster Barnes published his own newspaper - a one-side, single sheet, little bigger than the current B4 size. He called it Epworth Bells (there was no definitive article). Over the years there has been much speculation as to how Barnes came up with the name. Some believe he took the name from the custom of assembling residents by the ringing of church bells to disseminate essential announcements. Others liken it to the ringing of the town crier's handbell (Epworth's Town Crier's Bell, used until the late 19th century, can be found at the home of the Keith Cawthorne on Mowbray Street, a descendant of the last person to use it). Finally, some erroneously link the name to two lines from Alfred Lord Tennyson's poem, In Memoriam, that eventually formed part of the paper's masthead. Whatever the origin of the name, it was, and still is, the only newspaper in Britain to carry the supplementary title of 'Bells,' a unique accolade, given the Victorian propensity to come up with 'original' and often obscure names for their publications.

Surprisingly, the first Epworth Bells carried no news about Epworth or the Isle of Axholme. In addition to a piece of poetry, an idea Barnes took from the Epworth Herald, the report of a fire at Finningley and information on the price of corn in London and Wakefield markets filled the rest of the publication. It was, however, given away free with the other papers on sale. The second edition was little better, but it did carry a handwritten note from Foster Barnes stating that the next copy would 'have the markets etc. added to complete it'. True to his word, by the third edition, Barnes included details of prices from Epworth's Thursday Provision Market. The cost of butter was 1/6d per lb.; eggs 10 for 1/-; fowls 2/6d to 4/- with ducks priced at 5/- per couple.

Having established a tentative foothold in the weekly newspaper market, Barnes began expanding its scope. The edition for Saturday 23rd November carried a report on a severe storm in Scotland and an article updating news of Henry Morton Stanley's 'rescue' of David Livingstone. In it, he quoted Stanley prophesying Livingstone would arrive in London in eighteen months. It was a bizarre prediction as Stanley found Livingstone worn down by disease; so poorly that he died on 1st May 1873, a year and a half after he met with Stanley. He was right about one thing however, Livingstone did return to London for burial in Westminster Abbey, but the removal of his body took longer than the eighteen months he predicted!

The paper also carried its first report of a death, that of Laura Ridgill, aged one year eight months – no details or explanation, just a simple one-sentence statement. There was also a commitment to broadcast announcements, 'should the public wish to forward them for printing'.

From the outset, and for many subsequent years, it was the Bell family, who selected the poem which appeared each week in the Epworth Bells. Charles Bell, a chemical druggist, grocer and sub-postmaster in Church Street, also contributed stories to the newspaper. Later, their son, Sir Harold Idris Bell C.B. O.B.E. F.B.A. F. S.A D. Litt., born at Epworth on 2nd October 1879, took on the role. In 1897 he won a scholarship to Oriel College, Oxford, and graduated in Classics. He spent a year at the

Universities of Berlin and Halle studying Hellenistic History. In 1903 he took up an appointment as Assistant in the Department of Manuscripts at the British Museum. Much of Harold's working life centred around translating Romano-Egyptian manuscripts. He was awarded four honorary university Doctorates from Wales, Michigan, Brussels and Liverpool. Although he published many books and treatises and gave hundreds of lectures, he preferred to stay out of the limelight. Described as a 'spare figure with twinkling eyes and a kindly demeanour,' Harold became Keeper of the Department of Manuscripts at the British Museum from 1929 to his retirement in 1944. Two years later he received a knighthood. It seems Harold was a man of great charm and courtesy; someone who remained modest despite his high academic status. He had a lifelong interest in poetry, particularly that written in the Welsh language. Most, if not all, of the poems that appeared in the 'Bells' from 1900 to 1940 were products of Harold's research.

In the edition of 28th December 1872, the poem chosen by the family was the full version of Tennyson's 'Ring Out Wild Bells' from his elegy, In Memoriam. It was the first time the words; 'Ring out the old, ring in the new; Ring out the false, ring in the true' appeared in the Epworth Bells. It was an apt poem for a newspaper entitled 'Bells', and it must have resonated with Foster Barnes as he would have been aware of the accepted English custom of ringing church bells over midnight on New Year's Eve. At the first peal, bells rang muffled to signify the 'death' of the year past. With the muffles removed, the bright and cheering sounds that echoed across the land, heralded the 'birth' of a new time. The words gave Barnes the seeds of an idea, but they didn't find their way into the masthead - yet!

Over the next few weeks, the paper reported the murder of a policeman in Cardiff by a butcher named Jones; informed its readers about the origins of names for the days of the week and months of the year, and, contained anecdotes and amusing stories from around the world. There was even an advisory list of all British birds, from Avocet to Wryneck, that came under the Wild Birds Protection Act during the breeding season. There was still, however, little news about the local area though it was not that local news was hard to come by. Despite his request for advertisements, it took until Issue 15 for the Epworth Bells to publish one, a personal notice placed by Foster Barnes himself announcing the availability of Valentines Cards and Books from his printer's office.

The first item of what one could term, serious local news, appeared in the edition of 15th February 1873. It seems that for some time, locals had visited the Lawns Farm area to bring home lumps of coal that found their way to the surface. Picking up on this, a company from South Yorkshire began sinking a shaft to check on the viability of a coal mine (the unfolding story that ran in the Epworth Bells for several weeks). When news came that the company had found a thin seam at a depth of ninety yards; 'Amongst all classes there was thankfulness and joy, and a few flags were hoisted in honour of the event.' The news brought complaints from local sportsmen as the spot chosen for the shaft was in the corner of the cricket field (the club eventually decided to move to Thurlow Croft) but, the consensus expressed in the newspaper's reports was that; 'Epworth deserved success.' Sadly, the seam of coal was not sufficiently broad or deep enough for commercial exploitation, and the venture came to nothing.

During its fledgeling six months, in addition to Caldicott's Gainsborough News and Read's Epworth Herald, Foster Barnes' Epworth Bells had to compete with several other established newspapers for success. There was Thomas Beal's Epworth Weekly Herald, The Isle of Axholme Messenger, and, over in Crowle, Richard Wood's weekly publication, The Crowle Advertiser, and Tradesmen's Weekly Circular first published on 2nd December

1871. Wood's office was on the corner of the High Street and what is now Printing Office Lane. As it, too, settled on a readership, the next six years would see the newspaper retitled, the Crowle, Isle of Axholme, and Marshland Advertiser, and Tradesmen's Weekly, and The Isle of Axholme, Marshland, and Crowle Advertiser. Woods finally settled on the name it would carry from 1877 to 1986 – the Crowle Advertiser and Isle of Axholme News. The newspaper also sold for a halfpenny. Over the years, while many of the journals mentioned above would cease publication, like the Epworth Bells, the Advertiser would stand the test of time in the Axholme area. It was a completely separate title until the Second World War when it became a slip edition of the Epworth Bells. From 1974, however, it became virtually the same newspaper but with a different masthead. It was absorbed into the Epworth Bells altogether in January 1987 under the title, The Epworth Bells & Crowle Advertiser.

A mirror for Axholme life

Issue 26 of Barnes' newspaper, printed for sale on 19th April 1873, was a landmark publication. It was the first one to be entitled The Epworth Bells with the subheading of The Isle of Axholme Messenger. It signalled Foster Barnes' intention to widen his reporting of local events and heralded in a format that would serve the newspaper well for the next eighty years. Some 'purists' argued, and no doubt will continue to do so, that this is a more appropriate date for the founding of the Epworth Bells, as this was the date the paper came out under this title. There is some merit to the argument, but the fact that Foster Barnes did not change the volume number and carried on with a sequential issue shows that, for him, it was merely a continuation of the endeavour he started in October 1872.

True to his principles to make the newspaper a community

resource, there would be no sensational headlines on the front page. He determined to report news factually, free of bias or favour. There would be no editorial commentaries and no attempt to sway opinion; he would leave it for his readers to form their own judgements. In line with convention, in what became described by some as a 'wall of text,' he devoted the front page to informative columns of advertisements (inserted for a reasonable fee), market prices, public meetings, births, deaths and marriages. In this way, by appealing to an increasingly affluent middle-class seeking a variety of new products, Barnes tapped into the way local, and national newspapers made a profit. By advertising locally, manufacturers tried a more direct method to develop nationally known brand names. Even though Axholme was still a remote and isolated place, adverts for the latest London fashions featured in the pages of his regional newspaper.

To modern eyes, this 'wall of text' approach may seem little more than a confusing riddle of small print, with numerous columns and a lack of the kind of eye-catching headings seen today. Those well versed in the style would recognise it as being modelled on the Times, a newspaper that since its inception had spread its front page to six columns. The Western Mail went even further, managing to squeeze an incredible ten columns into its front page. To this end Foster Barnes' Epworth Bells copied these formats but, taking the substance of the Epworth Herald, he settled on three columns. To accommodate this extra information, Barnes' paper began its first move towards a 'Berliner' format, one that was slightly shorter and narrower than the broadsheet form used by several national dailies. It was a format he would use for the next twenty years.

Even allowing for the increase in size and an increasing number of readers, Barnes decided that the Epworth Bells would remain a free supplement with other local and national Saturday papers. There was, however, one subtle change. Those who wished to have just the newspaper could buy it separately for the price of one halfpenny. Although many did not realise it at the time, this was Barnes' first move to secure the future of the Epworth Bells as an independent and profitable enterprise.

By now the newspaper was well on the way to becoming a mirror of life in Axholme. Locals soon turned to it for an objective and impartial understanding of local news and a fair assessment of what was to come. For some time, publicans had seen the attraction of providing at least one newspaper for their customers. So it was that landlords of local hostelries such as The Red Lion and The King's Head included copies of the Epworth Bells in spaces set aside in their establishments for newspaper reading. For many of Axholme's working-class, the pub was an attractive, accessible and cheap reading place; it offered greater comfort than their cold and dimly lit cottages. Even those who failed to grasp the skill of reading could find corners where sections of the newspaper were being read aloud and discussed. This ability helped them keep abreast of local news without exposing their illiteracy. Those who preferred more temperate surroundings, however, could find copies at The Mechanics' Institute.

The Isle of Axholme may have been a remote and isolated place, but, like all communities, it had an incredibly efficient 'bush telegraph.' Some said that the people of Epworth knew what happened in Belton/Haxey/Crowle etc. before most of the population of those towns and villages. As with all mouth-to-mouth news, however, constant repetition often 'coloured' the incident as people added their interpretations, or omitted basic facts, to suit their agenda. In those early days, word soon got around that if you wanted the facts you could 'trust the Bells'. Sadly, it is not a statement that would hold for the whole of the paper's history!

Opening up a readership

In August 1873, Barnes published an article that offered sound advice to readers such as the importance of making a will, believing that such remarks 'kindly meant [would] be kindly received and [would] not be in vain'. He went on to explain that, 'if they are only the means of stirring up someone to duty in this matter, if only a wife or child, or friend, or good object be thus saved from disaster, we will not have written in vain'.

Two months later, the newspaper ceased to be a 'free' publication; no longer would it be an insert to other newspapers bought on the day. It had found its feet and was now a broadsheet in its own right. So much so that it began to carry more wide-ranging advertisements. One such announced that John Robinson, an Auctioneer from Haxey, was proud to be the agent for those seeking to book a passage to New York at a fee of £6 6s.

After inviting reader participation, on 22nd November the Epworth Bells published its first 'letters to the editor' the following week. The first letter to appear complained about people's 'bad order' at funerals, where mourners 'rushed to the graveside trampling on the grass, making noises and displaying a want of reverence'. The author, seeking anonymity from the outset, signed their self 'A. Sympathiser'. The second letter condemned the 'slumbering trade' in Epworth, likening it to Rip van Winkle, who after sleeping for twenty years, woke later to find nothing had changed. The author's main gripe was that Epworth lacked something, anything, to increase trade and prosperity. He suggested the formation of a limited company for the manufacture of some desirable commodity to revitalise the local community, such as happened with the boot and shoe industry in Northampton. What the writer failed to factor into his argument was that Northampton's population, being well served by the L&NWR, was at least twenty times that of Epworth's.

Perhaps the most telling letter of the time came from a resident reflecting on the sanitary arrangements in Epworth. His proposal to remedy the stench traps in the yards that brought mortality to the town, particularly amongst children, was to lay an 18-inch drain through the town with 12-inch branches at the short streets. The letter adds that 'whenever epidemic breaks out in Epworth, it spreads through the town, selecting its victims indiscriminately amongst rich and poor. I could name several yards in the town where the ash pits, piggeries and wells for domestic use are in close proximity to each other, which of course is highly dangerous; for the drainage of the former under such circumstances is certain to percolate through to the soil of the latter. At present, the whole of the sewage system runs into cesspools and ashpits, and the foul gasses generated in these places must find their way into the air, and thus become dangerous to the inhabitants. It is a fact that about seven years ago, from 12 to 15 children died at Epworth in a very short space of time and there is very little doubt that the unsatisfactory sanitary state of the town had much to do with it. The death of 15 children in a place of say 2000 inhabitants must be considered a very high death rate. Now nature has given Epworth every facility for an effectual system of drainage upon easy terms; indeed, nothing could be more easy to drain, as from the top of Epworth to the bottom, there is a gradual fall to land having sandy subsoil'. It was a letter far in advance of its time as it would take another fifty years before Epworth got its underground drainage system.

As his newspaper grew, so did Foster Barnes' mini-empire. Several of the books he sold to his customers can still be found in Epworth Mechanics' Institute. These include, Norah the Flower Girl, Blackie's Comprehensive School Geography Series and A Casket of Gems, - an anthology of famous poems. All the books carry Barnes' embossed stamp on the inner leaf. Not only did he undertake a range of printing jobs, but he became the local agent for an extensive cleaning and drying business that included hearthrugs, doormats, table covers, curtains, bed hangings and counterpanes. His most arresting advertisement, however, was for the French Cleaning of ladies' and girls' dresses and men and boys' clothing – a process invented by Frenchman Jean Baptiste Jolly. Today we know this process as dry cleaning.

Over the next few years, as his sphere of influence increased, Foster Barnes gradually widened the scope of his newspaper. 1874 saw a report in his newspaper recording the firing of barrels of tar in Epworth Market Place to celebrate the result of the General Election. The year also saw the first detailed cricket scores squeezed in amongst other local stories. Some made for poor reading, however, as several teams rarely exceeded totals of fifty runs; indeed, some struggled to make even twenty five! The year also saw the advent of small illustrations that added interest and inducement to some of the advertisements. On Christmas Eve 1874 the Epworth Bells office delivered its first Christmas greeting. In a measured salutation, there was a desire for a 'Christmas like ones of olden time [where] the feathery snow has fallen fast, and a thick white mantle covers [the land]'. Thoughts turned to the: 'Thousands of persons who at this moment are treading the white carpet on their homeward way, and they will soon meet those loved ones whom they have not met for many a day. The warm and friendly greeting, the blazing fire, and all the good things of Christmas combine to give a distinguishing charm to the eldest of the cold days of winter. But there are others to whom it will be a lonely Christmas. Their loved ones are gone, and to them, Christmas brings only memories of departed joys. To others, it is of want and affliction. Hence, while it is the season of joy, it is also a time for stirring up the noble heaven-born sympathy of humanity for those who mourn. To those who possess much, and to those who have little, and to all our readers, we wish A Merry Christmas.' It was a homage to the time but one that would not be out of place in our 21st century world.

1877 – The end of the Bells?

In December 1877 Foster Barnes announced that 'the publication of The Epworth Bells is discontinued for the present'. One can only speculate as to the reason, for there was no qualifying explanation. Perhaps Barnes had health problems; maybe he just wanted a break from the rigours of producing his newspaper; perhaps his other commercial commitments required more of his time. Whatever the cause, he did not stop publishing, however, because, for almost five months, he printed a news sheet he called, The Epworth Weekly Announcement. It was a single-sided, hymn-sheet sized paper of adverts and notices. There is a clue in issue 14 of the 'Announcement' that may throw some light on the reason Foster Barnes halted the publication of the Epworth Bells. At the very top is an advert, placed by Barnes himself, requiring the services of 'an intelligent, well-educated youth of good character to train as an apprentice printer'. Perhaps, during those months when he ceased publishing the Epworth Bells, Barnes, with an eye to the future, was taking stock. His newspaper was at a crossroads; it was either expand or abandon the enterprise. After twenty publications of The Epworth Weekly Announcement, he had come to a decision – the Bells would return!

In the top right corner of the masthead, Barnes placed the now familiar lines from Tennyson's 'Ring out the old'. He firmed up his layout further by returning to a front page of adverts. Still, the most significant change was the move to provide a newspaper of four pages, allowing more room for articles, reports, anecdotes and advertisements. Barnes introduced his relaunched newspaper with the statement; 'Five months have rolled away since we last had the pleasure of addressing our readers through the medium of The Epworth Bells. Since then Christmas and New Year's Day and the months of winter have come and gone, and now in the bright month of May, the month of springing flowers, we enter on the second issue of our little messenger, in the sincere hope that it may be a useful visitor in any home.'

Barnes and Breeze

In mid-June 1896 Foster Barnes placed one of his last advertisements in the newspaper he had established. He wished to announce that he had a fine assortment of fans, crinkled paper, in assorted colours; vases, ladies' companion purses, and other fancy articles, suitable for presents. By late July, however, it was with great sadness he informed his friends and his readership that he had disposed of his Old-Established business to Messrs. David Breeze & Son. He was anxious to assure every one of his complete confidence in the Breeze family to carry on publishing the Epworth Bells in the manner established over his twenty-four years in charge.

For their part Breeze and Sons '[begged] to inform [readers] that we have purchased the proprietorship of The Epworth Bells and the Printing and Stationery and Newspaper Business, also the Agencies etc. connected therewith which for the past years have been carried on by Mr. Foster Barnes. We have arranged that Mr. Barnes shall continue to edit The Epworth Bells and this fact will, we doubt not, ensure your continued interest in the paper. Having had practical experience in every department of the business, we hope, with prompt attention to all orders with which you may favour us, to give such satisfaction with our work, despatch and charges as to secure the continued patronage of all Mr. Barnes customers and others. We respectfully and earnestly solicit the favour of your patronage'.

The new publishing company traded under the name Barnes and Breeze. Whether by placing the name of the founder first was a clever marketing ploy to ensure continued support as suggested by some is debatable. It seems more likely that this was part of the contract, with Foster Barnes retaining a significant stake in the business. Perhaps it was just a sympathetic means of edging him towards retirement. Whatever the reason, the two names became cemented in Axholme history; so much so that even today, the more senior residents of the town refer to the old printing works and shop as Barnes and Breeze.

What the notice published by David Breeze did not state, however, was that he had little experience of the world of printing and publishing. He arrived in Epworth from Burslem, where for thirty years he was in the employ of Messrs. Edge, Malkin and Co., manufacturers of earthenware. Here, an unfortunate accident with a piece of machinery, saw him lose his left hand and although he carried on in a less active, but more responsible role, the loss of his hand took the sunshine out of his life. True to his Wesleyan principles, and to show his appreciation for the care he received at Haywood Hospital in Burslem, he set about collecting money to purchase a piano for the hospital so that music might cheer its sorrowing inmates in time to come. It was for this, and his devout Wesleyan ministry, that many remembered his time in Burslem. Many residents of Epworth found David's presence in the pulpit an inspiration, someone who was always prepared to look for the good rather than find fault. Others saw him as 'a fine soul lodging in a frail tent'. However, some found it hard to reconcile David Breeze's commitment to the church alongside what, for many, was an abrupt and at times discourteous manner.

To any but the eagle-eyed, the change to the masthead on the edition of 15th August passed almost unnoticed. The new cartouche signalled this as the first newspaper published by Barnes and Breeze, Epworth. In all other respects, the paper remained the same mix of local news, the odd story from a national newspaper and the usual round of advertisements and notices. What did disappear (for a while at least) as Foster Barnes' health began to fail, were the amusing stories and anecdotes he used to fill the pages of his publication. To those in later years who complained that the newspaper was full of advertisements, one glance at the Barnes and Breeze newspaper would surely be enough to disabuse them of that opinion. In a newspaper that ran to twelve columns over four pages, the Epworth Bells carried ten and half-columns of adverts and notices. Confirmation if needed that the Epworth Bells was, from the outset, a vehicle to publicise and broadcast businesses as much as a meaningful agent bringing community cohesion through the dissemination of news.

At 4.40 a.m. on Tuesday, 5th July 1898, aged 74, Foster Barnes died. It was not unexpected; his health had deteriorated considerably over several weeks. Not only did the district lose a renowned printer but also a revered local Methodist preacher. He was a founder member of the Epworth Temperance Movement and a prime mover in establishing the Temperance Hall as a centre for the group's activities. Foster Barnes' quiet influence had endeared him to all. Practical, down to earth and mindful of his audience, he'd developed his newspaper in his own image. Unashamedly independent, he was unmoved by pride, opinion or greed for power. His journalistic style was one of humility, and he invariably reported with courtesy and integrity, ever mindful of his aim to educate and inform.

And yet, despite his undoubted popularity in the district, the report of his death hardly filled one column of his beloved publication. No letters extolling his virtues or comments and anecdotes came from colleagues as one would expect for a man who had many friends and few enemies. The report of his death, however, did end with a telling and poignant sentence. It read: 'Today the Epworth Bells ring out no merry marriage peal but the solemn knell to a dear one departing.'

Although the newspaper appears to have made little of his death on Friday 8th July, the day of his funeral, residents closed their blinds, and nearly all tradespeople halted work at their shops and offices. Carried from the Methodist Chapel by associate members of the Oddfellows in a pitch pine coffin, the long procession, with his son to the fore, joined a large gathering at his resting place in Epworth Cemetery. The brass plate on his coffin carried the simple message - Foster Barnes aged 74, 1889.

As part of his epitaph, one of his closest colleagues asked for the following to be published: -

He was long-suffering, kind; he envied not;
He was not boastful, nor with pride up-blown;
In his behaviour no unseemly blot
E'er shewed. He did not seek his own
He thought no evil, nor in wrath soon moved;
Nor in sins triumph nor the sinners fall
Did he rejoice, but in truth he loved;
Enduring, hoping, and believing all.
There, where the simple and sincere have peace,
What shall our wisdom or our gifts avail?
'Tis charity alone that shall not cease,
Nor of their heritage her children fail.

To commemorate his work in Epworth, residents began a house-to-house collection to raise money to buy a Handsome Cab for the town. Reverend Greaves and Arthur Maw each gave 10/-. Eventually, however, the residents settled on three 'Tribute Seats.' One would be placed on the crest of Belgarthorne Hill (this seat has now been removed to the Beltoft Road end of Church Lane), another opposite Epworth Cemetery (again removed to sit on the border of Epworth and Haxey) and the third outside Lawns' Farm (long since missing). It was quite an apt proposal as some years earlier, Barnes had campaigned for several wayside seats to be erected (he suggested twelve places in the parish for these). He wrote; 'On these seats, the traveller might sit down as he passes on his way: here our bread-winners – our working men and women, might have a brief rest on their days of hard labour in the fields. And even to our gentry, a plain seat on the roadside would be a luxury not to be despised. For at Epworth our Fields are our Parks – and our Highways are our places of public resort, and so in our journeys of pleasure or of toil how pleasant would it be to have a seat on the highway!'

For his memorial seats, subscribers rejected wood as not being 'durable enough to withstand attention from boys and their penknives' and opted for wrought iron. When the money came in, there were many donations from Epworth folk, but others came from as far afield as Croydon, Manchester, Southampton and Leeds. From his home in Keswick, Joseph, Foster Barnes' son contributed ten shillings. The seats, made by Aldams of Misterton cost £4 each, excluding painting and fitting. They provided welcome relief for those making the journeys to West Butterwick, Belton and Haxey by foot. It seems the seats were not robust enough to withstand the worst the youths of the town could throw at them, however, as not long after the Epworth Bells reported one of the seats had been damaged by some 'evil disposed individual.'

The Bells Almanack (sic)

One major innovation David Breeze introduced to his printing business was the publication of The Epworth Bells' Almanack (sic). For years under Foster Barnes, the company had been a distributor for the most widely read almanac of all time – The Old Moore's Almanac, but Breeze took the decision to adapt this style to a more local and provincial audience. He advertised his publication as an 'amusing and instructive supplement to the year ahead'. The one penny publication, 'a price in the reach of everyone', began by listing all the residents of Epworth and then arranged these according to trade and occupation. To fund this, the publication relied on a plethora of advertisements, but what followed was handy information for farmers and rural dwellers alike. There were moon and tide times, predictions of weather patterns, dates advising farmers of the best time to plant their crops, and other tabular data relating to the calendar. Available from the office or other local agents, it also included a copy of 'A Pilgrimage to Epworth' by Arthur Bennett. Breeze's Almanack was a more pragmatic version than many of the time and studiously avoided some of the more idiosyncratic predictions made by its rivals. Taking evidence from the Almanack, at the turn of the century, Epworth had no less than four coal merchants, six butchers, six boot and shoemakers, seven joiners, twelve grocers and fifteen drapers/dressmakers. It seems remarkable that a town of fewer than three thousand inhabitants could support so many businesses of a similar type.

Lacking the gift of foresight, no blame could be attached to the individual who posted their wish for a 'Happy and Prosperous New Year' in the late December issue of 1913. No one could have predicted the sheer horror of what 1914 would bring. No one that is, unless one put their faith in 'Old Moore's Almanack'. For the price of 1d residents of the Isle could have read that August would begin under 'rather unfortunate circumstances', with the prospect of 'troubles abroad'. Had they followed this through and read the predictions for December they would have found the Almanac prophesied 1914 would be 'an eventful year, not of a reassuring nature'!

JUST PUBLISHED.
THE BEST LOCAL ANNUAL.
The " EPWORTH BELLS " ALMANACK
ONE PENNY. GET A COPY TO-DAY
Of all *Bell's* agents, or by post 2½d.

Advert for the Almanack.

Death of David Breeze

In December 1902, black lines separated the columns of the Epworth Bells. They commemorated the death of the owner, David Breeze, at the age of fifty-nine. From the outset, he had embraced Foster Barnes' philosophy of running a newspaper that 'while the cost is often forgotten, the quality is remembered forever'. At his funeral, in quite a sad adjunct, one mourner expressed a desire that his 'new sphere and occupation [would be] infinitely more congenial than the happiest he ever found on this terrestrial globe'. Twelve months later, his wife, who had been in failing health for quite some time, died. The couple left three daughters and two sons with William Breeze, their eldest son becoming the chief proprietor of the business.

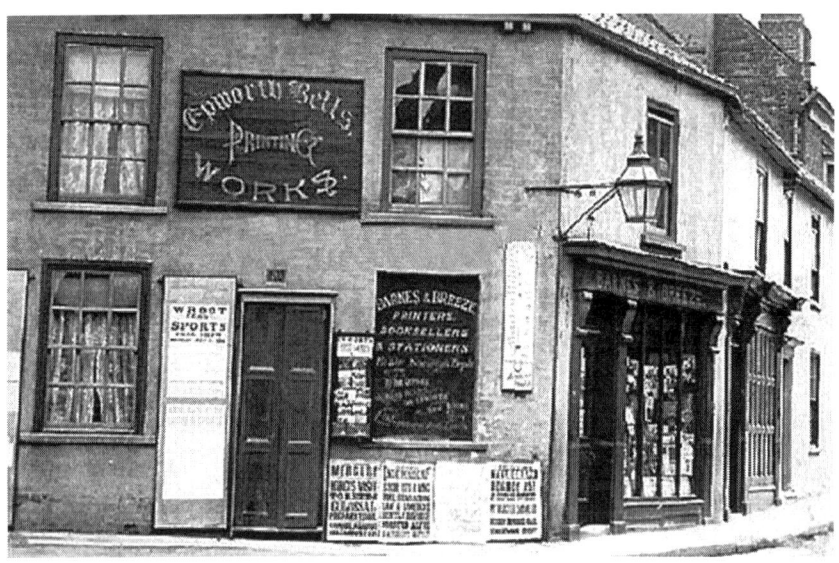

The Epworth Bells printing works

CHAPTER 6

Some people

The clockmakers of Epworth

Kelly's Directory of 1922 tells us that three clock and watchmakers were working in Epworth – Henry Marriot, Charles Robert Newbitt (his son, Alf, is on the town's Roll of Honour, having been killed at the Somme in 1916) and William Smith. But we have to go back to the mid-1700s to find the 'Golden Age' of Epworth's clockmakers.

Born in 1704 to Quaker parents Epworth man Benjamin Huntsman began his apprenticeship with an established Epworth clockmaker at the age of 14. Talented and inventive from the outset, he showed an aptitude for things mechanical. In the town, he fixed all things from locks to clocks to tools and spit roasters.

Face of a Thomas Kilham Longcase Clock.

He began his own clock making business, and he would probably have continued in this occupation had fate not taken a hand (more of that another time). Today Huntsman's long-case clocks are collectors' items and exchange hands for thousands of pounds.

The next clockmaker to gain a deserved reputation was Thomas Kilham, brother of Alexander who founded the Methodist New Connexion. Working from the mid-18th century into the 19th, Thomas produced long-case clocks of superb quality. He used oak for the case with mahogany inlays for his 8-day painted dial movements. Today, some local people still have Huntsman and Kilham clocks in their hallways and front rooms.

Taking up the mantle from 1826 to 1856 came Robert Pitts who worked on Church Street (later included in Market Place). He too specialised in Georgian long-case clocks with 30-hour to

Face of a Robert Pitts Longcase Clock.

8-day movements. Above the clock face, Pitts often painted an arch showing Britannia. The Pagoda pediment he used was typical of Lincolnshire Clocks of the time. John, one of his sons, was apprenticed to Charles Watson of Pepper Lane, Coventry (a city noted for its clockmaking industry) for 7 years. A disagreement saw John return to Epworth to work with his father. Clocks by Pitts of Epworth are in high demand on the antique circuit. Robert died in 1875 and is buried in Epworth Churchyard. One of Pitts' clocks can be seen at Normanby Hall; another is in Gainsborough Old Hall.

The final family in this illustrious line of 18th and 19th/early 20th century Epworth timepiece makers is the Clark family; Thomas (who worked in High Street) and Charles (on Belton Road). They are listed as farmers of 17 acres, and watchmakers and their clocks sell today for four-figure prices.

The cycle makers and sellers of Axholme

In June 1899, Richard Moody, described as a hale and hearty old gentleman, from East Butterwick, was something of ardent cyclist. A strict teetotaller, on one occasion at the age of 70, he accomplished a journey of 117 miles in one day. Having left East Butterwick about 4 a.m. he encountered some very tedious up-hill riding. It was very hot, the roads were dusty, and there was no wind, but The Crowle Advertiser reported Moody arrived at his destination as 'fresh as a daisy.' Apparently, he accomplished the feat thanks to several cups of his favourite beverage. It was the heyday of the bicycle, a two-wheel implement that had a liberating impact on the lives of both men and women. It empowered them with a freedom of movement which their ancestors could only have dreamed. For women, in particular, the bicycle allowed them to travel on their own; it gave them greater scope to meet with their friends away from the drudgery of home; to work beyond their immediate environs and join groups of like-minded individuals. At fairs and commemorative events, members of cycling clubs turned out in their cycling clothes, often on bicycles decorated with flowers, ribbons and banners. Most villages in the Isle had their own cycling clubs, but it was the one in Crowle that had by far the highest number of members. Several took part in fancy dress parades judged by local worthies. The meeting place in Crowle was the Market Place, usually at or around 5 p.m. In one fancy dress parade first prize went to Miss Lily Pacey, who was attired prettily as a schoolgirl, and the second to Miss Nellie Parkin, whose costume, which represented Harvest was much admired. Mr A Wheatley was awarded first prize in the Gentleman's Class, whose character represented 'The Red Rider'.

However, it was not all fun and frolics in the world of cycling. When Arthur Pettit, of West Butterwick, riding on the road to Kelfield, passed a police carriage at great speed, without giving an alarm, he set up a high-speed pursuit along the banks of the River Trent. When he appeared in court, the police thought they had a good case against him, and were astounded when the magistrates concluded there was no case to answer. Later, 'An Old Cyclist' wrote to complain about the dangers posed to cyclists by wagons and carts. The writer commented on several instances that happened during the past week, 'where cyclists have wanted to pass a wagon, and have rung their bells repeatedly and also shouted, but without avail'. He went on to say that 'when a cyclist does not observe the rule of the road or does not ring his bell when passing pedestrians or conveyances, an outcry is soon made, but the cyclist has to put up with many little annoyances and can get no redress. If cyclists will make a point of reporting such cases to the proper authorities, it will greatly assist in stopping this much complained of nuisance'.

Across the Isle, there was at least one cycle maker in the largest settlements along with several cycle distributors. Walster

Brothers of Epworth proudly advertised that their 'Isle Cycle' had won eight out of the ten races at Crowle Show. A unique selling point was their claim that they could build individual 'made-to-measure' machines for those over fourteen stones! The brothers, James and Edward, built quality machines and for many years their workmanship and reliability were held in high esteem. In Belton, the Axe family sold their 'popular' ladies' cycles for £6 10s, five shillings more than the machine for men! The price of the 'high class' model was two pounds extra for both sexes. Baileys of Epworth sold The Rudge Bicycle, while Brunyees of Crowle offered 'The Speedwell' for £4 10/- (again the ladies' model was 5s extra). F. J. Long of Crowle advised readers that for everything in the cycle and motor line they should; 'Go to the Cycle and Motor Man' where 'the best is cheapest'. Long's advertisement has the distinction of being the first to mention motor car sales in Axholme. Sometime later, all three of the above businesses, along with Clarks of Owston Ferry, stocked the Raleigh bicycle. Fitted with Dunlop tyres and a three-speed Sturmey-Archer gear ratio, it was, to quote the Epworth Bells' advertisement, 'as near perfection as human ingenuity can attain' for, 'of all the bikes that ride so sweet, none can beat the Raleigh'.

The state of those roads!

Before the year 1800, there was no reliable road network across or along the Isle. Stone for road making in the Isle came at a high price and much it had to be transported down the Trent by boat from Spurn Point. As a consequence, many of the 'highways' were left 'in a state of nature, the result being that, except in very dry weather, it was almost impossible to use them'. It forced those whose focus was on expanding their agricultural business to join together to come up with a cheap solution – they laid narrow causeways of Yorkshire flagstones from Garthorpe to Gainsborough and at all points in between. These created raised causeways, one Yorkshire flagstone wide that linked one village to another. Along these, packhorses carried goods to be sold or traded. This convenience led to an unwritten rule that 'whosoever should meet a laden horse along the way should step off, into the slush if needs be to let the animal proceed at ease'. Sufficient for pedestrians, men and women on horseback, and leaders of packhorses, they remained useless for carts and carriages! In wet conditions, drivers of farm carts would pick their own way through the morass; the result left the highways churned up even more.

The 'improvements' may have satisfied many of the residents of Axholme but visitors saw things differently. Dr. Adam Clarke, a noted preacher and theologian on his journey home from Epworth in 1821, wrote of the experience - 'We had no road for upwards of forty miles, but travelled through fields of corn, wheat, rye, potatoes, barley, and turnips, often crushing them under our wheels. In all my travels, I never saw anything like this: I feared we were trespassing, but the drivers assured us there was no other road.' It was an accurate if damning description.

A Mr. Peacock, describing a ride with his father from Beltoft to Epworth in 1858 concluded that had there been no flagged pathway, the journey 'would have been unsafe to venture.'

When, on 21st May 1916 King George V, performed the opening ceremony of a new bridge over the River Trent at Keadby, the hope was that this would help 'open up the Isle' and bring profound change to the network of roads.

The new replaced a swing bridge built by the South Yorkshire Railway Co. in 1866. Alderman Stephenson of Althorpe noted with pleasure the absence of drunkenness amongst the workers employed in its construction. He believed there to have been only one case directly traceable to the site. He was sure the absence of rowdyism showed a significant improvement in the morality of the

Keadby Bridge soon after its construction.

navvies, something that would benefit them in later life.

The bridge worked on the Scherzer 'rolling lift' principle and would carry both road and rail traffic across the river. Those responsible for its construction claimed it the most substantial lifting bridge in Europe. Two 115 horse powered motors, counter-weighted by lattice framed girders to add strength, powered the lifting span. The angle of maximum elevation, when fully opened, was 82 degrees to the vertical; this position being achieved in less than two minutes. To prevent too rapid a descent, the bridge came down on a pneumatic buffer that lowered it to its final resting position. It brought the roads leading to and from the bridge into sharper focus and led to some severe criticism. Some locals even questioned the use of the bridge, calling it a marooned curiosity and a museum specimen, served by roads that were 'so utterly vile of surface that a Ford van would jibe at them.'

A popular cycling and motoring journalist, describing a journey through part of the Isle commented on the terrible roads, particularly the misuse of tar upon them. He reported the 'road' from Keadby to Crowle as 'the most horrible road I have found in the land. Not by any torture of euphemism could it be called a road. After thudding and bumping for a mile or so, we came where the thing had been recently tar-painted and spread with fine gravel and chips. To treat a ruined road in that way is to waste tar, gravel and time. If you are forced to ride into a deep hole and out again is it made [better] by lining the sides with tar and chips? It took me exactly half-an-hour with a heavy pocket-knife to scrape [the tar] from our four tyres, and there seemed to be about 2 lbs. of resultant debris ...... my deepest sympathy to all road-users in the Isle of Axholme.'

It was, however, a proposal by Haxey Parish Council to 'interfere with the Green Hill, in the interests of traffic convenience' that drew acrimony and outrage from the residents. One solution put forward to combat 'careless driving' that saw the brick wall enclosing the green being knocked down continually, was to take away some of the green to widen the road. It did not play well, especially with those living close to the green! Several made their feelings known at a public meeting. One resident bemoaned the fact that 'in the South of England the benefits of attractive settings are cherished and cared-for; while in the North they are not appreciated until it is too late'.

A suffragette visits the Isle

Perhaps the most telling report in the Epworth Bells that highlighted the 'advancement of women' came with news of a visit to Epworth by Miss Adela Pankhurst, 'a member of the family now so well known for its activity in the cause of Votes for Women'. Targeted by the police throughout her period fighting for the cause, Adela was seen as a high-profile activist and her appearance at Epworth was something of a coup for the town. Recognised as the most courteous of the Pankhurst 'clan', like the others she was not averse to using violent means. Having disrupted a meeting attended by

Winston Churchill, she had been arrested just months before she arrived in Epworth for slapping a policeman trying to evict her from a building. Quite understandably there was unease in the area over the visit, and to counter any 'antagonistic behaviour' several constables were drafted in from surrounding villages. Due to arrive from Doncaster where 'disgraceful scenes marked [her] first meeting', it seems, 'the cause so far [had] very few enthusiastic adherents in the Isle of Axholme'. At the time of writing, there was uncertainty over whether Miss Pankhurst would speak indoors or in the open air as she had done in Doncaster.

On the night of the meeting, Adela spoke in the Imperial Hall. The Epworth Bells reports there 'was not a single interruption during her address, and the lady had her hearers closely attentive and deeply interested from start to finish. Of course, every precaution had been taken to ensure the meeting should be more orderly than some which the suffragettes have experienced in other towns. Boys were not admitted, and the "mere man" had to part with 6d. at the door. A portly man in blue was stationed at the entrance, and the doors were locked when the meeting had commenced. At 7.30 p.m. the hall was about half full, but there was not more than half-a-dozen men present until some five minutes later, when quite a procession of them came in, to the evident delight of the ladies on the platform, for though they desired above all to enthuse the fair sex they also desired to capture the sympathy of the sterner ones'. By the time the speeches began, 'the assembly numbered about 400'.

Miss Pankhurst reminded the audience that for several years her organisation had been working 'on orderly and constitutional lines to get their claim for a vote recognised in Parliament'. So far, they had not been successful and were now forced to resort to militant suffrage in their determined fight to correct this unfairness. Miss Pankhurst explained that 'they had laid aside party feeling and would fight whatever Government was in power.' She reassured those present that getting the vote would not see women 'lose their beautiful womanly qualities or forfeit the chivalry of men. Why should the possession of the vote make them lose these qualities? And were men always chivalrous?'

Miss Pankhurst went on to refer to the 'comparatively easy time all men have today'. By the time she left the area, 'this lady with the small but energetic frame which never rested for a moment while she was speaking, with an exhaustless torrent of speech, and a homely gift of humorous expression, made herself thoroughly popular with her motley audience, and many who had come to curse remained to bless'.

An old fox

On Saturday 4th February 1911 the Epworth Bells came up with one of its snappiest headlines to date. Under the title 'Robbers in the Roost - an "Old Fox" caught', it told the tale of Miss Standring's missing fowls. On Thursday 26th January, the good lady fastened her hens in an outhouse at about 6 p.m. After going to release them the following morning, she noticed some feathers lying around which aroused her suspicions. After counting the creatures, she calculated there were six missing. Having informed the police of her missing birds, she received a visit from P.C. Knipe who asked her for a description of the hens! With their descriptions firmly logged in his pocketbook, P.C. Knipe went to see the henhouse. In the mud, he saw two sets of footprints and traced them to the home of Charles Merrills in Scawcett Lane. After waiting for the arrival of P.C. Baker, the pair approached the house and spoke to Mrs. Merrills. She confirmed that her husband was out, so the officers entered the house and began a search. In the kitchen, they found the heads and feet of six hens wrapped up and thrown among some old paper in a corner. When they asked

Mrs. Merrills where the other parts of the hens were, she went to a cupboard and took out three dressed fowls. After questioning her further, she told the officers two hens had been sent to Balby, where her mother-in-law lived. When asked where the sixth bird was, she went to a cupboard and came back with the remnants of a bird eaten that day! The officers left with the heads and feet and took them to Mrs. Strandring, whose tearful acknowledgement confirmed them as the ones taken from her hen house. Returning to the Merrill's house, the constables arrested Mr. Merrill and his workmate George Gathercole of Belton. At their trial, Merrills and Gathercole (described as an 'Old Fox') pleaded guilty. It was Gathercole's twenty-sixth offence, and his sentence of three month's hard labour reflected this. It was Merrills' first appearance in court, and he received a month's hard labour. Mrs. Merrills testified that her husband had gone out on the night in question and come home drunk. Nothing was said about the fowls until he produced them the next morning. When she began dressing them, she noticed their necks had been broken. She did not dare ask where the fowls had come from as she knew Gathercole would tell her to mind her own business. As it was her first offence, the judge ordered Mrs. Merrill to pay a fine of 10/-.

Early morning sprinters and an odd challenge
In another amusing report under the title 'Early Morning Sprinters', the paper gave an account of a race to settle an argument between a Newland farmer and a well-known potato merchant. Apparently, each claimed to be the faster runner, so to resolve the dispute, the pair agreed to a race. One Friday morning, at six a.m. residents close by the Free School field, awoke to the sounds of loud talking and cries of encouragement from those who had assembled to witness the race. The Epworth Bells goes on; 'It could not be said that either of the runners was in the pink of condition - a month's

strict diet and training would have been necessary to reduce the rotund form of either to sprinting weight. Having stripped off his coat, the potato merchant toed the mark, anxious to be off, and appeared to be pretty confident of winning. The farmer divested himself of coat, vest and boots, not minding the wetting of his stockings on the damp grass, so keen was he of being first at the winning post. As the excitement increased, the starter gave the signal to go. Both men got off the mark well, but it was soon evident that the warp-lander was out-classed, and the potato merchant was easily first, winning by a good margin. This early disturbance appeared to be advantageous to at least one gentleman residing in the neighbourhood, who turned out and cut his lawn before breakfast'.

From the time of Foster Barnes, the Epworth Bells had always been a newspaper that revelled in quirky stories about Axholme, none more so than a report in the mid-1920s concerning a farmer from Althorpe, Mr. Reginald J. Stephenson. Reginald accepted a challenge from Mr. George Cummings, the self-styled World Professional Walking Champion, to see who would arrive at York from London first. Reginald would travel on horseback 'and may trot or gallop as he pleases', while Cummings, who was over fifty years of age, must keep to a walk. The terms of the race were that the competitors would leave Trafalgar Square at 4 a.m. and proceed to York via the Great North Road. The first to arrive at the Mansion House in York would be declared the winner.

The reporter for the Epworth Bells saw it as an unequal contest because Mr. Stephenson was well-known locally as an excellent horseman and proud owner of 'Griff,' a 'fine lightweight hunter.' However, in his last race, Cummings completed the journey in 102 hours beating the horse ridden by a Mr. Tyrhwhitt Drake by a couple of hours so too had cause for optimism. Stephenson took up the challenge 'in a purely sporting spirit as a test of the relative speed and endurance of horse and man.' He also wanted 'to bring down the record from London to York held by Mr. Bell from New Zealand, who rode the course in 80 hours 45 minutes'.

The report in the Epworth Bells continues; 'They started from Trafalgar Square, London at 5.45 a.m. on Wednesday. Mr. Stephenson was accompanied by a Ford van, loaded with fodder, etc. for his horse, a motorcyclist, also three push cyclists, two grooms and a blacksmith. Tasked with looking after Cummings, this entourage made for 'an imposing spectacle'. A good number of people assembled to see the start, and Mr. Stephenson was congratulated on his pluck by some of those who considered his chances of winning were minimal. Mr. Cummings swung off at a steady pace of six miles an hour. Mr. Stephenson decided to take the lead at once, and urging his mount into a steady trot, was soon well ahead. According to the Epworth Bells the horse and rider 'reached Biggleswade at 12.30 and Mr Cummings at 2.45. At 7 p.m. Mr. Stephenson arrived at Stamford, and after refreshment resumed the journey. On their arrival at Grantham just before midnight both horse and rider appeared quite fit. The pair had covered 110 miles in 18 hours. As the horse stepped into the yard, his ears were pricked, but he was quite cool. He swallowed a bucket of gruel and immediately afterwards ate heartily at the manger. When he left, he appeared quite fit. Retford (55 miles from York) was reached at 10.05 on Thursday morning, Stephenson 'passing through the town at a gentle trot'.

A good number of Mr. Stephenson's friends from this district witnessed his ride through Bawtry and Doncaster. The horse was walking at a leisurely pace and did not appear to be in any way distressed. They had made excellent progress, and Mr. Stephenson 'decided to nurse his steed in the later stages of the journey'.

After resting near Selby, the journey was resumed, and York reached at 1.30 a.m., the 200 miles ride having occupied only 43 hours and 45 minutes. Mr. Stephenson cantered up Coney Street, York, and was welcomed by a crowd. The Lord Mayor of York being away from home, was unable to receive Mr. Stephenson, who stayed in the city to welcome the arrival of Mr. Cummings.' He had a long wait; Cummings completed the journey in 102 hours!

An Epworth 'historian'

June 15, 1912, saw a report on the death of an Epworth bachelor named John Clark, aged 76. For a working man, John was exceptionally well-informed. He especially liked local history and local 'goings-on', though as pointed out in the Epworth Bells, he 'contributed little to parish affairs'. Over the past twenty years, John had provided the newspaper with stories and letters highlighting the Isle's forgotten past. His real passion, however, was writing about 'characters from long ago', and it was he who raised, and embellished somewhat, the story of Dick Towris, a well-known Epworth 'soak'. He, too, recalled the story of John Hall noted in the Epworth Bells as one of the first 'man-fliers', even though his attempts at powered flight from the top of his windmill ended in abject failure! Not everyone agreed with some of John's conclusions, however, resulting in several angry exchanges between him and his doubters in the letter section of the Epworth Bells. Even when these presented sound evidence that some of his claims were, at best dubious, he would not concede the point.

What was not in doubt, was John's fascinating past; one where, at the age of twenty, he and another Epworth youth called George Wressel, crossed the Atlantic to take on bricklaying jobs in the southern states of America. When the work dried up, John threw in his lot with the Confederate forces and entered the American Civil War. After fighting in twenty-seven engagements, a severe wound put him out of action. It weakened his constitution to such an extent that after the war he contracted Yellow Fever. He escaped from quarantine and would have died had it not been for the attentions of a negro slave who nursed him back to health. After making a near full recovery, John made his way home to Epworth, where he settled into his quiet life of work and study. A great many Epworth folk turned out for his funeral, where friends and relatives successfully petitioned the rector to allow them to sing John's favourite hymn, 'Rock of Ages,' by his graveside.

CHAPTER 7

Axholme at play

Football rivalries

The fixtures between Crowle and Owston Ferry played on Christmas Day and Boxing Day (Christmas time 'double-headers' were a feature of the league), saw both teams out to avenge previous defeats. Playing on Christmas Day may seem strange to us now, but in earlier times it made a lot of sense, as the day was a rare public holiday, and football was one of the few entertainments available. There was little Christmas Spirit in this fixture, however, as a large crowd of over 1,000 gathered at the Crowle ground and the 'keen rivalry on the part of the players and spectators' saw play at times becoming 'a bit rough'. The report goes on; 'Just before half time Crowle scored, but the referee decided the goal was offside and disallowed it. At half-time, a lot of people went on to the playing piece, and Wilfred Dodsworth threatened to strike the referee with a stick but did not strike him. A Crowle player named Salt said, "Let's finish the game and give him it when the game is over." In the second half, the referee (Mr. E Snowden, Epworth) found it necessary to order one of the Crowle players (Chamberlain) off the field for a foul tackle, and he also disallowed [another] of the Crowle goals'.

The match ended in a 3-3 draw but the referee's decisions 'brought great dissatisfaction to the Crowle men'. As he walked towards the gate, Dodsworth carried out his threat and hit Snowden 'on the back of his head twice with a stick, and Tom Slingsby struck him in the eye with his fist, blackening the eye and causing it to swell very much'. Many other blows were received by the referee on the ribs' but, because he had to hold his head down, he did not see who struck these blows. 'Some persons on the outskirts of the crowd came to Snowden's assistance, and he was led from the field under police escort to the house of [motor mechanic] Mr. E G. Whiteley in Cross Street. A crowd of 100 to 150 persons assembled outside Whiteley's house and threatened to smash the windows if the referee was not brought out. After being attended to by Dr. Alexander, Snowden was taken home in a taxi.' The Epworth Bells makes no mention of the Boxing Day game, so we are led to conclude that it either did not take place or it passed off without incident.

The incident did not end there as at the inquest, convened to examine the event and ordered by the Lincolnshire Football Association, Ernest Whiteley was summoned to give evidence. He told the hearing that he had been threatened as to what would happen if he gave evidence, but, based upon his testimony, those responsible received summary justice. A week later, his garage was broken into. Chamberlain and Salt received two-month playing suspensions for disorderly conduct and assault, and the league suspended matches at the Crowle ground for one month; the team being barred from playing within a five-mile radius of the ground. The council authorised Mr. Snowden to take out court proceedings against the two spectators who carried out the assault. It transpired that for several weeks after the event, Snowden suffered from spontaneous nose bleeds.

In another match around the same time, when the referee awarded a penalty to Eastoft, the Haxey goalkeeper refused to stand in the goal for the kick to be taken. When the referee asked for a player to substitute, none came forward, so the referee ordered the penalty kick to go ahead. It must have been one of the easiest penalties of all time. The goalkeeper then returned to his position, and the game played out to a one-all draw. Haxey complained to the league on a point of law that the kick should not have taken place with the goal empty and, somewhat surprisingly, the officials ordered that the match should be replayed. It came as a further blow to the Eastoft team as, having continued to play ineligible players, they now found their fourteen-point deduction increased to eighteen points!

When Haxey Town F.C. played a team from Thorne, it was, the 'thickness of the grass in certain areas that hampered their short passing game'. In other reports the correspondents described the game as a 'ding-dong of a struggle' It is, however, a report on a match between West Stockwith and Newells' Engineers from Misterton at Owston Ferry that has an unfortunate but amusing ending. Three minutes from the end of the game, the reporter recorded that T. Maw, the West Stockwith goalkeeper was 'following the ball out when he collided with Bramhill and Kellington, and his leg was fractured. The referee, Mr. Freemantle, Lincoln, at once stopped the game, which thus ended in a draw. Maw's accident was exceedingly unfortunate, because his wife in falling down some steps that morning, had fractured her shoulder, and while she is in the Coupland Hospital, Gainsborough, he is in the Doncaster Infirmary. The replay is fixed for Saturday, November 27th'.

The night before an important football match, 28-year-old Walter Rodgers had been helping erect the goalposts and nets. Upon returning home, he complained to his wife that he did not feel too well and decided to have an early night. She told him that if he felt unwell, it would be best if he missed the match. He said to her that he would be alright after a good night's sleep as he 'did not want to let the lads down'. The following morning, he declared himself restored and, after a late breakfast he set off to the match. Just before the kick-off Walter went up to the team's goalkeeper and asked him to 'feel his ticker' as it seemed to be beating oddly. The goalkeeper offered the same advice as Walter's wife the night before – that it would be best if he 'sat this one out'. However, nothing could dissuade Walter from taking up his position. After touching the ball a couple of times, and as the match entered the seventh minute, Walter was seen stumbling toward the touchline. Before he reached the white line, he collapsed. By the time some of his teammates reached him, he displayed no sign of life. As the referee abandoned the game, Walter's teammates lifted his lifeless body to the side of the pitch before conveying it to his house.

When several football supporters from Westwoodside decided to attend a match at Doncaster Rovers, Wallis Saville agreed to transport them to and from Belle Vue Stadium in his lorry. It was no hardship, as he was making the journey into Doncaster having been asked by his employers to transport some furniture to the Market from where he would return with 22 boxes. He had asked his employer if he could break the journey to watch the match and received confirmation. He took 30 people with him, but at the end of the match word that a free lift home was available saw 47 people pile onto the back of his vehicle. They vied for the limited space among the boxes with some 'clinging on to each other for support'. Things became particularly dangerous when the lorry swayed into and out of corners. Unfortunately, Wallis' antics drew the attention of the police, who followed him for seven and a half miles, at times marvelling how several people managed to stay in contact with the lorry as on several occasions both legs and arms could be seen flailing beyond the sides of the vehicle!

When the case came to court, the police charged Wallis with three offences – using fuel for purposes other than which it was granted, using a lorry which was unsuitable and believed to cause a danger to passengers, and using a motor lorry without a certificate of insurance. The bench found him guilty of all three offences and fined him £4 10s.

Fair days

For the children and adults of 1950s Epworth, the fair was a welcome distraction in what for some was a holiday-less year of drudgery. It was a cheerful, uncomplicated attraction that drew a good crowd to the town. Some children, risking the ire of both teacher and parent, skipped school to wait for the magic hour when the fair lorries pulled onto the show field. Crowle had their own fair company, Wroots, that operated in a field in Johnson's Lane. Crowle Fair, held on the last Monday in May and 23rd November often coincided with a carnival, gymkhana and children's sports day. In its heyday, the fair took place in the Market Place.

Like Crowle, the fair that visited Epworth originally used the Market Place, but it too moved to a field at the back of the Red Lion as the size and number of attractions increased. The company that provided most of the fairs for Epworth was Tuby's from the Stainforth area. They had two fairground circuits, rotating their attractions through the year and sharp-eyed truants would soon get the word out whether they had brought the waltzer or dodgems as their 'centrepiece' attraction.

A report on Epworth Fair from 1886 tells of the 'pleasure fair [being] largely provided for by attractions in or near the Market Place, the chief of which was what was known as the "The Great Sea on Land", consisting of six sailing vessels (with sails set) propelled on a circular railway by a central steam engine, the vessels rocking fore and aft, as at sea, and a powerful trumpet organ giving forth its loud sounds as the vessels move round. These were extensively patronised, there being a large number of visitors'.

Fair nights in the 1950s were filled with excitement: wide-eyed screaming youngsters; teenage boys keen to show bravado when sitting on the outer bars of the waltzer or walking the undulating inside floorboards; young men with sleeves rolled hurling wooden balls in an attempt to dislodge seemingly immovable coconuts and impress doting companions, and parents pestered into trying to win one of several sick looking goldfish. Anticipation and excitement were etched on the faces of all as they marched up Albion Hill and turned onto the strip of land leading to the fair field. The air rang with the sounds of tinny, ear piercing, music; the wailing crescendo of the slowing dodgems; the constant background hum of the vast generators and the hysterical screams of those intent on drawing every last drop of wonderment from the night's adventure. Starry-eyed children walked around holding their parents with one hand and a huge 'cloud' of pink candy floss, soon to be plastered from forehead to chin, with the other. It was a week when the fairground children would turn up at school, bringing their challenging view of authority into the classroom and playground. The local boys regarded them with a mixture of jealousy and disquiet; the girls with veneration or disdain.

Skating on thin ice

In the late 1800s, when the frost bit hard into the Axholme ground, the people of the Isle put on their skates and took to the ice. In the north around Crowle, this often led to several 'immersions' but fortunately, it seems there were no severe consequences. Robert Hall and Charles Fox had a severe ducking in the Old Moor drain. Joseph Cook, H Eyre, and C B Fish were skating together just below Pilfrey Bridge, on the Double Rivers, when Mr Cook fell through the ice in the middle of the river. This was where the river was the deepest, but with assistance close by, he survived his ordeal with little more than wounded pride.

Several residents used the drains as a means of reaching other villages, venturing beyond Hatfield. Others, unsure of skating the rivers and drains waited until the low fields froze over. In the area around Epworth, many headed to Newlands, where they displayed their skating skills and engaged in a variety of social activities.

Fifty years later the River Trent froze from the Humber to Gainsborough. The ice packs, some eight to ten feet high, jammed vessels in their moorings. Locals took the opportunity to walk from one bank to the other. A party of Hull evacuees arrived at the Trent and marvelled at several people doing 'fancy skating', - skating on one foot and cutting the figure eight. After watching this performance for a few minutes, they, too, ventured on to the ice, and walked right across the river, then came back to half-way. After coming together in a group, they had photographs taken and then walked back to Epworth.

Controversy at the Hood

The Epworth Bells of 1931 reported on the consternation in Haxey when the 'Hood' went 'missing' from its temporary home at the King's Arms. Reluctant to use the word 'stolen', the landlord put out a notice that he expected the item to be returned by 6 p.m. on the following day - failing that, he resolved to inform the police. When the deadline came, and there appeared no prospect of a return, it was to the police station he went. Upon his return, he found a man in his pub holding the hood. When questioned, the man declared he had not taken the leather tube but was returning

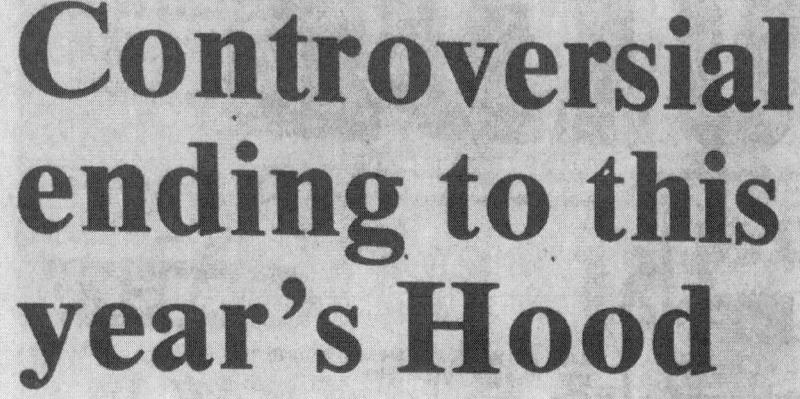

The Epworth Bells headline.

it on behalf of another who, fearing retribution, was apparently too frightened to bring it back. 'So, you know who took it?' said the landlord. 'I'm not going to say', the man replied. The hood was not damaged and the names of the original boggins and the money placed inside at the time of its making were untouched. As all seemed in order, the police took the natter no further believing the incident to be a joke.

In 1984, when Charlie Drewery tossed the Hood into the air to begin the ancient game, little did he know his actions would lead to one of the greatest controversies in its history. After an hour's struggle, the 'sway' was beginning to break up regularly. In the gathering darkness, as Stan Boor, Lord of the Hood, held up the Hood's progress to allow a car to pass the leather cylinder 'disappeared'! Despite a frantic search, no could locate it! What most did not realise was that in the confusion Reg Rockliffe and David Palmer, found themselves holding the Hood and under the darkening sky slipped away from the crowd unseen.

Eventually, word reached Stan that the Hood was behind the bar of The King's Arms – Rockliffe and Palmer were pushing for the King's. Stan went to the King's and asked the licensee, Stan Jarvis, to return the Hood so the game could continue. He reasoned that the Hood had not been 'swayed', so it was not within the spirit of the game. Stan Jarvis refused, and the Hood stayed!

As for Rockliffe and Palmer, when questioned they had a simple answer: 'While the rest of the lads were scrabbling about trying to find the Hood, we set off towards the King's Arms, and nobody challenged us. The object of the game [is] to get the Hood to our own pub, and that is what we did!' Despite their claim, the action brought stinging rebukes from traditionalists. Stan Boor declared that he would ensure everything would be done to prevent 'such a thing ever happening again'.

Not just one 'Hood'

It may come as a surprise to many, but Haxey Hood was not the only 'hood' game played in the villages of the Isle. Records show that at least Belton and Epworth had gatherings in early January when residents came together to compete in a 'rumble-tumble of a game'.

The hood at Belton took place across the open fields between Westgate and Church Town (an area now recorded on maps as Belton Fields). The one at Epworth saw participants heading to the open field north of the church (assigned the name 'Church Field' from early mediaeval times). Both Belton and Epworth games were similar in their rules and execution but differed substantially from the Haxey one played today. Their 'Hood' was not a cylinder but something approximating a ball. It was not a 'sway hood' either, the idea being to get the object to designated posts at either end of the field of play by any means – kicking (not just the ball!), running, throwing etc.

A report in the Crowle Advertiser dated 11th January 1896, tells of the 'rebirth' of the Belton Hood 'after fourteen years slumber. It brought back to some of the oldest residents the good old days of their youth. Old and young, fast and slow, wended their way to see and hear the conditions relative to the [game]'. The wyking posts were placed at Westgate, Grey Green and Churchtown. Then came the leader's speech, ending with; 'Gentlemen, I declare the hood open!' On this occasion, play commenced with the 'greatest vigour, but owing to the open weather and many fallows, the heavy horses could not stay the distance. Blood will tell.' The hood was run to the Sir Solomon.

At Epworth, the game began at 2 p.m. when posts were fitted into the ground at either end of the field before the commencement of activities. Once the hood touched the post (an action called 'wyking'), those supervising the game took it back to the midpoint, and the game began again. In this way, the contest continued until dark. The only involvement with public houses that I can find evidence for is that the Epworth Hood was held in the King's Head (that being nearest to Church Field) until the landlord released it before the game for the fee of one shilling. As the notice shows, there were prizes donated by individuals and businesses, but no money changed hands. The two hoods did not survive long into the 20th century if at all. All of which reflects great credit on those charged with perpetuating the custom in Haxey, to the extent that it survives and prospers to this day.

Racing the barrows

1958 saw the tenth running of Belton Barrow Race an event that according to reports began as a bet in a local hostelry. The first event saw five couples take part over a course that included 'calls' at the Crown Inn, the Steer Arms, Sir Solomon, the Wheatsheaf and finally at the Bridge Inn where the bet was laid.

At each stop, the contestants were obliged to 'quaff' a half pint of liquid – either beer, lemonade or water. According to the Epworth Bells; 'There was to be a small handicap according to age. The winners would receive a fiver if the organisers could raise it from the crowd.' Over 200 spectators came to see the contestants on their way with some 50 cyclists and several motorcyclists intending to follow the race. Eventually, every one of the competitors arrived [at the start] but not all with wheelbarrows! First off, followed by a horde of small boys on cycles, their elders by car, were partners in the local garage, Rupert Axe and Ben Naylor. Combined age, 74.

Last to start were R. Turner and H. Thompson, the youngsters with a combined age of 41. Crowds lined the route as though anticipating a Royal procession. Running and sweating, hopping in and out of barrows, pausing only to gulp down a rapid half-pint at each pub the lead competitors, Axe and Naylor, completed a mile at the Crown on the other side of the village. They were closely followed by George Sykes and Stan Cooney, the fourth pair to start. And that's how it stayed. Axe and Naylor covered the distance in 34 minutes, much of it over newly surfaced roads.

Cooney and Sykes finished fifty seconds back with Cooney, pushing his companion in a brickyard barrow, too heavy for such an event, but borrowed gratefully for the occasion. They worked to a plan - Cooney making the fast sprints, for about a hundred yards with Sykes plodding for about a quarter of a mile.

By 1958, both tactics and barrows had improved, and the event saw a win for a couple from Braithwell in record time. The highlight of the event was the appearance of Dick Spivey's 1902 Gladiator motor car, 'KKK Katie' the car he used to compete in the London to Brighton Veteran Car Run. George Stones claimed the barrow race to be the 'event of the year in Belton, one that was good for the pub and fish and chip trade in the village'.

Some years later the event would be dominated by Adrian Freebury and Malcolm Shipley on their specially constructed barrow which was little more than a sprung platform above a wheel. It was the 'barrow' they used when they pushed each other from John O'Groats to Lands' End, an undertaking that saw them listed in the Guinness Book of Records.

Born a cricketer

Compared to my father-in-law's exploits in the war, my dad's seem relatively mundane. He was a sergeant in the Royal Artillery, based in the Middle East. His commanding officer summed him up in a few words – 'A reliable soldier, not given to panic in battlefield situations.'

A sportsman from his youth, he played left-back for the regimental football team. However, the war robbed him of a career path he had followed since the age of fourteen.

Born in the Yorkshire village of Cawthorne he'd played for the cricket team since the age of 10. By 14 he was playing for Barnsley, and it was here he came to the notice of Yorkshire CCC. Taken to the training school, he made his way into the Yorkshire second team and played alongside Len Hutton, Johnny Wardle and Hedley Verity. He was approached by Warwickshire CCC who were looking for a left-handed batsman, but he turned the offer down – it was Yorkshire or nothing! He was on the verge of the Yorkshire first-team when his call up papers arrived.

After the war, he took up cricket again, but at 29 his chances with Yorkshire had gone. For several years he played as a professional in the Bradford League with Saltaire CC even though he had moved to Lincolnshire after marrying my mother. They met at a wartime dance in the Imperial Hall when stationed in Epworth. For a period, he held the record for the longest six at Doncaster when he hit the ball over The Rockingham Arms into Bennetthorpe Road. For a couple of years, he was the one professional allowed to play in the Lincolnshire CCC team in the Minor Counties League. He scored well, on one occasion racking up 120 at Trent Bridge.

Cricket did not pay well and, eventually, he abandoned his professional career and began work at Keadby Power Station when it opened in 1952. For several years he played for Epworth and also 'The Islonians', a select team drawn from players across the Isle.

No quick runs, right?

By the time I made the Epworth team, dad's knees had 'given out', and he took to quizzing me as to how I 'got out'. To him being bowled as anathema (to a Yorkshireman any other form of dismissal was preferable to letting the bowler knock down your 'castle'). After being out a few times LBW, he asked what guard I was taking. 'Middle and leg', I replied. 'That's it,' he said, 'get across to one leg, keep your legs out of the way.' Next match I was bowled, and when I told dad, he asked me my guard. 'One leg' I said. 'Ah' he replied, 'get yourself back on leg and middle! – better to be LBW eh lad?'

I thought my chances of playing with him had gone. And then …… in 1971, when trying to raise a team for a beer match, I managed to persuade him to make up the numbers. I opened the batting, and as wickets began to tumble, I began to think that if I hung around long enough, I might still be in when dad came to the wicket. He came in at number nine with me one run away from fifty. As he passed me, he nodded and said; 'No quick runs, right?' The third ball he dropped at his feet and he set off towards my end. 'One run!' he called. He made his ground easily; I was run out before I got half-way down the wicket!

Dad played a couple of classic cover drives before the innings closed. When he came back to the pavilion, he paused at the scorer's table and wrote something in the book. Following my name, the reason for dismissal said, 'Rob Fish run out 49' after which in brackets in my dad's handwriting were the words 'by his dad'!

CHAPTER 8

Going to the Cinema

The Palace de Luxe

During World War One, John Lovelace ran a cinema in the Market Hall area of Crowle called the 'Palace de Luxe'. He also sponsored films in other Isle villages. He was always at pains to ensure all those attending knew the theatre was disinfected throughout with Jeyes fluid. The movies included war presentations such as Lord Kitchener's visit to the Front. Sometimes John's wife would sing at the cinema before the films began. In Crowle, Althorpe and Epworth he would often offer 5/- for the best impersonation of Charlie Chaplin or other screen favourites and encouraged the audience to act as judges. He organised several musical concerts for Nurses' Associations, the Epworth Training Corps, the Prince of Wales Relief Fund, the Women's War Relief Association, the Red Cross, and the Women's Belgian Relief Fund. He billed his showings to include 'topicals'. Little wonder, then, that he received a public vote of thanks on many occasions for the splendid programme of events he provided, often at his own expense. Invariably, and where appropriate, children who attended did so for free; the only stipulation being that they arrive early. There were several occasions, however, when the halls were not big enough for the numbers attending.

Mr Lovelace had been working hard to secure a copy of 'The Little American' starring Mary Pickford for showing locally. When he managed this in September, almost a year after its release, the Epworth Bells advertised it as one of the greatest films ever produced.

It seems John's efforts did much to help with the recruiting of young men and, as such, in June 1915 he received the following citation from the War Office:

'Sir, I wish to express to you personally, and to those who have helped you in your recruitment work, my best thanks for the energy that has been displayed by you all in the matter of recruiting. I would ask you to take an early opportunity of urging all able-bodied men in your neighbourhood to come forward and enlist so that they may be trained as soldiers to take part in the war and help keep our forces in the field at the maximum strength. I shall be glad to hear of any reasons that may be given you by young and suitable men for not availing themselves of the opportunity to see service in the field, where they are so much wanted, I am, Sir, Your obedient servant, Kitchener.'

Despite his commitment, the war was not kind to the Lovelace family. Mrs. Lovelace's brother was drowned at sea, and their son Hugh was severely wounded. The family soldiered on, however, and in 1919 they organised sumptuous teas, good company, games, dances and entertainment for the Peace Celebrations in Crowle.

A 'Regal' gentleman

The early thirties saw the first mention of a licence being granted for a picture house in Crowle, for the public showing of 'talking pictures'. Joseph Spivey moved to Crowle in November 1921 to become manager of 'The Picture House Co.' in the Market Hall. In 1927 he acquired 'The Picture House' on a lease and began the move into talking pictures – one of the first in Lincolnshire. Some years later he built the Regal Cinema on the site of Mr. W. Bleasby's blacksmith's shop in High Street. With a seating capacity of 500, the cinema opened on Monday 6th September 1937. Known as 'Uncle Joe' by the children he put on matinees especially for them and each week gave a free show to the pensioners of the town. He was constant in his support for charitable organisations and allowed

The front entrance of The Regal.

free use of his premises for entertainment in aid of similar efforts. He was even known to buy shoes for needy children forced to walk the local streets barefoot.

Before his cinema business in Crowle, Joe's entrepreneurial spirit had seen him working in a variety of roles in the entertainment business. He entertained troops in WWI with sketches and jokes. He was on the bill at the Tower, Blackpool where he worked with George Formby snr., and had links to Charlie Chaplin. He organised roller skating rinks in Crowle, at the Flax Mill in Chancery Lane and the Assembly Rooms in Cross Street.

A motoring 'pioneer', he once bought a lorry to convert to a makeshift bus. As he drove around the Goole area, he would engage the passengers in sing-alongs. In later years, when he was confined to an electrically powered chair, the family had to have it geared down to its lowest speed!

His son, Harry, (better known by his nickname – 'Dick')

continued with the Regal until its closure as a cinema in 1970. Even then, Dick viewed the thought of giving up the family's role in the entertainment industry with horror. 'Had not the family gone into business not merely for what they got out of it financially, but with a spirit of giving? Had not fathers, sons, wives, daughters and grandchildren all combined in the grand design of making things move and swing in entertainment for over half a century?' Dick had friends in every part of the country and according to the Epworth Bells, 'knew everybody of note, mixed among the Knights of the Road and the gearboxes of the world's factories'. The family turned the premises into a motor museum. One of the cars on show was the 1902 Gladiator motor car, named 'KKK Katie,' the car Dick used to compete in the London to Brighton Veteran Car Run.

The Rio Grand

At the Imperial Hall in Epworth, the 'Talking Cinema' brought the audience 'Bob Steele, the fighting and singing cowboy' and Constance Bennett and Kenneth McKenna staring in 'Sin Takes a Holiday'. Its success brought the idea of a permanent 'picture house' for Epworth closer. In April 1938, Mr. S. York of Albion House advertised his intention to build a Civic Theatre on Queen Street.

Immediately it drew the attention of most people in the south of the Isle. The Epworth Bells carried advertisements for forthcoming films in the top right-hand side of the front page, a prime spot guaranteed to attract immediate attention. In addition, there was a precis of each film to be shown that week on the inside pages. Many of them were comedies, which featured artists such as George Formby; several focused on police inspector dramas; others such as 'Gunga Din' and 'Tarzan' told tales of adventure, while for those who yearned for a life quietly lived there was 'Goodbye Mr

Chips.' There was, however, a shock in store for cinema-goers; two days after the declaration of war, the government ordered the closing of all places of entertainment. It brought condemnation from all quarters and locally from Mr. Spivey of Crowle, who argued that the ban should not affect cinemas, 'not in danger of an air-raid'.

When the war ended, locals flocked to the Rio to see films that brought a more uplifting mood to the nation. One, in particular, was 'The Outlaw' starring 'the sultry and voluptuous Jane Russell'. Advertised as a film; 'Bold with primitive emotions', it generated long queues stretching back to the Market Place. Unsurprisingly (perhaps), The Epworth Bells reported that by far the greater majority of customers were male!

As the 60s came to an end, both Isle cinemas faced an uncertain future. For some years the Rio had functioned solely as a bingo hall, but when attendances began to fall, the owners offered the building to the parish council as a possible town hall, community centre or arts venue. It was an offer that may have met with success had the council been able to find the £15,000 to purchase the building and come up with further funding to secure a viable long-term plan. Someone even came up with the idea of turning it into a bowling alley! Less than a year later, it was the turn of the Crowle's Regal Cinema to close down. Under the heading 'Widespread Gloom,' the Epworth Bells reported on the 'melancholy thoughts [these closures brought to] many homes throughout the Isle'.

There had always been a healthy rivalry between the two cinemas, but it was a rivalry that had spurred each to provide the best service to its customers. When three local 'entrepreneurs', under the guise of Axholme Cinema Services, came forward with a plan to reopen the Rio to show films at weekends, it was the Spivey family who were among the first to wish them 'every success in your venture'.

For six years the Rio's revival continued but, as audiences began to dwindle again, and after the film shown on Sunday 28th August, the directors felt they had little choice but to close. Less than four months later, the Rio reopened, this time under the guise of 'The Rio Bingo and Social Club'. Attracting acts such as the Doncaster comedian, Charlie Williams, and Gerry and the Pacemakers, it would be trite to state that once again its flame burned bright, as, on the night of 22nd June 1979, flames engulfed the building. This time there would be no further reprieve - the Rio was gone!

The front entrance of The Rio

CHAPTER 9

Crashes and Explosions

On a dark Monday evening in January 1931, the area experienced the first aeroplane crashes that would contribute to a scarred landscape for the next twenty years. Lost in a severe Axholme mist, three reconnaissance aeroplanes attempting forced landings came down in the fields at Park Drain. One hit a telegraph pole, another landed safely, but the third, a Vickers Vimy, tore through a hedge and pitched nose-end into a dyke, killing three of the crew of six.

Moving into the war years; in August 1940, when flying over Owston Ferry, the pilot of a Handley Page Hampden (L4187) on a training flight, lost control after being dazzled by searchlights. He had initiated the correct recognition signals, but these were too weak to be seen by the searchlight crew. The aeroplane hit the ground at a very steep angle killing the four crew members.

Six months later, on 26th February and again over Owston Ferry, the pilot of an Airspeed Oxford had to make a forced landing when caught up in a severe snowstorm. He landed the plane safely, but the damage was considerable. The aircraft had to be dismantled on-site before being sent off for repairs.

Two days hence, on a night bombing exercise, when the starboard engine of an Avro Anson failed, the pilot had to make a forced landing at Westwoodside. Thankfully, the three-man crew exited the aircraft unhurt.

Moving on to February 1944, Halifax V9983 crashed close to the road from Graizelound to Owston Ferry five minutes after taking off from Blyton Airfield. The Australian pilot lost control after successfully evading a mid-air collision. All six crew members perished.

The year is still 1944. It's March, and two Halifax bombers take off, HR657 from Blyton and EB184 from Sandtoft. They are headed towards the greatest air accident to occur over the skies of Axholme. With both tasked to night flying exercises, the two planes collided over Misson bombing range. EB184 stuttered on but fell into a Graizelound field owned by Mr. Snell. HR657 didn't get quite as far, falling close to the Warping Drain on the road from Haxey to Misterton. Both crews died in their respective aeroplanes.

In September, Halifax DK133, airborne from Sandtoft on night circuit practice began a banking manoeuvre to the right three minutes after take-off. At 200 ft the plane went into a dive over Crowle out of which the pilot failed to recover. All seven members of the Canadian crew were killed outright. In the same month, on the 18th, a Spitfire crash-landed at Mason's Farm on Crowle Waste killing the Indian pilot. The plane's home base was RAF Kirton-in-Lindsey.

A month later, Halifax LK642 was returning to Sandtoft after a half-hour take-off and landing exercise, when it overshot the runway. The plane careered across the road and ploughed into a bungalow on the Westgate Road at Belton. All six members of the crew suffered mild injuries, but the inhabitants of the bungalow and a man passing by on a bicycle were not so lucky – all three died at the scene.

On 5th April it was the turn of Lancaster PB565 which is well documented in my Memorial Book. On the same day Lancaster ND639 also outbound from Sandtoft crashed and burned near Windsor Lane, Crowle. Investigators believed the pilot lost control due to ice on the wings. The crew of seven which included six Australians all died at the scene.

The final act in this two-decades of aerial tragedies happened in 1953 when a Meteor Jet crashed in a field at Low Burnham, narrowly missing three generations of the Smith family who were at work in the fields. The pilot, Flight-Lieutenant Tanbred, was killed outright in what was thought to be his attempts to avoid the plane coming down over Haxey. In 2003, fifty years to the day after the crash, family members came to the crash site to meet John Smith, one of those in the fields that day.

Flixborough

On Saturday 1st June 1974 I was playing cricket for Epworth at Messingham. As the tea interval approached, I watched from behind the wickets as suddenly the bails jumped in the air. There was no wind, and the batsman was away from the wicket – what caused the bails to dislodge was a mystery. That is until I got home and heard the news. The Nypro chemical plant at Flixborough had exploded. Of the 72 people on site, 26 died, and 32 received severe and potentially life-ending injuries. My friend from youth, Steve Musgrave, was on site that day. He and his team had agreed to go in early to complete the work assigned. They finished at 3p.m., and all were back home at the time of the explosion. The second fire engine to arrive at the disaster was the Epworth appliance. On the crew was Don Musgrave, Steve's father. He knew his son was at work that day but didn't know he had left early. The other members of the crew secured him in the engine for fear he might see something that would haunt him forever. Back in Epworth, Steve was frantically trying to get a message to his father but in the confusion getting a message to crews at the scene was virtually impossible.

Another resident of Epworth was on site that day. Ian Tune from Rectory Street heard the siren and managed to run before the explosion. However, the blast caught up with him, picked him up and bowled him down the road towards the River Trent. He ended up on the grass bank – another few yards on he would have ended up in the river. He always believed he had cheated death twice that day.

The blast left the site in 'corridors'. One headed across the river and the impact struck St. Mark's Church at Amcotts, lifting off the roof and dropping it back down to leave a gap of eight inches at the apex. It blew out the stained-glass east window and left cracks in the outer walls. For a time, it seemed the only solution was to pull the church down. A restoration did take place, however, and although it meant remaking the east window, the work was completed in two years.

It was the second incident concerning the church in Amcotts. On 14th August 1849 after the rector, the Reverend James Aspinall noted 'a yielding of the walls', the building dedicated to St. Thomas a' Beckett suddenly collapsed. In 1853 the rebuilt church was dedicated to St. Mark.

In another quirk of fate, I had been released from my teaching post at Haxey to cover for an absent teacher at Burton Stather school. Another 'blast corridor' struck the school, taking out all the glass windows on the west side. Huge shards of glass flew through the classrooms penetrating desks and walls. Had the blast happened on a school day the resulting carnage would have been immeasurable.

The 1880s – under the weather

In 1881 severely cold weather caused many children to be absent. Much of the Isle was enveloped by what became known as 'The Great Fog'. The days were cold and raw, and the fog lifted little for some weeks. Unable to see even a few yards ahead, people who knew their district and neighbourhood well lost all sense of direction. Perhaps the eeriest circumstance was to hear people both near and far calling out for help in confusion and alarm when faced with the 'prospect of abandonment'.

In July 1885, the newspaper carried details about one of the greatest storms to hit Axholme. Around half-past five on the evening of 9th July, Mrs. Major of Sandbeds, just off Church Lane in Haxey noticed an approaching storm. So violent was the sky that she reasoned the best thing to do was shut herself and her twenty month old child in her cottage and await her husband's return. He, on the other hand, decided the best course of action was to shelter while the storm passed and sought refuge in the Post Office. It proved to be a fateful decision. At around quarter past six, neighbours saw smoke coming from the Major's house. Running to investigate, Harrison Eastwood, looked into the front room and saw several wooden items on fire and Mrs Major laid on the floor with her apron alight. Close by was the child, blackened by soot that had fallen down the chimney when lightning struck the chimney stack.

Local surgeon, Dr. Eminson, arrived on the scene to find the fire extinguished, the child unharmed, but Mrs. Major dead. She had an abrasion on her neck and burn marks down her breast. He came to the conclusion that the 'electric fluid' had travelled into the room attracted by the steel sewing machine from where it glanced into Mrs Major's upper body.

On Haxey Carr, Mrs. Allen sat by the fireside relaxing after a hard day. Her two dogs lay either side of her. As lightning entered the house through the chimney, it also brought down a large amount of soot. The bolt of lightning struck the younger of the two dogs, killing it instantly. It then divided; one element tracking upstairs to enter a bedroom where it stripped the paper and plaster from the wall. The other exited the house through a downstairs window.

Over in Churchtown, Belton, Mr. Watson Stones and his family were also sitting by the fire. Here, too, lightning struck the chimney and burst through the brickwork into a bedroom causing damage to the walls and floor. It then split the oak door jamb leading to an apple store before bursting its way into the kitchen fusing a metal cleaver to a handsaw where both hung on the wall. From there it hit a copper warming pan, punching holes in the side. Finally, the electric charge struck the fire surround, stopping six inches from Mr. Stones' right foot but still leaving it numb. Though shocked, the whole family survived the experience unscathed.

What is significant about the reports in the Epworth Bells is the amount of detail elicited by those reporting the incidents. Given that there must have been a great deal of confusion and fear, it seems remarkable that each family was able to describe the route taken by the lightning as it tracked its way through their houses.

February and March 1888 brought extremely cold weather with very deep snow. Parents refused to send their children to school 'for fear of losing them in the drifts'. Some of these measured 9 or 10 feet high! Great storms throughout Europe brought shipwrecks, derailed railway engines and resulted in a significant loss of life. When the snow began to melt in late March, Axholme experienced what was referred to at the time as 'The Great Darkness'. The Epworth Bells reports that at 2 p.m. the afternoon sky turned a copper colour that darkened towards the horizon. The darkness lasted for 30 minutes when a hue 'as if a volcano was erupting' ended the blackout suddenly. The event brought much alarm to all villages.

In spring 1941 Britain entered 'double' Summertime! A few days after the alteration of the clocks, Axholme experienced its best-ever Aurora Borealis. The Epworth Bells reported that just before midnight, 'the sky turned blue and white as though highlighted by the searchlights of wartime'. The colours soon changed to green and finally to crimson as the cone-shaped lights 'apexed over Axholme'.

CHAPTER 10

An Axholme school - 1880

Like pupils across Britain, the school children of Axholme were encouraged to learn through 'object lessons'. In the school curriculum, there are 30 such lessons listed including the cow, the sheep, the squirrel, the rabbit, the dog, the lion, the tiger, birds, fowls, fishes, an umbrella, a railway station, a table, a kettle, sugar, bread, windows, baskets, a clock, harvest, haymaking, coins, the seasons, winter and clothing. For the lesson, each teacher produced an object, or the picture of an object, from a box or bag and told the pupils about it in minute detail. The object lesson was supposed to make children observe, then talk about what they had seen. Unfortunately, many teachers found it easier to chalk up lists describing the object, for the class to copy.

At this time, and when making decisions as to whether pupils would be submitted for testing, the headteacher had to list the reasons for exceptions for those pupils not considered capable of undertaking the test. Some reasons recorded for pupils in the village schools were wretchedly dull; defective eyesight; very delicate health; timid and nervous; away from school for long periods nursing grandmother who is ill.

At Owston Ferry in 1888, the school had the services of three pupil teachers. One teacher left suddenly 'to attend to her mother', another left to be married (females who married were not allowed to teach) and the headteacher, John Frewin, was absent for long periods. The three pupil teachers were his daughters, Sylthe, Kathleen and Beatrice Frewin. In Kell's Directory, John Frewin is also listed as a boat owner; in 1909 he is credited as being a collector of Crown taxes. It is this family, however, that gives us one of the most poignant periods in the history of the school. From May to October 1890, the school closed for a month at a time because the staff and pupils had a fever. In the school logbook for June, the headteacher writes 'Kathleen Frewin, third-year pupil-teacher died June 11th R.I.P.' Just a simple sentence in a 'relatively' obscure journal but one can barely imagine the anguish the headteacher must have felt having to sit and record the death of a daughter in such a manner.

A charitable pair

The Examination Schedule of 1864 for Owston School records: 'The general efficiency of the school is shown by the high percentages reached in every subject but spelling. The school enjoys considerable advantages from the liberty of the late Archdeacon William Stonehouse and Miss Frances Sandars.' Born in 1792, Rev. W. B. Stonehouse was the vicar of Owston Ferry from 1821 until he died in 1862. From 1844 he was also the Archdeacon of Stow. His wife, Elizabeth, Frances' sister, was responsible for the installation of the organ in St Martin's Church in 1835. Still, it is Rev. Stonehouse's benefactions in collaboration with Frances, which continue to define much of the village today. Thanks to their intervention, along with other subscribers, a Diocesan School was begun in the village in 1841 for the 'reception of fifty children of both sexes'.

The equally benevolent Frances, who was born in 1787, was to provide many bequests to the school and village. She paid for a parish clock to be mounted on the school building; she had a gaslight erected in the Market Place; she paid for the east window in the church, and in 1860 founded, 'for the benefit of aged females' six almshouses; each resident receiving an 'allowance for daily bread' totalling five shillings a week. Other stipulations included; attending church morning and evening, no quarrelling and keeping a neat house. The houses are still in use today.

Together they set up the 'Stonehouse-Sandars Charity' to provide funding for apprenticeships and to support students of the village. Upon his death in 1862 Stonehouse left the interest of £5,800 and when Frances died in 1868, she left the interest of £5,300. £2,000 from each went to support boys and girls of the age of fourteen attending the National School for 5 successive years. £1,000 each went towards the salary of the master and mistress. This period of benefaction coincided with the greatest increase in the population of the village that had trebled since the 900 inhabitants recorded in 1801.

Looking further into the history of the school, December 1926 saw the classrooms very cold as the coke supplied would not burn sufficiently well enough to get the pipes warm. An inspector's report from around this time gives us some indication of the building's layout and some of its deficiencies. He records, 'The school has three rooms, each separated by a light folding partition. There are three narrow cloakrooms with washing facilities. The playground is small and in a rough state. The pail closets have worm-eaten seats. Pupils do P.E. in the classroom and games on the recreation field. A system for pupils to change into appropriate clothing for this has not yet been established'. The inspector insisted that the fence between the boys' and girls' playground be retained to prevent the boys 'entering the female closets'.

This was the period of the Great Depression, with the full effects of poverty being felt throughout Northern England. As is sometimes the case, when things get bad, they often get worse. On Wednesday 24th September 1930, there were some of the worst floods ever experienced in the village. The heavy tides rose to over 35 feet, and boats became the preferred method of transport in the streets close to the river. Children could not get to school. The post office was flooded and out of commission for some time. A haystack and a number of chickens were seen floating away towards Gunthorpe! The school took the decision to provide all the pupils with a hot drink at playtimes. The drink chosen was Horlicks at the cost of a halfpenny a cup with the powder sprinkled into hot water heated in a boiler. The drink was so 'thin', and when the effects proved ineffective, the school abandoned the scheme. If pupils wanted a drink, they resorted to drinking rainwater collected from the roof in a metal tank. As dead bodies of birds were often be found in this tank, the boys referred to it as 'sparra watter'.

An inspector calls

School inspection has a long history. In its early days, its terms of reference were very limited, and the reports given could be quite brutal. Often, they were critical of the staff, the pupils or the school building (sometimes the inspector was scathing of all three). With the introduction of the state system of education, governments of the time needed to check that all schools met the statutory requirements. This usually involved inspecting attendance records, student discipline and basic standards of literacy and numeracy. To carry out this task, inspectors needed little direct experience of teaching or schools. They were government agents who policed, rather than supported, the work of schools. Unsurprisingly, they soon gained an unwelcome reputation. It begs the question - were their reports reliable? Well, they were writing an official report that was likely to be the subject of considerable scrutiny in Whitehall so it seems unlikely they would make things up.

On the other hand, some school inspectors had their own agenda, and even in official documents, their reports often set out to influence policy. Whatever their main findings amounted to, they had to be copied into the school logbook. Axholme schools had many problems to deal with; poor attendance, bad weather, illness, and shortage of money for equipment, being among the most pressing. Believe it or not, the most significant problem was convincing the inspector that your school may have some minor issues but overall, it sought to provide an acceptable level of instruction.

Reading some of these reports from the latter end of the 19th century in the logbooks is a real eye-opener. One states, 'I regret to report that I can see no signs of improvement. The children are backward throughout. The prospects are all the more hopeless as the infants and children in the first standard are so ignorant. In the first standard, 13 out of 21 children have failed in all subjects. A certificate was issued to the master last year by mistake, as must have been evident from the official letter which announced the annual grant. It has accordingly been cancelled, and another will not be issued until the inspector can report favourably on the school. A deduction of one-tenth is incurred in the present instance for faults of instruction (article 32b)'.

In another, the inspector finds that 'in class subjects children seemed listless, and the work was not as good as last year'. A few years later a report highlights that several changes in the teaching staff had 'somewhat retarded' the progress of Religious Instruction and grave irregularities and overcrowding were brought to the 'serious attention of the managers'. Around the turn of the century, one inspector concedes that 'a great deal of illness has kept the school back from doing its best'. One of the most damning reports of an Isle school goes on to say: 'The school is in a deplorable state. The buildings are dirty and unsanitary, and the school is lacking the common necessities. The fences are broken and the offices (toilets) are partly unroofed. The floors and seats are littered with excrement, the smell from which is most offensive and nauseating.'

On one occasion, when an inspector called and found the timetable was 'not in the right place', meaning that the children were not doing what they were supposed to at the given time of day, he left this to be corrected by the managers. A few days later, and in what appears to be a rather pompous manner, one of the managers called to check if the timetable 'was in its proper place'. He found the headteacher had framed the weekly timetable and hung it on the classroom wall. When the manager challenged the headteacher over this, the head pointed out that this was the right place for the timetable!

Over in Owston Ferry, a report from 1905 finds '... an improving school with creditable work and every prospect of the school becoming a very good one'. By 1912 the teachers are ranked as 'industrious' with pupils displaying 'good recitation, singing and behaviour, with the girls showing much interest in simple domestic lessons'. By 1914 the school was classed as 'very good' to the point that in 1939 an inspector is glad to report that, 'in spite of the evacuation problems and war conditions which naturally affect school life, very excellent progress has been made'. Inspections take something of a back seat for the years of the Second World War. There was a desperate shortage of men for teaching, and in a changing climate, inspectors became more the givers of advice than the writers of distasteful reports.

School in wartime

During the Second World War, it seems the headteacher placed a great deal of trust in his pupils to perform significant tasks that would aid the smooth running of the school. On one occasion, the headteacher sent two boys to a neighbouring school to deliver 30lbs of rosehips collected on nature walks during the week. These were to be made into Rose Hip Syrup – a trusted source of vitamin C in those austere years. Later on, two others were tasked with walking the four miles when their school ran out of exercise books and needed some urgently. In some schools, the postmistress prevailed upon pupils to deliver telegrams if she found herself too busy. In other local schools, when the school canteen ran out of potatoes, the headteacher often sent boys to his own home for a small supply he had in stock for personal use.

Absence

Of all the records of pupils found in the early logbooks, the most numerous entries are those that deal with absence. Of course, children could not learn if they were not at school, and there were many reasons why they did not attend. When children in school and performance in testing brought funding to the school, one headmaster noted in the 1870s that 'many children are kept at home for the most trifling excuse'. Historians of education know well that one of the main reasons for absence in the last quarter of the 19th century, was because their parents wanted them to be at work during periods of hardship as many poor people depended on a 'family income'.

In the late 1800s, in our logbooks, we find records of pupils (mainly boys) staying off school to work on the land: bean pulling and potato picking in the autumn, and potato setting in the spring. During late summer, haymaking, hoeing mangolds and fruit pulling occupied many a youngster's days. These absences, often in contravention to the Education Act brought much distress to the headmaster, and in one entry his exasperation can clearly be seen for he writes in capital letters, 'farmers simply ignore the Act and employ whosoever they will'.

One of the most popular reasons for absence was that of celery 'dropping'. This activity had gone on in Axholme for many years. In Haxey and Wroot, on the dark peaty soils, it was the principal crop, so much so that in one three-day period in 1927, 7,000 bundles of celery left Epworth station. On another occasion the head of a local school was shocked to learn that some pupils were absent from school 'New Year Gift soliciting', something he was at pains to dissuade, as it was a custom that was becoming ever highly prevalent and was little more than a polite way of begging! Later pupils attending the village 'Feast' at Owston Ferry caused the headteacher even greater anxiety. He had some concerns about them riding on Tuby's steam roundabouts, but his greatest worry was those attending sessions of fortune telling being run by Gipsy Lee!

In our Axholme logbooks, are entries cautioning older boys for 'late coming, truant playing and vulgarity'. Very often the children from Gunthorpe were admonished for 'late-coming' on account of the distance walked. On 24th November 1894, the headmaster writes that the Gunthorpe children returned to school for the first time since harvest. Fieldwork and very wet weather would keep the children of Gunthorpe off though it is somewhat odd to find them referred to as 'the outsiders' in several entries. On one occasion, and after several warnings about lateness, the headteacher saw fit to expel a pupil only for the vicar to countermand this and 'give him one more chance'. Schools 'lost' children to 'truant bathing', on Epworth Fair Day and to Butterwick Feast. The names of these truants were not only recorded in the logbook but put into a red book that had to be available for the School Attendance Officer.

By 1900, the School Board of Luddington had become impatient with the irregular attenders. Eventually, it recommended four of the worst cases to the court at Epworth. Three out of four were so sure of being convicted that they didn't bother to defend their situation; they just sent the required five-shilling fine. When considering the case against John Curry, the board was handed a letter from Curry, stating that 'the child could not possibly attend on the 17th, as on that date his wife was confined of twins, so he kept the child from school to run errands'. It was a case that would have elicited some sympathy were it not for witnesses stating that the child was seen running errands 'which were not likely to promote sobriety'. The Bench had no alternative but to convict, and ordered the required fine be paid.

It was not just children who were guilty of slipshod absence. On 29th May 1897 a report states '…. the master went home unwell for a drink of water, fell asleep in the chair and did not wake up until recess.' He apologised to the managers but found some quite unforgiving.

Back in the late 19th and early 20th century there were no long summer holidays. The new school year began in May, and the managers determined the holidays, often in collaboration with the local landowners and farmers, to ensure these periods of absence would coincide with the need for extra help on the farm. What we now call the Summer Holiday period would last for some two weeks, with three weeks being allocated in October for 'Potato Picking.' Schools were often open on 24th December and 1st January. Easter was a holiday of two weeks that could be stretched to three if sufficient children did not attend owing to land duties. In 1902 the school at Owston Ferry had to close from 1st August until 5th October for health reasons. No sooner had it reopened than it had to be closed again for three weeks of potato picking.

Some parents did go through the proper channels when applying for their children's absence. A gentleman farmer from Kelfield asked for his son to have time off to help with the harvest, and this was granted. Several children absented themselves to go flax pulling and, to the headmaster's disgust, they were employed by one of the school's managers! When the headmaster overheard two pupils say they were going potato picking, he informed them that it was illegal. He then records, 'they went anyway!' However, it seems the skills they learned came in useful as, when given the task of finishing the school potato pie, their work was good enough to '...[keep] the frost away all winter.'

In 1903 all the East Ferry children who attended school at Owston Ferry were away because they had gone on a trip to Cleethorpes. Later in the year the headmaster records that the 'East Ferry children could not be rowed across the river and the ice on the river was too dangerous to walk upon.' In 1908, when a headmaster's brother died, he had to have a week off school, so he closed the school. To make up for the lost time, the vicar shortened the Christmas Holiday from two weeks to one! Some years later another headmaster went to his garden to get some leeks during school time and records he was away from school for three minutes. Unfortunately, he was seen in the street by the vicar who estimated the time to be more like eight minutes and did not see the 'collection of vegetables as a legitimate reason for absence from school'. On another occasion a headmaster went home unwell at lunchtime and fell asleep in the chair, not waking until dismissal time. He was censured severely by the managers. Later, when the same headmaster had to account for lateness, he seems to have snapped and written, in red ink, a long entry in the logbook finally objecting to '.... having to account to people who have little or no idea of the work involved in school organisation'.

Infections

The poor health of many, and the continual reoccurrence of life-threatening diseases, brought repeated references to Scarlatina, Mumps, Chicken Pox, Diphtheria, sores on pupils' faces, Ringworm and, disconcertingly, illnesses grouped under the heading of 'the fever'. More likely, however, the infection came from another source; that of a girl who worked as a servant for Messrs. Harniess, roundabout proprietors. Having worked for the Harniess' family in Bradford where typhoid amongst textile workers was an ever-present danger, she fell ill. When the family heard of her condition, her brother brought her home to Epworth 'in a state of near collapse'.

The years of the Great War brought much illness – mumps, measles, bronchitis and whooping cough all took their toll and scarlet fever, in particular, brought death to Axholme schools. On 20th February 1915, the school at Owston Ferry recorded twenty cases of diphtheria that brought closure to the school. Later in the year on 14th August, we find a report saying – 'It is a considerable time since the health of this Trentside village was so bad as it is at present. Both schools are closed with Scarlet Fever, Diphtheria and Chicken Pox. Whole families have been laid low.' The school reopened on 7th September only to be closed on the 18th for six weeks or 'until conditions improved'. Parents had to pay for visits from the doctor, and the headteacher wrote to them to urge that they contact the physician to help alleviate the problem being faced by the village. In some weeks, illness reduced school rolls to a measly 48%.

The scourge of the 'flu pandemic of 1918/19 hit the community of West Butterwick hard, and the Pilsworth family suffered greatly. The first to be struck down was Thomas Ellis Pilsworth (25), and his death was followed quickly by that of his wife, Alice (27). The next to suffer was his father, Watson, aged 63, followed by the death of his daughter, Miriam, aged 22. Their funerals took place over six days. Their eldest son, George, had been killed in action in France on 19th September 1918. All in the village described the sadness as overwhelming.

In Haxey, the town doctor was one of the first to catch the disease and, though he sought to work through it and administer to his patients, the effort proved too much. The town was fortunate that two nurses arrived from Gainsborough to take on the doctor's workload. Nurse Graveson, worked by day and paid four hundred home visits in six days. Nurse Spacie worked through the night among the most severe cases. She, too, contracted the disease, as did a relief doctor sent in her stead.

In 1922 a manager called to criticise the closure of the school at Owston Ferry for the measles epidemic. His written comments to the headteacher were that, 'it was nice for teachers to have such long holidays' and that, 'there was no more illness here than elsewhere' and, 'something must be done to ensure ratepayers get value for money'. The headteacher wrote a stinging rebuke in response to these comments in his logbook; no doubt using it as a repository for the ire he felt towards the insensitivity of others.

On 2nd February 1935, three children died of diphtheria in Owston Ferry. The school was closed until 23rd February, but the disease continued. Twelve patients were sent away from the village for isolation. Some believed it was the lack of piped water in the village and that it was filtered water from the Trent that caused the outbreak. Others blamed it on an outbreak some weeks previously in Leeds. Some shunned the bargees claiming they brought it from Hull. Whatever the trigger, it brought an immediate closure to the schools in Owston Ferry. Books and paper were taken away and burnt, and the buildings fumigated. In the Mellors' family, four of their nine children caught the disease, and two failed to recover. Madge Mellors was not allowed to attend her daughter's funeral. She waited by the church lych gate and stroked the coffin as it passed into the churchyard. Anyone identified as a carrier was also excluded from entering the church. The vicar was so fearful of catching the disease that he conducted the funeral service from the other side of the building. Tom Platts of Gunthorpe buried three of his children in Misterton cemetery only to find on his return that his wife and surviving child had caught the disease – they also died.

The infection set in motion measures that we saw replicated in the recent Coronavirus pandemic of 2020. Dr Macbeth took swabs from most of the village residents and identified several carriers who he placed in isolation. Twelve patients were sent away from the village for isolation – four to each of Gainsborough, Market Rasen and Scartho. Later, in the local press, Dr. Macbeth received considerable praise for his efforts in keeping the disease in check. By 25th May the disease was abating and, as all swabs had come back clean, it was assumed that everyone at the school was clear. When the school reopened, however, there were no books for the pupils to work from or in. Those who died were named as; Joyce Lilian Mellors (7), Thomas William Torn (10), Alan Mellors (3), Kathleen Laister (3), her mother Alphonso and a small child named simply as Henderson.

In 1945 Dr. Macbeth was called to the school to inspect a girl who had done no writing for seven weeks. He suspected the onset of St Vitus Dance, a condition associated with rheumatic fever and characterised by rapid, uncoordinated jerking movements affecting the face, feet and hands primarily. He sent her home for two weeks 'to get herself right'.

The school garden

Gardening played a vital role in the Isle schools over the years. The National Society encouraged horticultural activities from the outset, but it is in the 1900s that the work done in the garden began to enter the pages of the school's logbook. In 1911 vegetables grown by pupils at Owston Ferry won first prize in Haxey Show. The school won awards for the best-looking turnip and for the heaviest turnip and submitted a four stone bag of King Edward potatoes for judging. The headteacher writes proudly of this new venture and speaks of the splendid job done by the boys. An inspector's report from the same time commends the work being undertaken and the energy and enthusiasm of the headteacher for the subject. He augments this by writing, 'the soil is being carefully cultivated and wise use is being made of domestic manure, increasing the garden's fertility. The tools are clean and stored tidily in the shed'.

Further positive reports were conferred on the school in recognition of its successful exhibits in local shows; the good work done in introducing grafting and the considerable amount of correlation between the garden and schoolwork. However, an unfortunate incident occurred sometime later. Whilst clearing a plot for cultivation a group of boys 'discovered' the school cesspit and, as this could not be cleaned out for some considerable time, it meant that work on the garden ceased.

In 1923 the Horticultural Adviser arrived at St Martin's School to advise on how school garden plots should be rearranged. Unfortunately, while he was doing this, a twelve-year-old pupil turned dizzy and put the tine of a fork through his boot, inflicting a slight wound to the foot. The injured part was bathed, treated with iodine and bandaged.

When the adviser returned 18 months later, he complimented the pupils on the condition of their plots and asked after the injured pupil. He was glad to hear that the injury soon healed and his fears that tetanus might result from the wound were unfounded. He was less impressed when he inspected the state of the tools in the garden shed. He left with an instruction that, upon his next visit, he would expect to see cleaner tools and a tidier shed! The headteacher at the time put it down to that fact that it was now 11 and 12-year-old pupils doing the garden, as opposed to the 14- and 15-year olds of previous years.

CHAPTER 11

Working the land

Retting it right

The growing and processing of flax and hemp in Axholme was an essential industry up to the late Victorian era. To peasant families of the 17th century, it was a prime source of income, so much so that in a settlement over Vermuyden's drainage in 1636 the inhabitants of the Isle won compensation amounting to £400 to provide employment to aid the production of sackcloth.

Harvesting and processing flax was a summer activity. Like so many other agricultural tasks, it was laborious and time-consuming, starting with either pulling up the entire plant or cutting the stalks down to the ground. Before anything else could be done, all of the seeds would have to be carefully removed so that they could either be used for their oil or saved for planting a new crop of flax.

Flax grown for its fibres can reach four feet in height. Its needs are simple; a reasonable length of daylight, cool nights, a damp climate and well-drained soil. Sown early to mid-Spring, it is ready for harvesting on sunny days in late July. Harvesting is done by pulling the plants from the ground before stacking them into bundles.

When these are sufficiently dry, they are pulled through a rippling comb and then taken to be retted in ponds of stagnant water for about three days. The water, penetrating to the central stalk portion, swells the inner cells, bursting the outermost layer, thus increasing absorption of both moisture and decay-producing bacteria. This process of retting was called 'rating' in the Isle, which gives rise to the names of areas today such as Lound Rates at Haxey and Rates Lane in Epworth. Because of the awful smell created by this process, retting invariably took place well away from the principal areas of habitation.

The plant fibres then go through a process called scutching (scraping the fibres) and hackling (where the cord-like strips are drawn out by an iron-toothed comb). The scutching operation removes the broken woody pieces (shives).

Visiting the area in 1790, Arthur Young, an English writer on agriculture and economics and a campaigner for the rights of agricultural workers, noted that Epworth had 'four textile factories providing well-paid work for many residents'. Pullers earned 2d per score for small sheaves. If it was a good crop they could just about manage to make 5/- a day (about £30 in today's money). In particular, the flax workers of the town were noted for their skill in producing linen tablecloths of quality and longevity. The young folk who worked in the factories, however, were seen by many as the most immoral inhabitants of the town. When three Wesleyans visited one facility, they had to contend with lewdness and hostility. It took a visit from John Wesley himself to bring about a change to their 'profane lifestyle'.

The Hiring (land work in the 1960s)

It's 7.30 a.m., there's a buzz in Epworth Market Place as a crowd begins to assemble. It's a motley bunch; wide-eyed youngsters who josh and jostle; older boys who swagger around or lean casually against the walls of shops, and further back, a group of women and girls dressed in pinnies and headscarves. Stern of face, the women stand as though rooted to the Axholme soil they have worked for years - arms folded they prepare for the day ahead. This is neither cavalier nor casual, it's serious; a welcome opportunity to supplement their family's meagre income. As the church clock strikes eight o'clock, the first tractor, a grey 'Fergie' TE20, chunters over the cobbles hauling a dilapidated wooden-sided trailer 'garnished' with straw bale seats. The farmer stands hard on the footbrakes; the machine and its attachment come to a juddering halt outside the Red Lion. Covered in spatters of farmland muck, the only shiny piece on the tractor is the chrome accelerator lever. He rises from his seat. The crowd edge forward, surrounding the machine, eager to hear his words and catch his eye. Not given to long speeches the farmer bellows, 'I want fifteen good hands!'

'What's t' job?' comes a reply from one of the women.

'Singling beet.'

'What ya payin'?'

A brief pause as the farmer surveys his prospective workforce. 'Shilling a row.'

'Is thar-all,' someone counters

'Best I can do – I've gorra family t'feed anor'll thee noors!'

'Where'll we be workin'?'

'Dook Mill Furlong.'

There's a short though barely audible groan from those who know the agricultural landscape of Epworth. Dook Mill Furlong is long - it'll be a hard-earned shilling!

As folk settle to making up their minds, a competitor enters the fray – a dark orange Nuffield Universal. The sound of its throaty diesel engine turns heads, and some of the crowd drift over to stand alongside. Once again the verbal pantomime begins; 'What's job?' 'What ya payin'?' 'Where ya workin?' etc.

By 8.15 a.m., and after the arrival of a couple more tractors and trailers, with decisions made, the farmers leave with their sombre cargo. For those 'selected' (for it is the farmer who has the final say on who mounts the trailer), it is a bumpy ride to the field. Those left behind, mainly the youngest of the lads, turn and trudge home. No 'extra money' today, just the task of explaining to mum why there'll be less in the savings jar for those precious few 'treats'.

Singling beet

The creaking trailer, with its ramshackle constituents, bumps its way into the field and halts. One young lad trying to perfect the skill of standing up on a moving trailer pitches forward and despite the outstretched arms of those nearby falls between the tractor shafts. Luckily he is more shaken than injured, but after receiving a tongue-lashing from the farmer, he claims to be ready for the work ahead. Out on the field, inching their way along the ribbons of green shoots are the 'strikers' – two men moving in almost ballet-like precision with their eight-inch blade hoes, cutting gaps between the cluster of plants. They have been at it for two hours.

The 'singlers' fan out and gather behind their allotted rows like Olympic sprinters pacing the track before the starter calls them to their mark. Speed, however, will not be the essence of the day; it is all about accuracy, removing extra plants to leave just one that will benefit from the space provided. The farmer allocates one row to the youngsters but allows the older ones to 'take up three' - the row they straddle and one either side. Most of the women opt to 'take up five'. It means progress forward is slower, but that's a willing price to pay to reduce the distance of crawl. Having said that, their experienced hands move so quickly that many outpace the youngsters only 'taking up' their single rows. It's repetitive work, but after a while muscle memory takes over and the whole cavalcade moves across the field like an automaton. As the heat of the day rises, so does the temperature of the soil, leaving those in shorts seeking relief by tying sacking strips to their knees. As each person reaches the end of their allotted row(s), it is left to them to record the number completed for its payment by piecework on this task. Some scribble their 'score' down on sheets of paper, others remove a penny 'marker' to a pocket or bag. I favoured the knots in string method. At the end of the shift it's back to the farmyard for payment – this time no one stands up on the trailer, not because of the accident earlier, but quite simply, because they no longer have the energy!

Picking potatoes

It's October. In Burnham Slough, the low mist clings to the soil, a ghostly blanket anchored to the red clay. Spilling from the trailer, some of the workers peer at the rows of potatoes, as they disappear into an infinity of grey. Somewhere out there the farmer is pacing out ten-yard sections (called stints) that he will allocate to the pickers. While the innocent stare, the more experienced saunter over to a pile of baskets, safe in the knowledge that they will secure one made of wire. Latecomers will have to make do with wicker baskets that become clogged with earth, adding significantly to their weight.

As everyone reaches their 'stints', the spinner begins its journey down the rows, casting potatoes and gouts of muck across the field. The pickers scramble to load the potatoes from their stint into baskets and then into the large hamper which the men upload into a following trailer. Then it's a quick dash across the rows to the other side, hopefully with a short period of rest, before the spinner comes trundling along on its return journey. It's backbreaking, continuous and monotonous work. Some pickers work bent double, resting a free hand on the handle of their basket. Others prefer to crawl on their knees and use both hands to pick. Occasionally, an individual rises and, placing mud-encrusted hands on their hips, leans back beyond the vertical in an effort to bring some relief to an increasingly painful back. The whole scene is played out under the pressure of not falling behind. To do so would hold up the rhythm of the day and elicit strong words from both the farmer and the other workers.

The grey clag refuses to lift and leaves the pickers isolated and seemingly alone. It's a damp, muddy group that leaves the field to head to the farmer's yard for the final act of the day – the handover of brown envelopes containing some of the most hard-earned wages one could ever expect to receive.

Happing, scoping and riddling

Until the late 1960s there were two ways of storing potatoes – in large hessian sacks or in 'clamps' (often referred to as 'taty pies'). These long low pyramid constructions on the field's headland could often stretch up to thirty yards. Tipped there by the collecting trailer, the potatoes are heaped up with a wide pronged fork called a scope. As the pyramid grew, teams of men spread straw over the pile and then cast spadesful of earth on top to hold the straw in place – a process called 'happing'. These potato pies have to survive the early frosts of winter – some not being opened until the following February. It is taken as a badge of honour if the farmer took you off the picking gang to help with the happing. But you had to do it neatly; the 'happers' do not accept shoddy lines of earth, or areas not secured firmly. If the frost gets into the pie the crop will be lost

Riddling potatoes.

and with it a vital proportion of the farmer's income.

When the time comes to open the pie, the land around resembles a concrete field of ruts as the frosts penetrated deep into the Axholme soil. It is no time do dawdle, the sooner you are consigned to work the better. Any 'spare' time is taken up by cross flapping your arms to keep the cold at bay. Close to the clamp stands the riddler, a moving flatbed that shakes the cloying soil from the potatoes. Supervised by a gang of women, resplendent in their neatly tied headscarves, the potatoes are cleaned and graded as they pass along towards the twin hessian sacks at the end of the machine.

Potatoes bagged straight from the field are carried to men who hold a circular hand-riddle. With the contents of the picking basket emptied into this receptacle, it requires a quick inspection to test for diseased and damaged ones, then it's a quick shake to release the worst of the soil before the riddler casually tosses the whole clutch into a hopper that feeds the hessian sacks. It requires great accuracy to ensure none of the potatoes succeed in their break for freedom. It is not a job entrusted to a fifteen-year-old youth.

On occasions you may bump into someone who hankers after 'the good old days'. Those of us who worked for 10 bob a day in the potato fields of Axholme will happily disabuse them of their rose-tinted spectacles.

Pulling

It's the summer holidays, and word gets around that a local farmer is looking for pea pullers. We youngster join the queue of women waiting to be employed. When we get to the designated crop of peas, we are met by the ganger, an uncompromising female with arms like shoulders of boiled ham and a voice as hard as the blade of a shovel. She directs us to our 'stand' with a grunt and a nod. There'll be no 'spare' words; no smile of encouragement;

no innocent chatter with her today or the opportunity to discuss local news and events. What these gangs do bring, however, is the cohesion of a common task, and for us youngsters the chance to merge with a different cadre of adults.

If truth be told, our young arms, knees and backs aren't really up to the job. Honed to a continuous motion of bend, tear up, lay out, and strip, each of us has our own way of consigning the pea pods into the paper sack. Some drop them casually, others cast them down as one might a lighted match about to burn the fingers. I swear my sack has a false bottom as it never seems to fill, no matter how fast I work. After what seems like an age, the peas reach the top, and it's time to take the sack to the scales to see if it meets the required weight. Those who seek to cheat the system by smuggling a few clods of muck into their sacks are soon rumbled; as are those who try to put their foot on the scales to help negate the effects of the 4 stone counterweight. Each full bag gains a ticket worth 4 shillings. Woe betide those who lose theirs; there is no other way to prove the number of bags submitted!

At lunchtime, the rasping voice of the ganger rings out across the field; 'No moor bags, we's havin we dinnas!' For many of the youngsters, it's a welcome interlude. Some, however, feel unable to eat having already munched their way through a fair proportion of the crop! In the afternoon, the bored and tired content themselves watching the women pullers at work as they argue and harangue each other and end up telling rude jokes that the more naïve fail to understand.

That pea pulling was seen as a means to earn quick but necessary money is illustrated in a story from World War One. When Gordon Clark, a farmer at Mosswood between Belton and Crowle, advertised for workers to pull peas, over 150 women arrived, instead of the expected 50. He had anticipated the work would last two days, but the job was accomplished by 11 a.m. on the first day. At 6d a bag the activity was not very rewarding, but the early finish saw the swarm of pullers head off to find further work to fill the day.

Bean pulling is a similar operation – the only difference being the beans are larger and full bags only bring in 1/3d. The one advantage it has over pea pulling is that the stalks grow to waist high and offered cover for those 'caught short' during the long day. When the cry goes up, 'Gerrout my row!' everyone's heads pop up so as to identify the miscreant slinking off to perform some undesirable bodily function among the unpicked stalks further up the field.

The hardest job for me is screwing red beet. It is a similar bend and rise procedure but finishes with the twist of a rapidly stiffening and swollen wrist. It's beet in the sack and leaves to the ground – any lack of concentration and you run the risk of reversing the operation. Beneath a flat cap that appears to have seen more winters than the warped oaks along the field's edge, the farmer stares mindful of the precious minutes that pass as you retrieve the leaves from the sack and the beet from the mud-clogged field. If there's a reckoning, it will come with the brown envelope at the end of the day!

You load, I'll stack!

My mother's side of the family were Browns, long established farmers in the district and consequently she knew most other local farmers. If I needed a job nipping along to a local farm invariably resulted in employment for a day, a week, or even longer.

One place I worked during several school holidays was Firth's egg producing unit at Holmes Farm. The tasks varied from collecting and grading eggs to mucking out the battery hens. The job involved winding the underlying reinforced belt and collecting the muck in a barrow that invariably slopped and slithered, turning the concrete yard into a shit-covered (sorry, there's no better word) skating rink. The hardest task was running the barrow up a plank to empty the foul-smelling effluent into a trailer. It involved lining up the barrow with the eight-inch plank, gathering enough momentum to ensure the barrow would arrive at the bed of the trailer, then tipping it up. Done from a dry base, with a dry load it was a relatively simple operation. But, in the wet, with a slippery plank – well, I'm sure you can guess at the many pitfalls!

Another job was taking feed across the farm to the outlying free-range fields. I worked with a chap called Jim and each time we had to load the trailer with the sacks of chicken meal he would jump up on the trailer-bed and declare – 'You load, I'll stack!' The cunning old fox would watch as I struggled to lift the meal bags onto my shoulder and dump them at his feet – a lift of 4 to 5 feet. He would then drag the sacks to their place on the trailer.

'You load, I'll stack' became a mantra that I carried through my working career whenever anyone asked me to help them do a job but left me doing the lion's share of the work! It seems an apt metaphor, as for me the world appears divided unfairly between those who struggle to 'load' and those take the easy route to 'stack'!

Bringing in the harvest

Here I am on Goose Pits Furlong watching a grey Fergie claw its way up the field pulling behind the reaper-binder, a device that chunters along like a huge sewing machine. The six-bladed reel turns continuously flattening the stalks of corn onto the cutting bed while from the side bound sheaves spew out onto the stubbled ground. Men in white shirts and dark waistcoats, their sleeves rolled to the elbow follow behind sweeping up four sheaves at a time and setting them in eight stook pyramids. Left to dry they will attract farm hens who find them ideal cover in which to lay their eggs. Each morning, a trip up the field is rewarded with a basket of fresh eggs – two for breakfast today!

When the ears are dry (the older heads reckon three Sundays if the weather is kind) it's time to 'lead' the hay. If you're lucky, this might entail a ride out to the field on the dray and a trip back on top of a springy bed of sheaves lugged from the ground by one of the farm's most dangerous implements – a two-pronged pitchfork. Don't get too near the edge mind; it's a long way to fall to the ground.

Arriving at the farm, we come face to face with a heaving, rattling contraption that almost defies description, a steam traction engine with a huge iron wheel that spins and whirrs, driving thick webbing belts that bring life to the pink threshing machine. Over in a corner of the yard comes the familiar 'pom, pom, pom' of a single-cylinder Marshall. I love the sound, but it isn't my favourite tractor. That accolade falls to the three-wheeler Allis Chalmers with its long steering column for no other reason than the name sounds like that of a young girl. Everywhere it's a hive of activity; men clamber over and on the threshing tackle, their shouts and calls competing with the chatter and clatter of the many moving parts. Had they been around it would have been the stuff of nightmares for a Health and Safety Inspector.

Suddenly a man breaks away from the throng and approaches us, his trouser legs bound with binder twine. 'Are you lads upfa earnin some cash?' he asks. 'Get thissen ower theer an pick up a bat. An' don'ts fa'git to tie up thee legs – don't wanna rat runnin up theer.' It's time to splat rats and mice that escape from the straw. As if acting to command, the ground erupts as a dizzying cavalcade of rodents break cover. Instinctively they head away from their current shelters in the straw and scatter to all four corners of the yard. We follow suit, matching their vigour, buoyed on by roars of encouragement from men taking time off from guiding and servicing the machines. It's a little light relief in a day of grinding toil.

It's sixpence for a rat and threepence for a mouse. To prove our kill total, we cut off the tails and tie them to our belts. At the end of the day we'll jostle and joke as we stand before the tallyman. The dead bodies go in a bin, but they won't go to waste!

Eating for nowt!

It's almost the end of the school summer holidays, and my mum, dad, aunty and uncle begin to plan their expeditions into the fields and hedgerows in search of blackberries. Out come the white enamel buckets and walking sticks (how else can you reach those high up berries that invariably are the sweetest?). Instructed to wear my oldest clothes, I put a pair of sturdy gloves in my coat pocket and wait for the call to action. We are going into the fields of our relations at West Carr; there'll be no fear of being 'called out' for trespassing!

When we arrive at the fields my aunty sets to deploying her 'troops'. Then men will operate across the dykes, the women and I set off for the headland where the bushes grow further out into the field. There's a lot of grunting, a bit of giggling and the occasional word not designed for a youngster's ears when the brambles strike back to attack the skin of those foolish enough to pick with unprotected hands. With our buckets full we head back to the car, but the day is not over. Mum knows where there are some crab apples - one of sourest fruits you could ever eat, but with such high levels of pectin they are great for making jam.

For the next few days the house will zing to the heady smell of boiled blackberries and I will be entrusted with the most important job – cutting out greaseproof paper circles to create an air-tight seal at the top of the jars. It's a job well done, there'll be enough jam to last the year – except there's one slight problem that I daren't admit to; I don't like blackberry and apple jam!

After a long day pea pulling mum took me off to do a spot of gleaning; going back to the pea fields in search of any pods missed by the pickers – 'a good boiling will suffice' she says but I know that once on the field she will not stop picking until it's dark. On one occasion we are on Yealand Flats when a car pulls up at the entrance to the field and a burly individual walks toward me and snatches up my gleaning bag. 'What are you doing here?' he barks, 'these are my peas!' Mum, watching from the other side begins her march across the field. She has recognised her cousin; she believes she has a family right to be on the field. He will feel the full force of her fiery annoyance and we leave with all our gleanings reinstated.

Field barns

A hundred years ago the agricultural landscape of Axholme would have been studded with brick-built field barns. These single-storey buildings set within or on the edge of a field away from the main farmstead are a relic from a time when landholdings were intermixed, such as areas of wetland grazing in fen or marsh. In the Axholme area, they are not found in the strip fields but on the enclosures of land reclaimed after the drainage.

Their uses varied – sometimes they acted as shelters for sheep, with their low doors and floor-to-ceiling heights; shelters for cattle and their fodder or combination barns for storing crops, and housing cattle. They saved on transporting the harvested crop (hay or corn crops) to the farmstead, and enabled manure from the animals housed in them to be carted back out to the distant fields.

In later years when farms became more mechanised, farmers often stored their ploughs, reapers and binders in the barns, leading their horses from the farmyard each morning to harness them to the equipment in the fields.

The inside walls of many of these barns had several coats of whitewash. Years of neglect and damp have left them mildewed and 'flaky'. Their heavy framed doors were planked, sometimes ledged and braced, with iron strap hinges and handles. Some of the more 'refined' had stone-flagged or cobbled floors with drainage channels.

Workers in a field close to one of these barns found them a useful refuge from storm and rain. I recall on several occasions sheltering among old and rusting ironclad machines, industrial fittings and ancient tools such as scythes and side hoes. We would sit out the bad weather with steam rising from our damp clothes and listen to stories told by experienced farmhands. Some made us laugh; others, we found mildly embarrassing but sat with these men and women of the land conferred upon us a kind of brotherhood with the landscape.

Today, only a few of these brick-red barns with their simple, resilient and robust materials survive. Even in their ruinous condition, they make a distinctive contribution to the character of the landscape.

CHAPTER 12

More people

Visitors

In the 1540s, at the behest of Henry VIII, John Leland, an English poet and antiquary described as 'the father of English local history' visited Axholme and found 'the wetlands rich in bog myrtle and the fenny part of Axholm berith much galle, a low frutex swete in burning'.

Sir William Dugdale an English antiquary writing in 1662 states: 'Being now come into Lincolnshire, I shall first begin with the Isle of Axholme, which for many ages hath been a fenny tract, and

John Leland.

Sir William Dugdale.

for the most part covered with waters; but more anciently not so: for originally it was a woody country, and not at all annoyed with those inundations of the rivers that passed through it, as is most evident by the great numbers of oak, fir, and other trees, which have been of late frequently found in the moor, upon making of sundry ditches and channels for the draining thereof: the oak trees lying somewhat above three foot in depth, and near their roots, which do still stand as they growed, namely, in firm earth below the moor; and the bodies for the most part N.W. from the roots, not cut down with axes, but burnt asunder somewhat near the ground, as the ends of them, being coaled, do manifest. Of which sort there are multitudes, and of an extraordinary bigness – namely, five yards in compass, and sixteen yards long; and some smaller of a greater length, with good quantities of acorns near them; and of small nuts so many that there have been found no less than two pecks together in some places.' He was less complimentary about the locals, describing them as 'an obstinate, ignorant peasantry, clinging to a miserable life'.

Daniel Defoe, a university contemporary of Samuel Wesley writing in the 1700s, says 'from Rhetford, the country on the right or east lies low and marshy, till, by the confluence of the Rivers Trent, Idle, and Don, they are formed into large islands, of which the first is called the Isle of Axholm, where the lands are very rich, and feed great store of cattle: but travelling into those parts being difficult, and sometimes dangerous, especially for strangers, we contend ourselves with having the country described to us, as above, and with being assured that there were no towns of note, or anything to be called curious …'

In the 1800s, local botanist William Harrison described his view from Thorne where once he 'could stand on [the] threshold of [his home] and see Crowle Church across the Moors, but such had been the rapid rise of the surface in a comparatively short time, that the sacred edifice has become obscured from view.'

Rider Haggard wrote in his 1906 book on 'Rural England' of the Isle's 'almost inexhaustible richness [saying] it will produce magnificent crops of wheat, potatoes, celery, or whatever it may be desired to grow'. He reported the farmhouses were clean if plainly furnished. The main diet consisted of potatoes and bacon; sometimes bread and potatoes, with a little dripping. Being a mainly arable district there was little milk, and what little was produced, was not drunk but used chiefly for cooking potatoes. He described Epworth as 'the great home of smallholders [with] long bands of various coloured crops lining the plain and the slopes of the hill, all aglow with the rich light of evening'. His closing impression was 'of a prosperous and bountiful' area.

The story of the 'Wesley ghost' attracted the attention of Andrew Lang, a Scottish poet, novelist and literary critic, known for his publications on folklore, mythology and religion. Lang came to Epworth as a guest of Canon Overton in the late 1800s, ostensibly to ask local inhabitants for any family recollections of the haunting. He drew no conclusions other than the predilection of people in the area to believe in goblins and sprites and that the disturbances followed a quarrel with 'cunning men'.

George Rhodes

When William Rhodes (1781-1869) a prosperous tenant farmer met and married Theodosia Maria Heaton at Epworth on 15th April 1805, little did they know their sons would go on to help found a nation. William farmed at Epworth and later at Plains House in the Levels district. From the outset, they were an enterprising family who encouraged and financed seafaring expeditions, principally for

George Rhodes.

their eldest son, William (born 1807). William went to sea at an early age and soon became the second officer on a vessel trading in the Orient. At the age of 19, he had his first command, and after sailing to South America, Africa and India, he settled in New Zealand. Here he acquired land from the Maori and established cattle runs and trading stations. His success acted as a magnet to other members of the family, but he warned them if they joined him they would need to be 'enterprising, obliging, and not afraid of hard work, nor show any improper pride. Above all things [they should] avoid Public Houses and whores'. George, born in Epworth on 14th July 1816 and the family's seventh child and fourth son, was, by the time he joined his brother in December 1843, an established pastoralist. He helped William manage his property on South Island. In 1847, in the first recorded sale of station property in New Zealand, the brothers bought an area of land known as Purau, on the Banks Peninsula, close to Canterbury. A third brother, Robert, joined them in 1850 and later that year another brother, Joseph, travelled to New Zealand. The following year, George drove his flock of 7,000 sheep southward and established a sheep station at Timaru (Maori for 'place of shelter') which he named 'The Levels' in honour of his family home. On 31st May 1854, he married Elizabeth Wood from Hodsock in Nottinghamshire. The couple raised a family of five sons and a daughter at their house on the Levels, which they called 'Epworth Grange'.

William went on to become a prominent member of the Wellington community. He entered local politics, served on Wellington's Provincial Council and stood as a candidate for the first Parliament of New Zealand. Upon his election, William represented the Wellington district for several years. When he died in 1878, he had the distinction of being one of the richest men in New Zealand. It appears William never forgot his Epworth roots as he left a sum of money to be invested for the benefit of the poor.

Each year the interest from this paid for shawls and flannels for twelve deserving poor people in the parish. One of his grandsons, William Barnard Rhodes-Moorhouse became the first aviator to win the Victoria Cross on 27th April 1915. He died the next day from his wounds.

George died of typhoid fever at Purau at the age of 47. Like his brother William, he was strict and stern in business but seems to have been a more gentle and reticent man filled with 'integrity and honour'. An influential colonist, George avoided public life, but through the hard, uncertain years of a fledgeling nation, he helped establish sheep farming in New Zealand. His obituary in the Timaru Herald speaks of him being 'one of the founding fathers of the province' and someone 'not afraid to remove (his) coat to engage in physical labour when the necessity arose'. In Timaru, there are streets named Rhodes Street, George Street and Elizabeth Street in honour of the family and to the north of Timaru is Rhodes Bay. In a further claim to fame, it seems one of his ancestors was among those who helped rescue John Wesley from the Rectory fire.

More about Joseph Barnes

Foster Barnes' son, Joseph, was born in 1855. For a time, he worked as a letterpress printer on High Street with his father but left Epworth to study art in Paris. He toured various continental countries and in 1880 became an exhibitor in a Paris Salon. On returning home to England, he saw his pictures hung at various exhibitions in London and the Walker Gallery in Liverpool. After marrying Annie, the couple went to live in Carlisle, where he became an Associate of the Cumbrian Academy and received the patronage of H.R.H. Princess Louise, Duchess of Argyle. Joseph met John Ruskin when painting at Coniston and so impressed the art critic that Ruskin invited Joseph to show his sketches at his home at Brantwood, overlooking Coniston water. After giving him 'kindly advice', Ruskin insisted on buying some of Joseph's landscapes at much more than their commercial value. He went on to show Joseph some of his 'Turner treasures' and presented him with several etchings to further his studies.

He returned to Epworth for short periods to take commissions from 'Gentlemen's Residences in the Neighbourhood' He also brought a selection of his paintings of English and Swiss Lake Scenery that he exhibited at the offices of the Epworth Bells.

George Stovin

Born at Tetley Hall around 1695/6, in the parish of Crowle, George Stovin lived the life of a country gentleman. He married the daughter of James Empson of Goole in 1735. His primary interest was researching the topography and antiquities of Axholme. He inherited his father's estate of Hatfield Chase and devoted his life to the area, becoming a Commissioner of Sewers. Indeed, it is said that he rarely left the Levels, regarding 'no part of England comparable to the Isle of Axholme, and no town equal to Crowle'. Late in life, he did leave the Isle to live in Winterton, 'in a little cottage which he had made Arcadian with honeysuckles and other flowers, where he was to be seen with his pipe every morning at five, and where he was accustomed to amuse his neighbours with the variety of anecdotes with which his memory supplied him'.

It was Stovin who heard tell that out on the barren wastes around Amcotts, John Tate, a labouring man, came across the partial remains of a foot encased in a sandal. Taking his gardener, Thomas Perfect, with him Stovin set off to find the place. When they arrived at the scene, they found the sandal with the bones and gristle of the foot in it. Further digging revealed a second sandal that Stovin later likened to a pair of moccasins. As he excavated further, the 'esteemed historian' found the thigh bones, the skin of the lower parts of the body with 'fresh hair' on it, and a hand, with well-preserved fingernails – described by Stovin as being, 'firm and fast on the fingers as fresh as any person living'. It was the body of a woman lying on her side. Apart from the arm and hand, and the tawny coloured sandals, Stovin took the remains of the woman to Amcotts' chapel yard where he buried them. So-called 'experts' at the time concluded that the remaining objects dated from a time 'earlier than Edward IV, but not before the time of Edward I or Henry III'. Their estimate was incorrect but 'only' by some thousand years - the sandal came from the late Roman period A.D. 200 - 400. There were no apparent signs of burial, so perceived logic dictated that the woman had perished on Axholme's marshy plain having lost her way amid the desolate landscape. However, there was some suggestion that the body may have been a sacrifice to appease the gods.

In 2017, a local project initiated by residents of Amcotts and part-funded by North Lincolnshire Council, resulted in the return of the sandal to the local area where it went on display at North Lincolnshire Museum.

Samuel Wesley – the arrival

In 1697, when Samuel Wesley, short in stature but high on ambition, arrived at the door of the rectory in the small Lincolnshire farming town of Epworth hopes were high that this move would signal an upward shift in the family's fortunes. With him stood his wife Susanna and their four children: Samuel, Susanna, Emelia and Mary.

The family's journey from Samuel's previous post at South Ormsby to Epworth took them over the gently rolling hills of the Lincolnshire Wolds to Lincoln and from there north-west, to cross the River Trent at Gainsborough. It was a journey of about sixty miles over coarse, poorly signposted roads until ahead of them they saw their new home rising above the surrounding flat and frequently marsh-sodden ground. The building in front of this weary family group was a humble structure. It did, however, contain three acres of glebe land, a barn, a dovecot and a hemp-kiln. Though not without significant structural problems, compared to the 'mean cot composed of reeds and clay' at South Ormsby, it must have seemed positively palatial to the Wesleys.

Their arrival in this isolated and somewhat inhospitable area in the north-west corner of Lincolnshire caused a little stir. The previous incumbent, Dr. Robert Gale, had held the post for fifty-five years and the locals were neither used to nor accepting of change. Gale had 'fed his flock of God' and attended to their spiritual needs in a benign and benevolent manner. It would not be the style adopted by the studious Samuel whose adherence to ceremony, academic disposition, and Tory zeal were in complete contrast to those of his predecessor, and his illiterate parishioners. A man ahead of his time, he found himself in a place where there was little or no interest in the social movements occurring in the country, nor in the verbosity of an Oxford academic. Only a few of these 'morose and in-bred' inhabitants ventured further than their own parish boundary and many of those who did rejected a world they found alien and hard to comprehend. They saw nothing in this righteous idealist who spoke in an open and forthright manner, 'seeking to bring justice to all who offended by adultery, whoredom, incest, drunkenness, swearing, ribaldry, usury or any other uncleanliness or wickedness.' He considered it his duty to right the morals of these base parishioners and insisted on public acts of atonement for those who failed to meet his high moral standards.

So it was that, misunderstood and misrepresented by many, Samuel spent the rest of his life as Rector of Epworth, working in his study on sermons and poems and preaching to, at times, a hostile and uncomprehending congregation.

Ahead of him lay prison, fire, hauntings, eloping daughters and their failed marriages. Perhaps coming to Axholme was not Samuel's best move … and yet! Given the law of unintended consequence, had he not, the world could have been denied the presence of one of its greatest religious reformers.

Sir Robert Sheffield and Mulgrave Castle

The Sheffield family were devoted crusaders in the reign of Henry III. Robert Sheffield was knighted by Edward I and went on to marry the daughter of the owner of West Butterwick, Alexander Lound, which made him the largest landholder in Axholme. A descendant of his, another Sir Robert Sheffield, born in 1470, was one of the commanders of the King's army against John, Earl of Lincoln, in the battle of Stoke. He fought for Henry VII in 1497 at the battle of Blackheath, became Recorder of London and then Speaker of the House of Commons. Sir Robert married Helen, daughter and sole heir of Sir John Delves, and built a 'great tour (tower) of brick' at West Butterwick. His son, also called Robert, also resided in the tower at West Butterwick. His grandson Edmund was created 'Baron Sheffield of Butterwick' by the will of Henry VIII. On a 1778 map of West Butterwick, four fields to the south side of the village have 'Park' in their names: Low Park, Park Hill, Pond Park and Upper Park. Apocryphal evidence suggests the location for the tower house might have been on land between Park Hill and Upper Park. In 1616, Sir Edmund Sheffield who lived at Butterwick Castle, was appointed President of the Council of the North. In 1625 he was created Earl of Mulgrave, and his castle renamed Mulgrave Castle. It is possible that prisoners were held in the tower as a great many corpses were found near to the house. One theory is that these burials were of prisoners from the Mulgrave Castle. Some few years later, Dr Goel, one of the partners of Cornelius Vermuyden, paid several visits to the

Sheffields at West Butterwick with his daughter.

Eventually, the Sheffield family left West Butterwick for their new home, Normanby Hall, north of Scunthorpe. Samantha Sheffield grew up on the estate and later became the wife of David Cameron, Prime Minister of the United Kingdom from May 2010 until July 2016.

The Earl Manvers

Robert Pierrepont, 1st Earl of Kingston-Upon-Hull acquired the Manor of Crowle, early in the 17th century. Sydney William Herbert Pierrepont, 3rd Earl Manvers became Lord of the Manor in 1860 on the death of his father. His coat of arms can be seen in a window at the back of St. Oswald's Church. He oversaw a significant rebuilding of the church in the second half of the 19th century. His grandson, Evelyn Robert Pierrepont, 5th Earl Manvers and Viscount Newark suffered a mental breakdown at the age of 17 which left him unable to service the estate. After being place in trust his cousin, Gervas succeeded to the title on Evelyn's death. When Gervas died in 1955 the Manvers' title ceased to exist.

John Langley

Originally from Althorpe, John Langley went on to become a London Goldsmith. He served as Lord Mayor of the city in 1577.

I wrote in detail about the following people in my previous book (M,M,M and M) but, owing to the important role they played in the history of Axholme it would be disingenuous not to mention them again briefly.

William de Mowbray

Born in Epworth in 1172 and described as being as small as a dwarf, (which must have made mounting a horse in full armour difficult) nevertheless biographers describe William as being 'very generous and valiant'. Having been at odds with King John over disputed land, it is hardly surprising that he joined with other barons from Northern England who rebelled against John, as William had little to lose. He became one of the most resolute of the twenty-five executors who, in 1215, compelled King John to agree to Magna Carta. Contemporary sources refer to William's death aged 51 at his manor house in Axholme.

Augustine Webster

In mid-April 1533 Augustine Webster, the prior of Melwood, felt unable to compromise his faith and accept Henry VIII's Act of Supremacy. He approached Thomas Cromwell hoping to be exempt from the royal decree. Cromwell refused to listen, and eventually ordered him to Tyburn to be 'hanged with great ropes' beheaded and quartered, and the parts 'placed in public places on long spears'.

Augustine Webster was canonised as one of the 'Forty Martyrs of England and Wales' by Pope Paul VI on 25th October 1970.

Richard Bernard

Born at Epworth on 11th April 1568 Bernard gained a BA in 1594 and an MA in 1598. A Calvinist Puritan, and for a time a parson in the town, he wrote 'The Isle of Man' an allegorical story believed to have inspired John Bunyan to write 'Holy War', a precursor to 'Pilgrim's Progress'. In all, Bernard's religious texts and allegories stretched to over thirty works. Later he worked with William Brewster (1567–1644), a passenger on the Mayflower, and John Robinson (1575–1625), who organised the Mayflower voyage. In this way, his teachings and discussions on individual freedom influenced the Pilgrim Contract, established by the Pilgrim Fathers on the Mayflower. This contract would become the basis for the

American Constitution and help establish a nation. He died in March 1641 leaving a wife and six children, some with unusual names such as Cananuel, Besekiell, Masakiell and Hoseel. His daughter Mary married Roger Williams, co-founder of the state of Rhode Island.

The Mowbray Lion

CHAPTER 13

The First World War

You can take my men but don't take the horses!

On the Monday following the declaration of war, Axholme farmers having taken their livestock to Doncaster market, found the military authorities waiting for them at their hotel conveyancing yards. They were there to commandeer their farm horses! After an open and robust discussion and with the Axholme farmers unyielding in their resistance to comply, the authorities allowed them to return home with their beasts in tow. They left with a signed promise to take them back in the next few days, after arranging transport home. When some still refused to hand over their horses, men in uniform arrived in the Isle villages. They had not come just to pick up the farm horses; they had come to root out those who had not heeded the call to deliver them to the military stations. This time the instruction was, surrender your livestock or face imprisonment. As most, if not all, forms of transport in the Isle relied upon horses, it left landowners facing a dilemma. For them 'ordinary' life would just not function without being able to call upon the strength, power and adaptability of their thoroughbreds and shires. Some even admitted that losing their men to the war was infinitely more palatable than losing their horses. As one local commented, 'the men volunteered for the hardships they faced, the poor horses had no say in their fate'. Mr. Dale of Sandtoft Grange Farm declared that, whilst he approved of farmers being called upon to supply 'a couple of horses', he felt it unfair to take all their horses, especially at a busy time like Harvest! When the men in khaki rounded up the 'unsurrendered horses', they tied them all together on a long rope and lead them out of the villages. The sight broke many a stout Axholme heart. Farmers found little solace when it was discovered later that the feet of their heavy farm horses were vulnerable to the wet ground in the fields of France and were of little use!

Don't panic!

In late August 1914, the Epworth Bells exhorted its readers to – 'Keep your head. Be calm. Go about your ordinary business quietly and soberly. Do not indulge in excitement or foolish demonstrations. Try to contribute your share by doing your duty in your place and your own sphere. Be abstemious and economical. Avoid waste. Instead of dwelling on your privations, think of the infinitely worse state of those who live at the seat of war and are not only thrown out of work but deprived of all they possess. Do what you can to cheer and encourage our soldiers. Gladly help any organisation for their comfort and welfare.'

The demon drink

When Patrick Whelan, a trawlerman from Grimsby, appeared before the court in Epworth, his foul language and wild conduct led Alderman Blaydes to admonish him severely. He reminded the prisoner of the place all men such as him should be! Taking the hint, the defendant said he had not attempted to enlist, as yet, but was willing to do so. To this end, the magistrates sent him to Lincoln gaol for three days, under a promise to report for enlistment upon his release. Insobriety in the war years was not just confined to seafarers. When John Malia of Luddington leaving the pub one night came across men in the street talking about the war he heard them 'speaking in favour of the Germans'. In his 'less than sociable state', he was in no mood to forgive any perceived indiscretions against his beloved country. The fracas he created and the 'number of [his] previous convictions', saw the local magistrates commit him to seven days hard labour. It seems he learned his lesson as some time later he and his brother, Charles, were involved in another disturbance in the street. John went home when advised by the police, but Charles insisted on being locked up. When he appeared before the magistrates, he faced a 5/- fine with 3/- costs added. It was another of the countless instances of war-time, drunken behaviour Isle magistrates had to resolve and of the many who sought solace through drink, several of those appearing before the courts were not always male!

Working on the Home Front
In most Isle villages, the manner of fundraising for the 'War effort' followed a familiar and universal pattern. In Crowle, The War Relief Fund, under the chairmanship of Mr. J. Franks J. P., C.C. stated that all persons willing to give and work for the Fund were 'heartily invited to join the Committee at their meetings in the Upper Room of the Market Hall'. Here it was decided that 50% of all funds raised would go to the Prince of Wales' National Relief Fund and 50% would provide materials for the Ladies' Sewing Committee which had already undertaken war relief work. The Market Hall, however, proved to be too cold for meetings to be held in comfort, so members voted to approach the managers of the Council School to see if they would grant the use of a schoolroom for any future meetings. At one of Crowle's fundraising concerts, the town's Choral Society and the Council School Boys' Choir provided magnificent entertainment to an appreciative audience.

Older scholars at the Council School spent their spare time making garments for soldiers, under the direction of the headteacher, Miss Hodkinson. In addition, the school appointed four pupils to undertake house-to-house collections. On successive Saturday evenings, Crowle Town Brass Band paraded through the main streets for about 45 minutes and took up collections, raising on one occasion a total of £4/4/2, which all agreed was a 'most satisfactory sum'.

The ladies of Luddington divided the village into four regions to facilitate door-to-door collections. Their first 'gift' to the four Luddington recruits was £1 for sets of fresh underclothing. In West Butterwick, the school building hosted a 'capital concert', the proceeds of which helped provide for six pillowcases, five shirts, two nightshirts, thirty-four body belts, thirty-one pairs of socks, eight pairs of mittens, nine vests and a muffler. Members of the football club agreed to undertake collections every Saturday night and the War Committee allocated a 'liberal sum to send tobacco and cigarettes to everyone from the village serving with the colours'.

House-to-house collections began well in Keadby and Althorpe, and on several occasions, the War Fund helpers managed to raise enough money to send £5 to the Prince of Wales' Fund at Buckingham Palace and £3 to the local ladies' organisation to help buy wool. This helped provide a limited amount of wool for those willing to work on garments in their own houses. By the time the ninth house-to-house collection took place, however, residents were disheartened to find the amount collected had dipped below £5 for the first time. This disappointment was more than made up for though when the ladies' committee published details of their activities. Their enthusiastic endeavours supplied blankets, bed jackets, shirts, pillowcases, socks and mufflers to the Red Cross and helped secure a large quantity of wool for many willing knitters in the villages. In addition to providing practical support for the boys abroad, knitted garments proved to be an effective means of maintaining morale, both at home and at the front. In Epworth, when another meeting was called to look at ways the town could help support the National Relief Fund, there was a disappointing turnout - the result of a serious counter attraction in the form of the circus! When news of this filtered around the town, however, it became the catalyst needed to spur residents to action; it was acknowledged that never again would they put their own pleasures above national interests. Over subsequent weeks and on throughout the war in a variety of imaginative ways the Axholme towns and villages raised significant sums of money.

As further draconian measures began to take effect, some residents of Axholme, in keeping with towns and villages across the land, resorted to panic buying. In no time at all, the shelves of local shops were emptied of meat, sugar and other essentials. Some folk went out shopping with the prime aim of bringing back all they could physically carry; others, afraid of invasion, began systematically stockpiling. The Epworth Bells tried to reassure its readers that it was highly unlikely there would be an invasion, but the hoarding continued. Workers at Marshall's, Gainsborough, were immediately put on short-time working as the management announced that, owing to the hoarding of silver coins, they would find it impossible to pay their 5,000 members of staff! Special Constables initially appointed to assist parish constables with their duties, were asked to be on the lookout for those squirrelling away essentials. They took to their responsibilities with a zeal bordering on fanaticism.

When the Government introduced the Summertime Act in 1916, the Epworth Bells sought to mitigate the confusion this caused by advising residents of the Isle that there was no need to wait up until 2 a.m. (the official time for the changeover) as no harm would come to anyone altering their clocks before going to bed!

A refugee crisis

When the call went out to provide food and accommodation for Belgian refugees, the people of Graizelound and Haxey sent two cartloads of fresh vegetables to the Belgian Refugees' Committee in

Leeds. There were over 850 Belgian Refugees in Leeds alone, 539 arriving on one night. Later on, the Lord Mayor of Leeds wrote to the people of Graizelound to convey his 'sincere gratitude' for the Axholme potatoes, onions, carrots and other vegetables. Epworth set aside the yard of the White Bear Hotel as a collection point for potatoes and other produce to be collected and sent on. Most of the Belgian refugees arriving in Leeds were smallholder farmers, so these gifts of vegetables were particularly well received. Thousands more were expected in England and committees in the Isle began to look at where best they could help by providing homes. By 7th November the residents of Haxey resolved to support the vicar Rev. Sheppard's commitment to provide three homes for a minimum of 6 months. In Owston Ferry, a cottage offered to a refugee family could not be vacated immediately, so Mr. and Mrs. Knight kindly agreed to take in refugees from Ostend until the cottage could be made ready.

The residents of Belton looked to provide seven homes in response to an illustrated lecture in the Public Hall given by Mr. Charles Everatt. He spoke of the great duty the British owed to the heroic Belgian nation. The talk focused on Belgian towns and cities, showing them before and after they were laid in ruins by 'the brutal German invaders'. Mr. McNamee, the headmaster at Temple Belwood, offered the use of the coachman's lodge and agreed to educate refugee children free of charge. Colonel Senior promised one rabbit a week for every member of a refugee family over the age of eight years old. Sometime later the village held a concert for the arriving refugees. They, along with other residents, listened to songs by the choir; to dramatic and humorous verse by Miss Gladys King and to 'melodies' from Miss Annie Whiteley. The event concluded with a supper at the Wesleyan schoolroom.

When 24 refugees arrived in the Isle by rail, there were tears of sorrow that, 'so many mothers, infants and grey-haired old ladies should have had to leave their own fireside'. Some arrived with nothing more 'than the poor clothes in which they stood'. In an attempt to raise their spirits, 'luxuriant motor cars' carried some of the refugees to their billets. One poor woman, on the verge of collapse but clinging desperately to her two little girls, was taken to Owston Ferry. She had 'witnessed the cruel butchery of her brother-in-law and had her husband ruthlessly torn away to dig ditches.' She and her girls had spent two months walking to Ostend before being evacuated to Folkestone. The residents of the village resolved that 'now she has come to be our guest all that careful nursing and nourishing food can do will be done to restore her to health and vigour'. Scholars from the Wesleyan School gave the proceeds of their annual concert to help with the plight of the poor family. When some Belgian refugees attended the show, members of the audience gave them a 'very hearty round of applause'.

Crowle offered up to 50 homes for refugees, though some residents voiced their dissatisfaction that the refugees were from the 'artisan class and not country people more in keeping with their hosts'. Mr. Sanderson, headmaster of the church school, responding to this claim, contended that the committee was entirely within its terms of reference, as no particular class of people had been identified at their meetings. When eleven of the twenty refugees arrived, they were lodged at Morely Cottage, Proctor's Cottage and at the home of Mrs. Layden in North Street. These Belgians had arrived at Folkestone and been taken to Alexandra Palace before being moved on to the Isle. The news of their arrival in Crowle spread quickly and, once the residents saw them, they put aside their misgivings over class as 'their appearance elicited such great sympathy'.

Nursing sisters

If you look at Misterton's War Memorial, at the bottom of the list of men from the village who died in the First World War, you will find the inscription 'Nurse K Jollands'. Before anyone claims that Misterton is not in the Isle, Catherine (Kitty) Jollands originated from Haxey Carr where she was born in 1894. By the age of 20, she and her sister Agnes (Nan), volunteered to nurse wounded soldiers at Fir Vale Hospital in Sheffield. In early July 1915, Kitty complained of feeling unwell, but the ward sister refused permission for her to leave her position. Kitty completed her shift but fell dangerously ill over the following hours. She died a few days later on 8th July having contracted double pneumonia. She is buried in the graveyard on Haxey Road. Her death appeared to galvanise Agnes to commit further to the war effort. She went to the front to serve as a VAD nurse at casualty clearing stations. Although not at the front, these stations repeatedly came under shell fire. In recognition of her work, Agnes was mentioned in dispatches and later received the Military Cross. After the war, she worked as a school nurse until her health broke down. She died at Haxey Carr on 24th September 1923 from tuberculosis she had contracted during the war. She is buried with her sister.

 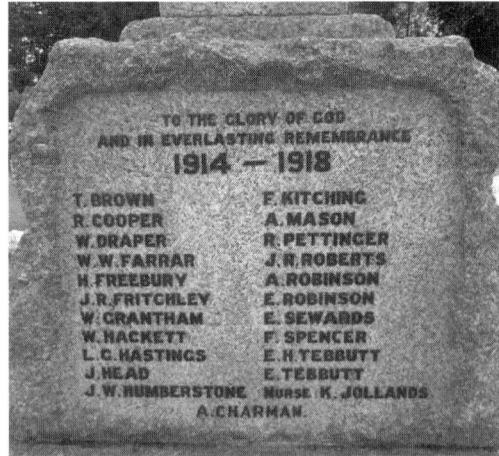

Kitty Jollands, and name inscribed on the Misterton War Memorial.

An Epworth V.C.?

William (Willie) Chafer was born in Bradford, but by the age of six, he was living with his grandfather, William and grandmother, Amelia in Studcross. He was admitted as a scholar at Epworth Church of England school on 28th August 1899. He left school at the age of 14 and later moved to Sowerby Bridge. He moved to Rotherham and worked at Silverwood Colliery. At the outbreak of war, he joined the East Yorks Regiment.

His citation reads; 'For conspicuous bravery: During a very heavy hostile bombardment and attack on our trenches, a man carrying an important written message to his company commander was half-buried and rendered unconscious by a shell. Private Chafer, at once grasping the situation, on his own initiative, took the message from the man's pocket, and, although wounded severely in three places, ran along the ruined parapet under heavy shell and machine-gun fire, and just succeeded in delivering it before he collapsed from the effect of his wounds. He displayed great initiative and a splendid devotion to duty at a critical moment.'

Severely wounded, Willie Chafer was removed to a hospital in Glasgow where attempts to save his badly mangled leg failed. His war was over! Seeking to use his disability as a rallying call to others, Willie spent the rest of the war at recruitment meetings and talking in schools. He became a leading figure in promoting the Thurlow Croft Field as Epworth's War Memorial.

In recognition of his bravery, the citizens of Epworth raised the sum of £50. They presented it to him at a concert in the Imperial Hall where, quite rightly, he was the guest of honour.

Cynics will claim that his eight years in Epworth hardly qualify as a reason to link his act of bravery to the town. He was not born in the area and was not living there when he enlisted (the criteria accorded to those whose names appear on the War Memorial). However, in the bleak days of that awful conflagration, one can understand the need to celebrate a heroic deed no matter how tenuous the connection to his place of residence.

Conscripted

The introduction of conscription did not sit well with the British sense of honour and fair play. Some argued that men who joined voluntarily would fight better than those compelled to. What conscription would do, was highlight further those who refused to fight on the grounds of conscience, with the inevitability that they may be called upon to kill. Nationally some 16,000 men objected on ethical or religious grounds and refused to join the forces or at least serve in a combat unit. This debate of conscience over duty played out publicly in the local papers, particularly in the Crowle Advertiser. Writing as 'A Christian' one correspondent felt challenged to attack those who took as their text, 'Thou shalt not kill'. 'Where would England be today if this was the motto of every able-bodied man?' the author argued. 'Why have so many brave lads laid down their lives? Have they not done so to save England from the sin with which Germany is so impregnated?' He went on to say, 'What a glorious day for the Allies when peace is declared, and what a glorious awakening, too, for all those brave lads who have gone to meet their God. Which shall receive the greater reward? The soldier who gave his life for his King and country or the Conscientious Objector whose plea was - thou shalt not kill. Surely all Christian people will agree with me and say with one accord; "Why! Tommy Atkins, of course." If this letter should come under the eye of a Conscientious Objector, I hope he will think it over and put aside his shirky feelings and go and do his bit.' That all Christian people did not agree with him is evidenced by the reply published a week later. Quoting other lines of scripture this correspondent, who titled himself 'A True Christian', attacked those who were 'blind to the sin of killing'. As the debate raged, the debate intensified. Under the heading; 'A word to cowards', the Advertiser published a letter that questioned where we would be if 260 brave lads from Crowle had not gone forward to defend Britain. 'Are they murderers?' the correspondent argued because, unlike you, 'they are not staying at home and hiding behind the fifth commandment!'

Torpedoed!

There was some disheartening news in May 1917 when a report confirmed the transport ship, Arcadian, had been torpedoed and sunk in the Mediterranean. On the ship were Second Lieutenant Reg Stephenson from Althorpe and Trooper Henry Lindley of Epworth. An eyewitness to the tragedy wrote; 'The Arcadian had been dogged throughout the night by a "U" boat when, without a moment's warning, a terrific explosion occurred. Everyone realised that the old Arcadian had received a 'Blighty' one and was shortly due for Davey Jones's locker. After one convulsive shudder from end to end, the great ship began to settle down on her port side with the loose deck paraphernalia slithering about in all directions and dropping into the sea.' As the ship went down the fear was that an inrush of water to the funnels would cause danger to those left on board. The Chaplain was, indeed, sucked down the funnel and subsequently, 'vomited out again like a rocket'. Remarkably he suffered no ill effects. Large numbers of those drowned, the survivors, and a quantity of wreckage were left behind after only six minutes as the ship slid away beneath the waves. The chilling wind and turbulent currents led to the survivors drifting apart. When all seemed lost, as if from nowhere, the words of the hymn 'Nearer my God to Thee', wafted across the waters, and reached the ears of the survivors. 'Every poor devil, more than three-quarters drowned, did his level best to swell the chorus on that awful night.' After a night clinging to the wreckage, the 'Q' ship Redbreast arrived on the scene and picked up the survivors. Amongst them were Reg and Henry who managed to swim until the rescue ship arrived. Second Lieutenant Stephenson was an expert swimmer, and Trooper Lindley offered 'thanks to the Old Torne' for his ability to stay afloat.

The gun is coming to Crowle!
In Crowle, the first coordinated celebration to mark the end of the Great War was termed 'Thanksgiving Week'. This began on 23rd November 1918 with a gun captured from the enemy at the front. Sponsored by the War Savings Committee, the gun was towed from the railway station to its site in the Market Place. The hope was this would encourage the residents of the town to raise funds to help the recovery from war. Patriotic flags hoisted on poles surrounded a barricade, erected to hold the 18-pound gun during its time in the town.

Unfortunately, the planned arrival turned out to be less

Advert for the coming of the Crowle Gun

spectacular than planned. Insufficient military horses could be found to pull the gun, so draught horses were pressed into action. The organiser failed to confirm a band for the proceedings; the weather was vile, and, although a reasonable number of ex-soldiers and town worthies turned up to process the gun around the town, the bad weather led to the abandonment of the parade. Despite this inauspicious start, the inhabitants of Crowle rallied round and the following week's activities raised over £11,000. This exceeded the town's target by £3,500 and averaged out at almost £40 per head of the population (2853). The amount qualified the town for one of the souvenir shells given by the National War Savings Committee. The gun left the town seven days later.

Going home!

On Friday morning 29th March 1919, 'the people of Owston Ferry bade goodbye to Madame De Ceye, who has been in the village since the last week in October 1914. When she fled the German onslaught was at its height, and she barely escaped with her life. She brought with her, her two children, one a baby in arms, and for a little time, it was feared that she even then might succumb to the exposure and dread to which she had been subjected. However, careful attention brought her back to her usual strength, and she has been able to some extent to assist in providing for herself and her family. The forty subscribers who from the commencement have paid their weekly contributions towards her support will be glad to know that she and her children left Ferry well provided for in food and clothing'.

Celebrating peace 1919

The Isle of Axholme Rural District Council rejected out of hand a suggestion to join with Gainsborough to celebrate peace. The Isle, they said was 'perfectly capable of organising its own celebration!'

On 5th July to start 'the ball of peace rolling' Belton played Crowle at cricket on the ground at Hirst Priory. In tandem with the match was bowling at skittles, bowling at a wicket, guessing the weight of a draught horse and an open-air whist drive. Buses to the ground ran from Belton and Crowle to ferry the large numbers of spectators wishing to attend. Much to the chagrin of both teams, the result of the game was declared irrelevant!

The day set aside to celebrate 'The Peace' saw all towns and villages begin proceedings with a Church Service. At Althorpe the fun started at 11 a.m. with a procession of decorated wagons and drays, that included an Indian sledge with a wigwam and family, decorated bicycles and horse riders. The committee provided tea in the Memorial Hall for about 250 children, demobilised soldiers and, most poignant of all, war widows. Entertainment in the evening included a married versus single tug-of-war, a comedy football match, a ladies' tug-of-war, a skittles competition and children's sports. Unfortunately, medals to be presented to the children did not arrive in time and had to be distributed later.

Celebrations in West Butterwick were extensive for a village of such size. The children paraded through the village singing patriotic songs, each child receiving a gift of money. Mr. and Mrs. J. Wall each gave a large ham and Mr. Barnett, the landlord of the Ferry Boat Inn, provided all with salmon sandwiches.

At Crowle Wharf, and Ealand, the events were declared 'a resounding success'. Decorated drays depicted the 'Dove of Peace', the Red Cross, the D34 Airship, Gipsy Fair, etc. conveyed children to where Mr. J. D. Foster presented them with a Peace Mug.

On 19th July, the day set aside in Epworth, houses throughout the town were decked with streamers, flags and bunting, and the church bells rang out from early in the morning. At 11 o'clock all the children assembled at the Council School and received commemorative silver medals (made by Fattorini, silversmiths of

Bradford) with ribbon and pin attachments. At one o'clock an impressive procession left Mr. Richard Selby's farm where a large arch bore the words, 'When can their glory fade?' on one side, and 'To the Silent Legion: Love, Remembrance, Honour', on the other. Superintendent Weston led the procession, followed by a comic band of discharged and demobilised soldiers, cyclists in fancy dress, children in their best attire, riders dressed as famous characters and cars, traps and drays all decorated in bright and illuminating colours. The demobilised soldiers entertained spectators to a comic cricket match and enthusiasm for the day continued through to its close at 9 p.m.

The programme of events in Gunthorpe ran over two days. Residents took part in 42 events that included two, three-mile, handicap bicycle rides and a whole variety of amusing sports. The children received peace and victory mugs. On the two evenings it was time or the adults to 'let down their hair' as they attended concerts and dances.

Three celebrations took place in the Parish of Haxey; one in Haxey, the others in Westwoodside and Burnham respectively. At Haxey there were prizes for the best-decorated dray and horses in the procession; for the best comic turnout and the best-decorated bicycle. The whole event was accompanied by a large jazz band and concluded with a bonfire and an excellent firework display. The church, draped in the flags of the Allies, provided an inspiring finale. At Burnham, the celebrations included a tea for all inhabitants followed by sports and dancing. The menu for the day in Westwoodside followed similar lines.

In Owston Ferry, the streets were decorated with flags and bunting, and residents turned out in their best holiday clothes. The day was given over to 'healthy pleasure, fun and frolic' as the children processed around the village singing patriotic songs. Following this came two hours of sports and tea at the schools and the Coronation Hall. Those who could not attend had their meal sent out to their homes. The day ended with fireworks.

Belton Peace Celebrations began on 2nd August with every child in the village receiving a Victory Mug. As a special treat, they were then given free rides on Messrs. Smith and Warrens' Galloping Horses at a field belonging to Mr. Hackney. Two days later, the village held a 'Monster Procession' featuring tableaux on the theme of the 'Trial of the Kaiser'. Headed by Crowle Brass Band, the procession (including a parade of comic cycles) set off from Grey Green at 11.30 a.m. and moved through Westgate, Carrhouse, Churchtown, Moss Lane, Bracon and Crowle Road. The day ended with a 'Victory Firework' display.

Belton peace celebrations 1919

CHAPTER 14

Letters from the Front

Private William Spencer of Albion Hill, Epworth, with the Canadians in the trenches, wrote to his mother: 'I guess you will have read in the papers that the Canadian Division is making a name for itself. Our regiment - the Seaforth Highlanders - is doing its share. About the beginning of March ... half a dozen of us were quartered in an old farmhouse, about a quarter of a mile from our first-line trenches. We had scouted round and found wood and potatoes and had got a nice stew nearly ready when we heard noises in the air, followed by a loud explosion behind us. Two or three more came along, each one getting nearer, so we decided we had better move somewhere. We ran out behind a couple of stacks about twenty yards away, thinking we would be safe there.

All the time the shells were getting nearer, but as we were getting hungry, we dashed across the open to the house, fetched the stew and served it out behind the stack. I know the potatoes were bolted whole and big pieces of meat swallowed without being tasted, for the shells were dropping each side of the stack by this time. A few of the men were like ostriches, for they had buried their heads in the straw so as not to hear the shells coming. The stack next to us was used by the artillery as an observation post, and an officer told us to "beat it", as that was what they were after. Some of us stayed, and some "beat it" to headquarters - dugouts. In a little while, they ceased firing, and we left the stack to look for pieces of shell. The nearest shell hole was about six yards to the side of the stack, and it was a wonder none of us were hit. The artillery officer told us that if they had used a different kind of shell, we should have been blown to pieces. That made us think we were rather lucky to be still alive, but we were complimented when he told us that all we thought about was our blooming stew. The worst of shrapnel is that you can hear it coming and you spend anxious moments wondering where it is going to burst. Since then, I have been in the trenches several times and up to the present have come out untouched.'

It was to be his last letter home as he was to die on 22nd April in an attack at the Second Battle of Ypres (St Julian). On the very day that Mrs. Spencer of Albion Hill, Epworth received the letter from her son telling her he had gone back to the trenches but was all right, she received a telegram informing her of his death from wounds to the stomach. The stretcher party had rescued him during a lull in the fighting but had been unable to get him to a dressing station in time.

In a letter home, Private R. S. Greaves, son of the Epworth baker described the threat from continuous shellfire and of several of his 'lucky escapes'. When under fire he recalled one lad, 'kept on calling for his mother and who could blame him'. On another occasion, he wrote of shrapnel tearing through his coat in two places and through his cap, taking with it part of his ear! He seemed more concerned, however, with a 90lb bomb that dropped on the cookhouse as the regiment was just about to eat breakfast. 'Of course, breakfast was spoilt', he wrote, 'in fact, where the fires were, there was now a hole about 12 feet in diameter and about the same in depth. Needless to say, curses were both loud and deep over it, but the fact remained, our breakfast was gone, nothing remained but bully beef and biscuit'.

Private Alf Newbitt of Epworth wrote to his parents about the privilege of being allowed to leave the front line and go 'shopping' in the nearby village. On other occasions, he had asked to be excused a lack of correspondence owing to the trench not being 'an ideal place to write letters'. In another letter, Alf wrote about the Germans 'giving us musical selections on the cornet and flutes. They played our National Anthem one afternoon. I don't know whether it was meant as a slur or otherwise, but the music was all right'. On another occasion, he spoke of it being, 'A1 here. We are billeted in a town and shall be able to enjoy ourselves a bit. Everyone wondered what the matter was when we awoke to hear the Church bells ringing for service. It is Sunday morning. I could fancy I was in bed at home listening to the bell going for 8 o'clock service. Excuse mistakes, everybody's making such a noise - they are so pleased. No wonder! The Germans gave us such a gruelling last Sunday, with all sizes of shells, aerial torpedoes, rifle grenades, whizz-bangs - I think they used nearly everything but gas, and the smoke from the big shells was nearly as bad as gas. It's the biggest wonder in the world we were not all killed, but luckily not one of our platoon got worse than a bad shaking. It was such a strain on the nerves that half of our chaps had to report sick that night. We had some very narrow escapes. One large shell burst about five yards in front of our dug-outs, nearly choking us with dust and smoke; another dropped between two of our dug-outs and buried our water-can. Another hit a dug out which luckily was empty - there was nothing to be seen of it after; a large hole marked the spot where it stood. When these aerial torpedoes burst they shake the ground like an earthquake'.

When Alf's death was reported some time later, his parents received this letter from Pte. Johnson Coggon saying; 'It was not until I received the Bells that I learned of your sad bereavement. Just before Alf went into action for the second time during the advance, I saw him as they swung along, cheerful as usual, but little thinking that the greeting he gave me was to be his last farewell. His regiment relieved ours after the first attack on July 1st, and probably he was within speaking distance then, but I was relieved to see that he had come through that glorious but terrible ordeal, and with the pluck and courage of the real British soldier was going up to strike another blow or die for England. People at home may read of the indomitable courage of the British troops, but if they could have seen how they fell yet shouting their triumph with their dying breath, they would have cause to be proud of those who have paid the great sacrifice.' Alf's memorial service in the Parish Church was held in tandem with memorials to Private Francis Brett and Private Herbert Thompson.

Private E. Dale of Belton, on active service in the Dardanelles, cautioned those at home about the dangers of trench warfare. 'The snipers are good shots', he wrote, 'if you show your heads above the trench they have you!' Private W. Johnson of Epworth, serving with the Lincolnshire Regiment, spoke of his spell in the trenches and things being, 'a bit lively at times – bullets, shells, bombs, and whizz-bangs knocking about all over the place, especially when we are cooking our meals. We are having some very funny weather out here, and it is up to the knees in sludge and water in some of the trenches. We were in the trenches for sixteen days for a start, and we were told we stood it as well as the regular soldiers. We have now been in four days. The night before last we got word that the Germans were using their gas on our side near Ypres, but later we heard that the gas had turned back on their own men. We can always know when it is mealtimes because the Germans start sending us a few whizz bangs. We laugh and joke and say that it is a few more iron rations for Tommy. We are about 200 yards from the German lines but cannot see anyone as they keep down in the daytime, all the firing – except artillery – being done at night.'

The parents of Albert Maddison received this letter from his commanding officer. 'Although I know the subject of this letter must be a painful one for you, I feel impelled by a strong sense of duty to write to you. Therefore, if this letter causes soreness, I hope you will forgive me and give me credit for the best intentions. I would have written before, but I was rather badly wounded and am only just beginning to feel myself again. I have no doubt you will, by this time, have received the official intimation of your son Albert Edward's death from wounds whilst a prisoner of war. First of all, let me offer my heartiest sympathy to you in your bereavement. I occupied the next bed in hospital to your son, and I feel sure you would like to learn a few details of the circumstances surrounding his sad death. Of course, you will have heard he was wounded in the leg whilst advancing on July 1st. It was at first thought to be a straightforward case, but complications set in with what unfortunate results you have heard. I am sure it will be a great consolation to you to hear that he received the utmost possible care and attention. Everything possible was done in the attempt to save him. I feel certain you will bless the sisters who nursed him with gentleness and kindness. It must certainly lessen the great sorrow you feel when you learn these facts. When I get back to Manchester after this war is over, I would only be too pleased to pay you a visit and give you a personal account. Anyhow, I hope you will write me. I shall be pleased to answer any questions you care to ask.'

Sgt-Major Arthur Goulding of Keadby wrote; 'We have been in the thick of it, and shrapnel humming hourly around our ears. Still the boys advance gaily along and as cheerily as on manoeuvres. I could make your hair stand on end, if I wished, with true stories of heroic deeds witnessed by my company at different times and in various places. When we think we are safe, along comes an aeroplane, and the positions are then disclosed. About an hour afterwards the shells are bursting right and left, but, thank goodness, the enemy have some inferior ammunition to ours, and the boys can time a good many of them, so "down flat!" is the order, except when we are in the trenches, which is another thing altogether, for then it is, "heads up and stick it out". When the boys see the uniform in front (German) then they see red, and one would think it was prize shooting instead of killing another human being, and the lines in front become thinned out; but as fast as one life is knocked over another one comes along. When we retired for a day or two it took a bit of the life out of us, but when we commenced to go forward everything was bright and gay, and forward they go with a good heart and with a relish at that. You could send some cigarettes along if you would, or cigarette papers: that's about all I require as we have plenty of food issued to us in the field. The army was never better fed than at present.'

I'm no shirker!

The fear of being labelled 'a shirker' led to Charles Staniforth of Crowle feeling obliged to re-enlist at the age of 37. In 1895 Charles had joined up for 12 years in the East Yorkshire Regiment and fought in the Boer War but had been invalided out. When war broke out in 1914 he felt compelled to 'do his bit' again. He enlisted in the labour battalion and spent several months in France. On December 1st 1915, in a somewhat rambling tome, he wrote home:

'Dear Father and all at Medge Hall just a few lines hoping they find you all in good health as they leave me middling only that I am stuffed up with cold and right hoarse. We have had a week of rather wintry weather snow and frost it is very cold here at nights we are on the top of a big hill ever so high, but I like it better than where we were before we came here. I have not heard from Claude yet I wrote nearly a fortnight since but he has not written back he has never wrote to me yet and I don't think I shall write to him any more unless he writes and I have not heard from Tom since a long while before Claude came on leave but I hope they are both of them all right. I have just had a letter from Frank Burkinshaw I saw him just before we came here, and he says I should see in the paper about (D) and Fred Chester being wounded but I have not

received the paper with it in yet. Tell Ethel she is to send it every week and a letter too she has wrote to me more than any one yet though I had the Gazette week before last but no letter, so I think I have told you all with best love to you all I remain your son.
C. Staniforth

P.S. we shall soon have Christmas now – I would like to have my dinner at home (there) but I begin to think I (shan't) but I hope to see you all soon.

Charles would write one more letter, thanking the ladies of Crowle for the parcel that contained the 'very things that are needed, especially the towel and socks, as we only have one towel and we have to do our own washing, and you cannot always get them dry as the weather out here is simply awful. We scarcely ever have a dry pair of socks on. I am in good health with the exception of a cold. I am in a labour battalion, as I am rather deaf'. Charles was discharged from the army in 1916, ostensibly because of his defective hearing, though the family recognised he returned from France in a poor mental state. He went to live with his sister in Balby but was unable to shake off his dark moods. One day he went for a walk in the fields but didn't return. His suicide, at the age of 39, was received in Crowle with great sadness.

George Dale of Crowle wrote the following to tell of his experiences in the trenches; 'We set off from our trench about six o'clock at night to go up to the reserve trenches. We had then nearly a mile to go to the communication trench before reaching the firing line. Having got about half way, bullets started whistling in all directions as there were a lot of snipers behind the lines at this particular part. However, we arrived at the firing line without anyone being hit, and when morning came we were able to have a look round and see where we were, and I was surprised to find that we were only about 200 yards from the enemy. I thought I would have a look over the parapet, so I just had a peep and I had just got down when a couple of pieces of lead came and skimmed the parapet where I had been looking over. I can tell you I did not look over again …. now we have got used to the trenches you would be surprised to see us moving about as bullets come from all directions. We are ready for the enemy as soon as they like to come, and I guarantee they will go back with a rattle'. Unfortunately, George's prophetic words did not come true. On 1st July, his battalion advanced from their trenches with 680 men and 23 officers. George was not among the sixty-eight men that returned.

Commemorating Axholme's fallen

In 2014, to mark the centenary of the beginning of the First World War, a party of students from South Axholme Academy, visited the battlefields and memorials in France and Belgium. As a mark of respect, they laid wreaths at The Thiepval Monument, The Menin Gate and the cemetery at Tyne Cot. The students also placed British Legion Crosses beside the following names of Axholme men commemorated at each site.

The Thiepval Monument

William Hughes	Belton
Herbert Everatt	Belton
Frederick Hill	Belton
Alfred Watlon	Crowle
Albert Wilson	Crowle
Arthur Rose	Epworth
Herbert Thompson	Epworth
Harold Johnson	Haxey
Lawrence Leggott	Haxey
George Hammond	Westwoodside
George Brown	Owston Ferry
Walter Glew	West Butterwick

The Menin Gate

Albert Broderick	Crowle
Frederick Key	Crowle
Lorrie Prince	Crowle
Frederick Wroot	Crowle
John Webster	Crowle
Arthur Winter	Crowle
Thomas Parkin	Epworth
Ronald Wrench	Epworth
Joseph Atack	Westwoodside
Joseph Fielding	Owston Ferry

Tyne Cot

Wilfred Kirk	Belton
Arthur Watson	Belton
William Bellamy	Crowle
Walter Fretwell	Crowle
Charles Hill	Crowle
Dennis Richardson	Crowle
Robert Brown	Crowle
Alfred Holmes	Crowle Wharfe
Edwin Keall	Epworth
Thomas Stones	Epworth
Arthur Hather	Haxey
Ernest Keightley	Haxey
Herbert Coggon	Haxey
James Ward	West Butterwick

CHAPTER 15

The Second World War

Evacuees

In a change to plans for evacuees from Leeds and Sheffield to be housed in the Scunthorpe area, the authorities decided against this for fear of air attacks on the iron and steel works. It had no effect on the three thousand or so, selected to come to the Isle from Hull. They arrived with their teachers and assembled at local schools before volunteers allotted them to the schoolrooms of Methodist Churches to await their billets. Once assigned, private motor cars conveyed them to their new homes. Having settled into their new surroundings, the Epworth Bells commented on the novelty they found from seeing the 'farmyards, fields, green lanes, corn and haystacks' around them. Everything was 'new to many of the children, and the way they roam about and gaze at windmills, farm carts and farmyard poultry is particularly noticeable to the country dweller. They enjoy being in the harvest field. It is no uncommon sight to see three boys riding on one horse. They love to go with the farmer's wife into the poultry run, or watch the farm labourer milking the cows'.

Under the terms of their employment evacuees could work as and when they liked and for as long as they wished, keeping 2d of every shilling earned to help pay for clothes and shoes. The scheme taught the evacuees many things about rural life; on occasions, they attended the local blacksmiths to see Mr. Harris shoeing horses and marvelled at the 'good grace' with which the animals seemed to accept 'iron rings being nailed to their feet'. Many locals noted that the refugees' time in the fields had brought 'colour to the children's pale cheeks leaving little to choose between the appearance of the Hull children and the healthy, fresh looks of the those born in the country.

As their first Christmas away from home approached, the evacuees were looking forward to a happy time. The Epworth Bells reported on a forthcoming re-union, 'arrangements having been made for a large party of mothers to come by motor coaches from Hull. They are expected to arrive at Epworth at about 10 a.m., and the children will be assembled at the Council School to meet them there. The visitors are bringing food for lunch; the children will return to their billets for dinner. At 3 p.m., the visitors will return home. The boys will give a concert in the Imperial Hall on Wednesday next, to help meet the expenses of the Christmas party they will have on December 29th. In order to show their appreciation of what has been done for the children by local people, it has been decided to invite all children of school age living in houses where there are evacuees to be present at the party.

Gifts of food, games, crackers, paper hats and other things which will add to the enjoyment of the children will be greatly appreciated by the teaching staff. If anyone has a Christmas tree they have done with it will be very acceptable. Now that the boys have the use of the Thurlow Schoolroom for recreation, they need a small billiard table. If anyone has a table, say half-size, to dispose of, the headmaster or any member of the teaching staff would glad to hear of it'.

There were minor difficulties over billeting some children, but on the whole, the evacuees settled down quickly. Although the paper reports positively on the new arrivals, some months later on 15th March 1940, when a second appeal to take in another round of evacuees was broadcast, of the 4000 circulars sent to homes on the Isle requesting help, only a small number of households came forward with offers. This could have been due in part to the heading 'Evacuees Must be Clean', under which the Epworth Bells offered a word of caution as allegations of uncleanliness among evacuees billeted in Lincolnshire began to surface. The Town Clerk of Hull wrote to assure the councils on the Isle that 'all children registered were being examined by the school nurse and steps were being taken to clean any who were verminous. They would again be examined before their evacuation, or on the actual day of the evacuation, and no child would be allowed to leave Hull until they had been properly examined'. The hope was that this would 'allay anxiety on the part of people who have undertaken to receive evacuees and make them more willing to have children in their homes'.

Eventually, however, 517 new evacuees, arriving from Hull on the Axholme Joint Railway, found homes in all the towns and villages of Axholme - Amcotts took in 13, Belton 57, West Butterwick 30, Crowle 126, Epworth 44, Garthorpe 20, Haxey 82, Luddington 13, Owston Ferry 46, and Wroot 19. The Epworth Hostel admitted 17; the one in Crowle 27. Residents of the Isle set up clubs and societies to help them assimilate into Axholme life, such as a cricket team, a gardening club, a stamp club, a debating society, a Young Farmers' club and a cycling club.

Three years later the chief billeting officer arrived at schools in the Isle to give the evacuated children, 'gifts from the people of America'. Several of these came in the form of sweets, though alongside these and on a more practical note, it was not unusual for wellingtons and clothes to be included. There were gifts of money in the form of postal orders to provide presents at Christmas time. In Owston Ferry, Father Christmas brought each child an orange, a quarter pound of sweets and a chocolate bar.

Take cover!

Local builder Reginald Hill advertised his air raid shelter stating, 'Don't wait till the balloon goes up, you can use your shelter in peacetime as a shed for your perambulator or bicycle'. The Bells printed Air Raid Precautions for residents, advising them that warnings of impending raids would be given by a fluctuating or warbling signal of varying pitch while a continuous signal at a steady pitch meant 'raiders passed'. Should there be concerns over poisonous gas then wardens had instructions to cycle around the town with hand rattles. When the danger passed, they would ride the same route ringing a handbell. Some Isle residents found it very confusing; others felt it was irrelevant!

A Haxey soldier's war – taken prisoner

Thursday was a special day in my boyhood years. It was the day 'The Victor' came out. Part comic, part storybook it told tales of human endurance, resilience, bravery and sacrifice. It fuelled my passion for 'escape stories' – I read them all The Colditz Story, The Wooden Horse, The Great Escape. Little did I realise that I would marry the daughter of a real-life WW2 escaper.

Sid Sedgwick's background in mechanics at the family's Central Garage in Haxey made him a typical candidate for the Royal Engineers. At the outbreak of war Sid was in the Territorials but was soon in the 106th Unit (West Riding) A T Company R. E. In June 1942 he was captured at Tobruk when it fell to the Axis forces. Herded like cattle onto a prison ship, with only a tin of corned beef and a small quantity of rusty water, his destination was Taranto in Southern Italy. From there he was moved to concentration Camp 53 at Sforzacosta a converted sugar beet factory. With little food, a small crude toilet block and three standpipes that spewed muddy water, several men viewed escape as the best option. This went against the orders of British officers who determined that with the Allies advancing, a 'wait it out' policy was the best option. They misjudged the speed of the advance and the determination of the Nazis who took over the camp and began moving the prisoners

Sid and Marjorie

north. On 8th September 1943, Sid found himself sixty miles north of Venice on his way to Stalag VII A when there arose an opportunity to escape. With his friend Enoch (Knocker) Round from Doncaster and three others, he jumped from the moving train. The five of them lived rough for a while until 'Knocker' developed a severe abscess on his backside. In desperate need of treatment, Sid helped his friend to a nunnery near Costa Di Aviano. It was a dangerous gamble for neither of them knew whether the nuns would inform the German authorities in the valley below.

In hiding

The nuns did not reveal the escapees to the Germans, but Sid had to leave his friend 'Knocker' behind while they treated the abscess. Joining up with the others again, the four made their way up into the mountains. In the region of Visinale, exhausted after a long climb, they took to hiding in a woodpile at the back of a farm. It could not have been a very successful hiding place as the farmer, an Italian called Bepi, discovered them when collecting logs. He took them to one of his barns and brought them food each day. Looking after four PoWs proved too much for Bepi, so his friend Cencio agreed to take two. Over the winter of 1943/44, the escapees helped look after the village livestock and took on various other jobs around the village. They soon became familiar faces in the area. Sid reckoned they even got some of the young girls to darn and mend their clothes, but that may just be an embellishment! As the Germans began to move through the mountains, the danger of discovery increased, so Cencio's son Giovanen showed them to a chamber under the patio where they hid on several occasions. It was a cramped existence that often lasted for many hours – the only toilet being a metal bucket that the men had to pass from one to another. There were spillages!

As the Germans increased the frequency of their 'visits' to the village, there came the very real threat that those harbouring escaped PoWs would be shot. So as not to expose the villagers to reprisal, Sid made the decision to leave Visinale. On the day of his departure, there were tears as many from the village turned out to wish him well. He had arrived as an 'enemy', but he left as a friend. For a time, he wandered through the mountains until he bumped into a German patrol. Using his basic Italian, he tried to convince them he was an Italian woodcutter. They didn't believe him - he was a prisoner again!

Behind the wire

The Germans took Sid to Stalag VIIA at Moosburg in Bavaria, the largest of the PoW camps in Germany. It served as a transit camp and at any one time held up to 110,000 prisoners. Conditions were dire; there was little food, and the guards displayed an aggressive and belligerent attitude. He was glad to be moved on to Stalag

The Polish watch that cost Sid a loaf of bread.

VIII-B in Poland. It was a relocation camp in Cieszyn built as an overspill camp from the original VIII-B in Lamsdorf. On the prison records, he is listed as a Sapper with a PoW number 128668. Unfortunately, conditions here were little better. The rules of the Geneva Convention which laid down protections and standards for the treatment of PoWs were often ignored, especially for Polish prisoners. Although rations were meagre, the British did manage to access Red Cross Parcels that contained food and personal hygiene items. They used some of these items to help support and barter with prisoners of other nationalities. On one occasion Sid swapped a loaf of bread for the pocket watch of a Polish soldier – he must have been exceedingly hungry to part with such a personal item.

Stalag VIII-B had six large wooden barracks, each housing up to 240 people. There was a field hospital, a prison, a disinfestation barrack, a kitchen, craftsmen workshops and a sports field. The whole camp was surrounded by double barbed wire and guarded by six watchtowers. When full, the camp housed up to 1650 prisoners: the largest groups being soldiers from the USSR, Italy

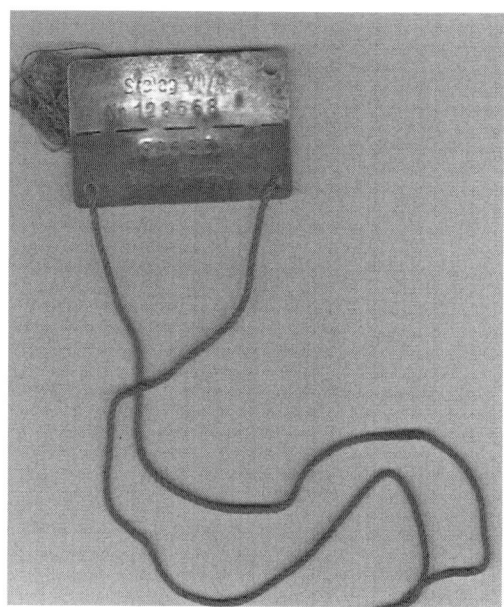

Sid's PoW Dogtag

and Britain - followed by smaller numbers from Canada, South Africa, New Zealand, Australia and Poland.

There is no record of Sid being involved in any escape planning at Stalag VIII-B, but knowing his restless spirit, it is hard to imagine him sitting out the days in fruitless activity. However, as the war moved towards its conclusion, he had no idea that in the weeks to come he would face the sternest test of his life!

Marching to death!

In January 1945, with the German Army in retreat to the approaching Eastern Front the decision was made to evacuate the prisoners from Polish camps to prisoner of war camps in Germany. The evacuation at Stalag VIII-B began on the 21st January in what was one of the coldest winter months of the 20th century. The occupants of the camp assembled in groups of 250 or so in preparation for the journey south through the German-occupied Czech Protectorate to their new 'home' at

Weiden in Bavaria. The groups would march up to 40 km a day, resting where they could find cover – in factories and barns but often under hedges and trees. There was little food provided and nothing in the way of clothing or medical care. Already weak and underweight from years behind barbed wire, the 'Long March' (better termed by many as 'The Death March') proved too much for many and hundreds of Allied prisoners died along the way. In addition to starvation and exhaustion, the prisoners had to contend with pneumonia, typhus, diphtheria and frostbite from sleeping outside on the frozen ground that in its severest state required the amputation of fingers and toes. With so little food, the only way to survive was to scavenge for food. Many took to eating leaves and berries; some ended up eating dogs and cats - and even rats and grass - anything they could lay their hands on! Those that fell or lagged behind faced being encouraged along by a rifle butt to the head or a bayonet in the back. As Sid exchanged places to help the soldier behind who was struggling, one of the guards stepped forward, casually raised his rifle and shot the poor man through the head.

In their ragged and emaciated state, the surviving prisoners who finally reached western Germany had one thing in common – shiny cap badges. Throughout all the privations they've suffered, it is the one thing the men have been able to do to maintain pride in their regiment. With the sound of Russian guns behind them and American ones in front, little did Sid realise that fate still had one more hand to play!

Freedom

As winter drew to a close, suffering from the cold abated, and some of the German guards, realising the war was almost at an end, became less harsh in their treatment of PoWs. With German morale collapsing, some even gave up trying to control the lines of prisoners. It was left to the Allied officers to advise and instruct their men. Those in Sid's column decided to push on and try and connect with the advancing Americans instead of waiting for 'liberation to arrive'. It was a wise decision; others were not so lucky! Those with guards who refused to accept Germany's impending defeat found themselves being marched towards the Baltic Sea where the Nazis used them as human shields and hostages.

Those who sat it out ended up under the control of the Russians – their journey back to freedom would not happen for months, even years. According to Nigel Cawthorne in his book 'The Iron Cage' many 'disappeared' into the endless wastes of Siberia, never to return.

Sid told me that when he presented himself at his home in Haxey, he had lost so much weight, his mother did not recognise him at first. It would be a long road back to fitness. Released from the army on 27th November 1945, he was judged 'Class C' - unfit for active service.

Postscript

Sid arrived in Haxey with another PoW who had been in Stalag VIII-B (reported in the Epworth Bells as Stalagate B) and on a 'Death March' – Lance Bomb. G.W. Dawes. He had been in PoW camps since 1940, having been captured at Dunkirk.

In the mid-60s Sid, 'Knocker' and their wives made the journey back to Visinale. As they approached the village, one of Bepi's sons recognised Sid and ran to spread the news. By the time they got to the centre, with the villagers turning out to welcome them, it was as though they had never been away. Once again, there were tears, but this time they were tears of joy.

In 2004, Sid's son Ivan and his wife Jane holidaying on Lake Garda also drove to the village. After knocking on several doors, they found themselves at Giovanen's house. The whole family turned out and communicated through an English-speaking member. The couple were shown where Sid hid from the Germans and were asked to sign a book written by a local historian about the war which included a chapter about hiding the English. He signed it 'Ivan son of Setimo', Setimo being Italian for Sid. The family sent a copy of the book to Ivan and Jane on their return home.

Make do and mend

Over the years, with the war taking its toll on the nation's food, the Epworth Bells provided ideas for Axholme families to keep well-fed. In one article, entitled 'Sandwiches for Supper', suggestions included sandwiches made from flakes of fish, tomato and onion, haricot beans, ginger and chocolate, banana and honey, and nut and raisin. Later on, the newspaper would extoll the virtues of dried eggs (just add water and treat like a fresh one), corned beef stew, bean sausage and dried egg pie, and coleslaw (a treat Americans had been enjoying for many years).

The instruction to farmers was to 'plough by day and night to beat the weather' as a successful ploughing was 'equivalent to winning a mighty naval battle'. Prosper de Mulder of Doncaster, offered to pay the best price for live but worn-out horses, 'for killing purposes' while Cheval Meat Supplies of Silver Street Doncaster, advertised for fat horses, cobs and ponies of super quality. The modern reader might find this disquieting but, up until the 1930s horse meat had been part of the British diet.

Throughout the war, the Epworth Bells advocated public commitment to the many organisations raising funds for the war effort. The first was the 'Spitfire Fund' and all settlements in Axholme appointed Spitfire Committees to come up with exciting ways to raise funds towards their 'own' Spitfire. In Epworth, one enterprising individual organised for a captured Messerschmidt 109 to go on display in the Market Place with the public paying to view it. By April 1941, Epworth's fund stood at £372.

In the years following, other campaigns such as 'Warship Week' (which raised £130,000) 'Wings for Victory' (which saw Axholme folk raise £200,000, enough to buy two Lancaster Bombers), 'War Weapons Week' (£170,000) and 'Salute the Soldier Week' saw over half-a-million pounds raised in support of the war. With the population of Axholme standing at 13,000, this equated to £39 per head. In addition to this support, there were saving schemes such as National Savings Certificates, National War Bonds and Mrs. Churchill's Fund to provide aid for Russia, and countless other adverts seeking to attract money from the civil population.

By 1942 the effects of the war were biting hard in Axholme. Fashion advertisements disappeared from the pages of the Epworth Bells to be replaced by a 'make do and mend' mindset. Even Bell Bros. Jewellers in Doncaster, used the newspaper to announce their regret that, having disposed of their quota of items for the year, they would only be open for repairs pending a relaxation in the directives on selling precious metals and stones. The Epworth Bells' office operated a paper salvage facility but, found themselves apologising for having to use paper partly made from straw which caused the pages to fade to a burnt bronze colour days after purchase.

In the early hours of Saturday 30th December 1944, residents of the Isle could be forgiven for thinking the area was under attack from the air. Buildings shook, floors vibrated, and people were shaken out of bed. It was not an air raid (as some feared) but an earthquake with its epicentre in the Skipton area. It proved a frightening experience for light sleepers; children woke up screaming, and adults and children alike wandered into the night streets expecting to see considerable damage to their property. Others, dismissing the incident as that of a passing army truck, turned over in bed and went back to sleep. The morning revealed there had been little damage, apart from the odd loose chimney pot. The 'quake' had a local magnitude measured at 4.8 on the Richter Scale and remains one of the most powerful earthquakes ever recorded in Britain.

New homes and no rats!
As the months of 1945 headed to a successful conclusion of hostilities, many reports reflected the mood in Axholme and that of a nation looking towards an uncertain future. The Isle Planning Officer was grappling with a housing shortage and under orders from the Ministry of Health to increase provision. Over the next two years the expectation was that Althorpe and Keadby would provide 32 extra homes; Belton and Beltoft, 22; Crowle 40; Eastoft 16; Epworth 20; Garthorpe 14; Haxey and Westwoodside 30; Luddington 7; Owston Ferry and Gunthorpe 24; West Butterwick 8, with Wroot not yet determined. In total this came to 213 new homes in the ownership of the council and available for rent. The Ministry of Health agreed to provide the sub-structures, paths, fences and connection to services, but responsibility for maintaining the homes in a good state, both inside and out, fell to the local authority.

Axholme's problem with rats also took up space in the newspaper. In Epworth and Crowle, the call went out to every man, woman and child to be a 'Rat Reporter'. The Ministry of Food calculated that nationally rats caused fouling or destruction to two million tons of food a year, and farming areas were the worst affected. The 'Bells' begged to inform 'farmers, owners of ricks and threshing contractors [that] any rick of corn, rye, beans, peas, linseed or clover must be surrounded by a fence of material impenetrable by rats', before commencing threshing. Farmers were under an obligation to take effective steps to kill rats inside this fence. Failure to comply with these instructions would see the offender, upon conviction, liable to a heavy fine or a term of imprisonment, or both'.

V E Day

On the evening before V E Day, the army billeted to the town left Epworth under cover of darkness - lined up in Queen Street, the soldiers departed so quietly residents didn't realise they had gone! One resident from the time recalls; 'The tanks and heavy vehicles just seemed to melt away!'

In the Epworth Bells, there were no triumphal headlines, no jingoistic slogans or fervid proclamations. In simple terms, the newspaper reported on the celebrations taking place across the Isle in an ordered and positive manner. In Althorpe there were reports of 'the village [being] gay with flags and bunting. After a service at the Methodist Church, Mr. G. F. Stones laid a beautiful wreath at the War Memorial in memory of those from the parish'. The people of Amcotts laid on a tea for the children, followed by sports in Mr. Belton's field. Later on, the village held a dance in the schoolroom where the Grammar School Quintette provided the music, and Mr. J. A. Ellis provided a 'comic turn'. In Belton, a large congregation gathered for a united service and sang 'suitable hymns and prayers'. Another united service took place in Crowle. Here, members of the Parish Council joined in the singing of the Hallelujah Chorus. Following the Prime Minister's announcement, the bells of the Parish Church rang out across the town. The next day, at Holy Communion, the congregation joined in a Requiem Mass for the Fallen. The community of Crowle set themselves the task of collecting a 4d levy to provide for some 300 returning men and women. The committee appointed, resolved to use some of the money to provide for any subsequent, and separate, peace celebrations.

The pupils in Owston Ferry were given a two-day holiday and celebrated with a tea in the Crooked Billet. Once again, this involved carrying school tables through the village, which 'the older boys did with enthusiasm'. For some children and for many adults the celebrations went on late into the night. There was singing and street dancing to the Blue Lyrics Band in a floodlit High Street. Mrs Todd was so grateful for the safe return of her son that she gave all the school children a 3d piece. Rations that had been saved up for this special time were brought out, and there were sandwiches and cakes galore, especially enjoyable for a nation that had been starved of sweets and treats.

At Epworth, thanksgiving services took place at the Parish Church and the Wesley Memorial Church. The news saw the residents take part in a torchlight parade around the town. The following day 'a long night-dance was held in the Imperial Hall'. The women of Rectory Street organised a tea for 80 children in the garage of Mr. J. P. Tune, with home made teas being sent to the homes of the old-age pensioners. The children received 9d each and an orange given by Mr. Tune. At the hurriedly organised sports events, there was even a married women's race! The Epworth Bells reported that all the competitors did well, although some finished in 'low gear'. The report declared it to be, 'a day that will long remain in the minds of both old and young'.

The community on Epworth Turbary provided a 'sumptuous tea' for everyone, followed by sports and a bonfire on the Common. In tug-of-war contests, 'the girls won handsomely .... and the old buffers pulled the "young 'uns" round the field'. Children under 5 received a bar of chocolate, and everyone agreed that the occasion was 'the best ever - like old times come back again'. Over 400 residents from West End (from the Railway Bridge to Nineveh) attended a tea in the dining hall of Sandtoft Airfield. It appears the three long tables were so laden with food that it made 'rationing appear a dream'. A huge Victoria sponge cake alone weighed in at over three stones.

V J Day

Belton was quickly off the mark when it came to celebrating the official end of World War Two. On Thursday 16 August about 30 children in the Churchtown district were entertained to a Victory Tea organised and arranged by Mrs. Kelsey in the Parish Room. As the day closed with a huge bonfire, each child received a gift of 1s. 6d. On 17 August, the Epworth Bells reported; 'The splendid news that the terrible World War had ended was received with feelings of thanksgiving by residents in the Isle of Axholme who heard the Prime Minister's broadcast message at midnight on Tuesday and in the early bulletins on Wednesday morning, and early on the latter-day the houses and other buildings were gaily bedecked with flags and bunting. Everyone appeared to be in a joyous mood, and there were various forms of rejoicing everywhere. Many of the shops and works were closed for the two day holiday specified by the Government in celebration of V.J. day, only essential services remaining in operation. The 'bus service in the Isle operated by one of the Scunthorpe motor companies was also partially suspended'. On the 18th the Imperial Hall, Epworth, hosted a 'Grand Victory Dance' with dancing from 8 to 12 midnight. Admission was 2/- (although any members of the military still in the district were admitted at half-price. Two days later the Epworth Bells reports that 'about 60 children and old-age pensioners, ranging from Melwood to the end of Mowbray Street, were entertained in Mr. J. P. Tune's garage. An excellent tea and supper [were] provided, and old people unable to attend were sent their tea and supper. Each child was given 1s. and very small children were presented with a beaker. Sports were held in Mr. Mell's field, and a good time was enjoyed by everybody'.

Later children from Belton Road and Burnham Road came together for a 'sumptuous repast' at the Cemetery chapel. 'They then adjourned to Mr. Lindley's field [for] sports. Towards dark the huge bonfire which had been prepared by the young people during the day was set alight, and the flames lit up the countryside for a considerable distance until nearly midnight. The skill and enterprise of the housewives in preparing the provisions was so successful that sufficient was left over for a second feed for the children on [the following] night.'

In Crowle, the children of the town, along with those from Ealand and Crowle Wharf, and Medge Hall, attended the Regal Cinema for a free programme of pictures. In the afternoon there were sports and a baby show. Tea was served in the Market Place, where the tables 'presented a most tempting spectacle, and full justice was done to the sumptuous repast provided. There were a large number of entrants in the fancy-dress parade for children, which took place in the Market Place during the evening, some very original characters being on view. The remainder of the evening (until midnight) was spent in dancing by the adults, in the Market Place, the Square again being floodlit by Mr. H. Hornsby, and altogether a most enjoyable time was spent'.

Victory celebrations at Beltoft were 'an outstanding success [that] will long be remembered in this hamlet of some 100 residents. No one was forgotten from children in arms to old people up to 93 years of age, and a thoroughly enjoyable time was spent by all'. The proceedings commenced with an evening of fireworks and a bonfire. The following day everybody enjoyed a free tea, with 'tables ladened with a tempting variety of food to which the youngsters did ample justice'. Later, both children and adults took part in a variety of sports. The day closed with an evening dance followed by a midnight supper.

Keadby and Althorpe's celebrations included a dance in the Memorial Hall, Althorpe. In Dolphin Street coloured lights were put across the street. There was a large bonfire on the riverside, with dancing in the street until 2 a.m. Later in the week, the

Women's Institute held a whist drive in the new clubroom.

The Epworth Bells carried an eye-witness account of the 'gala' celebrations in West Butterwick. 'A splendid organisation had arranged a fine programme, including a tea for the whole village and, happy thought, also all visitors. The first event was the fancy parade—not large, 'tis true, but what a parade; what ingenuity, what a sense of humour had been brought into play. This had to be seen, I can't describe it. What a task for the judges, Mrs. Bramhill, of Althorpe, and Mrs. R. Clark, East Butterwick. That task very graciously and satisfactorily accomplished, away went the parade all round the village to the accompaniment of appropriate music from a loudspeaker van (more ingenuity). Back to the Day Schools, the children were the first to sit down to tea, and oh, what a tea! Tables groaning beneath the weight of the good and varied things so liberally provided by a grateful village, and how tastefully were those tables decorated and arranged. After tea, the children had sports and games, ice-cream, 1945 sixpences, a bonfire, and then some of them danced with their elders until midnight, after which came the National Anthem. Then, young and old went home, tired, but happy. It had been a memorable day.'

He went on to make three further observations -

'First: farmers and men ceased harvest operations at 12 o'clock, midday: The weather had been bad, now it was good. It was a mighty act of faith.

Second: one of our young lads was in hospital at Gringley-on-the-Hill. He hadn't been home for three years. His parents knew he would love to come home, if only for the day. The organisation fetched him home and took him back the same night. Two words stand out throughout the whole day's efforts — sacrifice and love.

Third: almost in the midst of all the fun and gaiety, time was found for one minute's perfect silence in memory of those lads who will never come back to us, but who have made the supreme

Entrance to dummy airfield shelter, Low Melwood, Owston Ferry

sacrifice so that we had been privileged to live to see this day. The challenge to us is: Are we going to be worthy of that sacrifice in days unborn? If so, war is ended for all time.'

There are few signs left of those war days in Isle now: the remains of the Observation Post on Belgarthorne Hill, Epworth and at Eastoft; the army cookhouse in Epworth High Street; places where the iron railings were taken for use as bullets; a couple of Commonwealth War Graves in the graveyards of Epworth, Haxey and Eastoft Churches and Crowle Cemetery; an inscription left by prisoners of war on the site of the camp at Crowle and the remains of Sandtoft Airfield and the dummy airfield buildings at High Melwood, where each night a team of men would light flares to mimic those of an active airfield.

Gone is the army dump just beyond the Ellers' Tavern, the

practice shooting range in the cutting at Black Bridge, and the crater left by the doodlebug that fell near Thompson's Mill. There may be few physical signs left of the war, but as in all communities in Britain, the war left an indelible imprint in the hearts and minds of the people of the Isle. Indeed, after the activity and involvement, many found it hard to return to 'normal' life. My mother, who worked the fields during the day and walked the streets as an ARP warden at night, declared the war years to be, 'the most exciting time of my life'. It brought her husband-to-be to the town, and their union in 1947 produced one son - me!

PoW camps in Axholme

The main prisoner of war camp for the area was at Pingley Farm, Brigg. There were satellite camps in the Isle at Sandtoft, Crowle and Keadby (North and South). During the war, they housed Italian prisoners of war. After the war, they provided rehabilitation facilities for German prisoners.

At the Sandtoft camp for a time, the German leader was described as an ignorant type not suited for the position. The deputy was described as arrogant and, as a consequence, the camp was listed as Nazi-tainted. In fairness to some of the prisoners they had been picked up in Germany, and those with certificates showing they were Russian couldn't understand why they were prisoners in England.

Keadby South housed Austrians from 4th August 1946. They had limited access to such things as films and concerts and were denied the use of the football pitch. However, inspectors judged the leader, who spoke excellent English, to be doing a good job!

The camp at Crowle on Mill Road, just east of the cemetery, was small by comparison, and used to house Italians during the war. At the end of the conflict it was a 'hostel' for German prisoners. Inspectors reported that, although the leader was not

Evidence of removed railings at Wesley memorial Church

Replaced railings at Pashley Walk, Epworth

imbued with a 'democratic ideology', he kept up a reasonably high morale. Today in front of the house at Crowle Grange on a concrete apron, there is an inscription written by Italians dating from the end of the Second World War.

Bill Goldthorpe (on the Crowle Community Forum) recalls; 'Late 1941 up Mill Trod, now known as Mill Road, [and] following the early successes against the Italians in North Africa, a camp holding about 100 prisoners had been built. The matinees [at the Regal Cinema] were cancelled so that the Italian prisoners could go to the pictures on Saturday afternoon. The local urchins' animosity to prisoners suddenly knew no bounds.

The prisoners had to be exercised, so they were taken on route marches 2 or 3 times a week. A hundred prisoners with a platoon of infantry and a sergeant, all armed with bayonets attached to their rifles. It remained like that for about 6 weeks, then size of the platoon began to shrink, the bayonets disappeared, and then the rifles until at the end an elderly sergeant with a walking stick accompanied them. They started to work at the local farms and then farther away so that they had to be accommodated on the farms. Gradually they were all living on the farms and the camp was virtually empty.

Then the process began all over again this time with German prisoners of war. Route marches with numerous armed guards who gradually disappeared. Until the Germans themselves were running the camp with an elderly British captain and sergeant in charge. The Germans were employed locally on the farms and businesses, but unlike the Italians they were not distributed about the area. In order to make some spending money they started small businesses, a group started to weave slippers out of rope, which were tastily decorated. Others did part time gardening or helped out in local garages or joiners at the weekend. Many were adopted by an English family and allowed to stay with them on a Sunday. They were just ordinary

German soldiers no fascists or SS among them. They knew which way the war would end and were glad to be out of it.

A few of both groups never went home. The Italians married some of the Roman Catholic girls. Some of the Germans stayed, skilled and reliable workers were offered partnerships in local businesses and eventually married locally.'

In all Isle camps, inspectors noted a lack of progress in re-educating the prisoners and suggested they needed better recreational and educational facilities such as newspapers, libraries, lectures, discussion groups and a wireless providing access to Nuremberg trials.

Where morale was high, it came from civilian contact though evidence showed that some families treated the prisoners as little more than slave labour.

Post war problems

The winter of 1947 brought much disruption and disorder to Axholme. The bad weather began on 21st January and lasted until mid-March. Large drifts of snow blocked roads and railway lines. Snow fell continuously for 26 days and the high winds created drifts up to 15 feet. Vegetables were so frozen to the ground that they had to be 'dug up' with pneumatic drills. When the thaw came, and the snow-melt ran off the frozen ground, the River Trent burst its banks bringing more misery to the villages along the riverbank. When Lindsey Health Service reviewed the year they found that, across the district, there had been 33 deaths of children aged between 5 and 16 in the North Lincolnshire area. Twelve of these were put down to 'accidents'. 7% of children in the area were found to be undernourished. Schools locally were in desperate need of repair and poor sanitary arrangements and washing facilities were seen as contributing to the poor health of the Axholme's children.

A place to stay

In another notable event in the first full year after the end of the war, squatters moved into the buildings on the searchlight site at Owston Ferry. Later on, twenty families from Thorne and Thorne Moorends, moved into the now redundant R.A.F. station at Sandtoft and christened their community 'The New Village'. The men were mostly colliers from Thorne pit. Claiming the facilities at Sandtoft were excellent, the squatters agreed to reserve five shillings a week for each hut should any rent be claimed. The group appointed the oldest member of the 'camp' - a seventy-year-old pensioner - as an outside cleaner, with each 'tenant' paying him one shilling a week. Three families also moved into the huts on the searchlight site at West Butterwick.

CHAPTER 16

An Axholme Miscellany

The fair ladies of Axholme

There is something about an isolated community such as Axholme that raises the contribution of the womenfolk to a level at least equal to, if not surpassing that of their menfolk. That the females of Axholme played a significant role in steering forward the area's causes is beyond question. During the riots that led from the work of Vermuyden, one of the principal leaders was Robert Popplewell of Belton. However, it is noted that the rioters were much happier to be led by his wife for there was always the prospect of her sanctioning greater brutality! When she, along with others, was indicted at Lincoln Assizes, Popplewell applied to the court for leniency. He agreed to pay damages amounting to £600, saving his wife and the rest from further penalty.

Two hundred years later, the women of Epworth rioted. Led by Tommy Wrigglesworth a bricklayer of the town, they risked transportation if caught. Successive harvests on the Isle had been poor, and the women determined that somehow they had to feed their families. Entering the granary of Jacky Maw, a wealthy bachelor farmer, they each took a bushel of his 'good' corn. Each woman laid a sovereign on Jacky's desk to compensate him for the loss - it was, after all, not a theft borne out of poverty but out of need. The riot would go on record as one of the most orderly ever to have taken place.

During World War One, several farmers complained that women assigned to land duties were unable to accomplish the work assigned to them by their employers. Some deemed women not to be good with horses, as 'they taxed a man's whole energies'.

One can only presume that those who subscribed to this view were referring to the horses! One Trentside farmer, who applied to the Labour Exchange for 'any number of female labourers', felt compelled to point out that some turned up for work in high heels and 'peek-a-boo' blouses! Equally, many farmers amused themselves by giving their women workforce the dirtiest and arduous of tasks. At an Axholme War Agricultural Committee meeting, held in Epworth, Mr. Duke of Sandtoft Grange countered these complaints. He spoke of the great assistance he had received from 'ladies' assigned to him to help with potato gathering. 'It was not expected that these young ladies, many of them of good family and position, and who never knew what hard labour was before, could possibly hold their own with women of the district who have been at agricultural labour all their lives,' he said. He went on to praise the ladies for 'having done their best, potentially giving up their holidays for rough living and hard work, when they might have spent them in luxury in refined homes'. These ladies were contracted to farmers to work for 50 hours a week, with Saturday afternoon and Sunday free, at a weekly wage of £1-12 pence. In practice, some received less pay as farmers could, and often did, deduct significant amounts for board and lodging. When seasonal pressures dictated work patterns, many women found themselves in the fields from dawn until dusk; their weekly hours far exceeding the number set.

In truth, many women just resigned themselves to the hard labour, the inherent dangers of machinery, the sparse living conditions and the low pay. What they found harder to accept were the prejudices of their male employers. Government propaganda showing rosy-cheeked ladies buckling down to their chores on the farm was just that, propaganda! In the Isle, as in other rural areas, much of the work was done, as it always had been, by countrywomen well versed in country ways. These women had an open attitude when it came to balancing the daily grind of home chores with rural labour. They were simply grateful for the extra pay on offer.

In 1900, The Crowle Advertiser did not mince its words when it came to identifying 'the most deluded mortal in the world'. This they decided was 'the woman who fancies that much is gained by scolding or whining or complaining. She may seem to gain her ends for a while (for at first, one will do almost anything to avoid swallowing a bitter dose); but if she would stop to consider, she would discover that every day she has greater cause for scolding or whining or complaining, as the months roll by an ever-increasing amount is required to accomplish the same result. The scolding woman never has things her own way without a vast expenditure of nervous strength – much more than the object to be gained is worth. Why cannot she realise that, and adopt some pleasanter method?'

The Wesley tree

In the 1800s the sycamore in the north-west corner of Epworth Churchyard was a favourite spot for the people of Epworth, who came to sit beneath its 'fine expanding branches'. Unfortunately, by mid-century, the tree was 'old and much decayed' and had to be cut down. This proved a boon for William Read of Albion House who acquired most of the fallen wood, dressed it up and sold it on - for this was no ordinary tree! The tree had always been called 'The Wesley Tree' and reputedly had been planted by one of the Wesley family (some thought it was John, others claimed Samuel did it). It was to have a piece of this relic from the renowned family that folk flocked to Read's Emporium. In his Memoirs of the Wesley Family, Dr. Adam Clarke, a noted British Methodist theologian and biblical scholar, wrote after a visit to Epworth 'I have only to add that a sycamore tree, planted by Mr

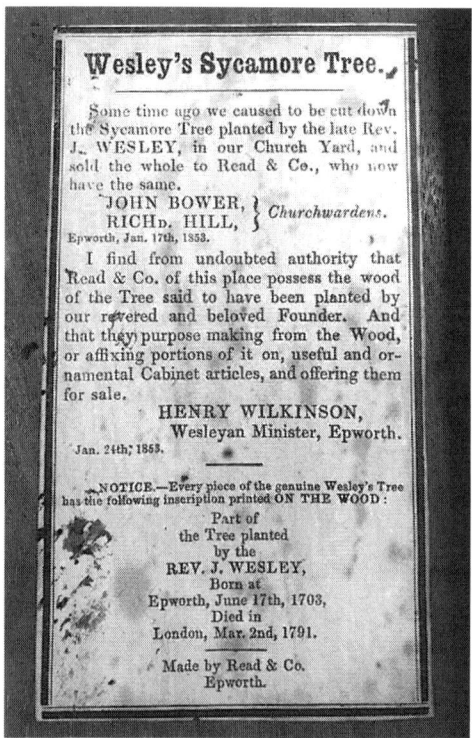

Verification of the Wesley tree

Wesley in Epworth churchyard is now (1821) two fathoms in girth and proportionably large in height, boughs, and branches; but is decaying at the root, where the tree is now becoming hollow – a melancholy emblem of the state of a very eminent family'.

Unfortunately, there is a flaw in this claim to the tree's greatness. As Clarke points out, the tree was old and decayed. Allowing for his allegations to its size, it must have been growing for more than 150 years or so, which would not have been the case if a Wesley had planted it!

A stately home and two pubs

In 1086 William the Conqueror sent a commissioner to John de Belwood. It was part of the 'Great Survey' whose results would form 'The Domesday Book. In 1144 Roger de Mowbray gave an area of land in 'Belwode' near Belton to the Knights Templar of Temple Balsall in Warwickshire. Later on, they built a monastery here and gave it the name Temple Belwood. In the early 1300s, the order fell out of favour, and the site was handed over to the Knights Hospitallers. After the dissolution, the land was taken over by the Vavasour family. What is missing, however, is a reference to John Ferne, the eldest son of William Ferne and his wife Anne, the daughter of Robert Sheffield of Beltoft. The family owned Temple Belwood. John married Elizabeth, the daughter of John Nedham of Wymondley Priory in Hertfordshire. The couple had ten sons and two daughters. In 1586, he wrote Blazon of Gentrie, a book written in dialogue form between six speakers, representing a herald, a knight, a divine, a lawyer, an antiquary, and a ploughman. It was a concise, yet explicit discourse of Arms and of Gentry, but a book that today is considered bizarre. He became Sir John Ferne on 30th May 1604, the same year as his election to serve as the Member of Parliament for Boroughbridge. Ferne's other claim to fame was that he played an active part in suppressing the Gunpowder Plot.

Early 19th century print of Temple Belwood

The history of Temple Belwood from the 17th century is rather complicated as it involves the tenure of the land by Popplewell, Johnson and Steer families. Richard Popplewell, a mercer and woollen draper of Belton, acquired Temple Belwood through a claim on the estate of his brother-in-law. His son Robert had two daughters who married into the Johnson and Steer families. There is even evidence of surnames being changed to continue the line of ownership. Over subsequent years, Temple Belwood has been a high school, a hostel for Borstal boys during World War One and a boarding house. Either side of the Second World War the house fell into disrepair and finally vanished under the M180 motorway. The two gatehouse cottages at the entrance on King Edward Street were removed in the 1960s.

What is more evident, however, is that the families at Belwood were responsible for naming two of the public houses

Obelisk to Sir Solomon

in Belton. The story of Squire Johnson and his favourite horse 'Sir Solomon' is known to many; how it fell breaking a leg and had to be put down. Some believe he buried the horse and two of his hounds beneath the obelisk to the north of the Belton to Beltoft road, but there is no foundation for this. What we can be sure of is that the public house that stood at Grey Green carried the name of the horse.

The other public house at the entrance to Belton from Epworth, known colloquially as 'The Steers' but actually named The Steer Arms, carried the name of the Steer family. Ironically, like the house of Temple Belwood which now resides beneath the M180 motorway, both the pubs bearing names connected to the families from Temple Belwood no longer exist either. The only clues to the existence of the house today are the walled garden and the obelisk and a legend that Squire Johnson buried a stash of gold somewhere on the site.

Fire on the moors

Fires on Crowle moors were a constant and continuing problem throughout the 20th century. Small ones sprung up at regular intervals, but with prompt action, they were soon extinguished. Two of the most severe fires happened within two years of each other. In 1909, 500 acres of peatland ignited in the hot weather and in 1911, fanned by a strong wind, the fire engulfed many stacks of drying turf.

In the 1930s, when a huge blaze erupted over seven miles of moorland, hundreds of beaters set out from the towns to try and halt its spread. Men from Medge Hall joined the Crowle workforce as they resorted to digging wide trenches to create a fire break, but with flames leaping to 30 feet these proved ineffectual. According to reports from the time, the fire devoured saplings like matchwood and left huge trees charred. The glow in the sky could be seen in Hull, Grimsby and Sheffield. As the fire headed towards paraffin wells close to the town, it seemed nothing could stop a major disaster. When all seems lost, a few tentative drops of rain brought hope to the exhausted workforce. By 4 a.m. the rain fell in torrents and halted the spread of the fire. Next day, the people of Crowle gazed out over a cauterised landscape and reflected on their lucky escape.

In the early 1980s, when a drill broke through into a natural gas field under Hatfield Moors a major blow-out occurred, which ignited and destroyed the drilling rig. The fires spread to the moors at Crowle, and after 17 days of burning, the Texan oil fire specialist Asger 'Boots' Hansen arrived to bring it under control. He finally managed to extinguish the flames but the 38-day burn, saw around 1 billion cubic feet of gas consumed.

The curse of the 'spirit'.

One has only to look at the court proceedings reported in the Epworth Bells and the Crowle Advertiser in the 19th century to see that in Axholme drink was king. In the Isle villages and towns, what social life there was centred mainly on the local inn. Coach transport used some of these inns as staging posts; coroners held inquests in local hostelries, and auctions of property took place both inside and out in the courtyards. It is hardly surprising that many succumbed to the 'evils of drink' as the Isle had a ratio of public houses to population of 1:265, a figure that would be even lower (or is it higher?) if we include the number of unlicensed brew houses.

The Temperance Movement began in Epworth in the late 1840s. Those who took the pledge of abstinence did so by putting their names in a register in a local shop. By the mid-1860s the movement had grown to such an extent that the call went out for a building where members could meet and further the organisation's aims. This was realised in 1868 with the construction of the Temperance Hall in the High Street. In 1833 members of the Crowle Wesleyan Sunday School acquired the copyhold to the property of Thomas Pettinger in Fieldside. It would become the site of Crowle's Temperance Hall. There was some confusion over the deed of trust, but this seems to have been settled by the mid-1800s. Although the building no longer stands, there is a plaque that signifies its position. In Keadby the Temperance Hall was in Chapel Lane close to a Primitive Methodist Chapel and a Wesleyan Chapel.

The Temperance Movement in Axholme had the following aims:-

Total abstinence from all intoxicating beverages.

The absolute prohibition of the manufacture, importation and sale of intoxicating beverages.

The creation of a healthy public opinion towards abstinence.

The election of good, honest men to administer the law.

Persistent efforts to save individuals and communities from the 'direful scourge' of alcohol.

Charity begins in Axholme

The Relief of the Poor Act in 1597 appointed overseers of the poor to administer relief to the parishes of Britain. It became their role to distribute essential items such as money, food and clothing. Churchwardens and overseers of the poor were tasked with allocating rents from cottages and parcels of land to provide funding for cloth, usually distributed to the poor on New Year's Day.

One of the Isle's significant benefactors was Richard Brewer, of Gainsborough, described as a 'gent'. In 1687 he left the rents from Town End farm in Crowle to be used for the learning of 20 needy children to read English and to buy books for their use. He left an annual rent of £4 10s for the poor of Epworth to be taken

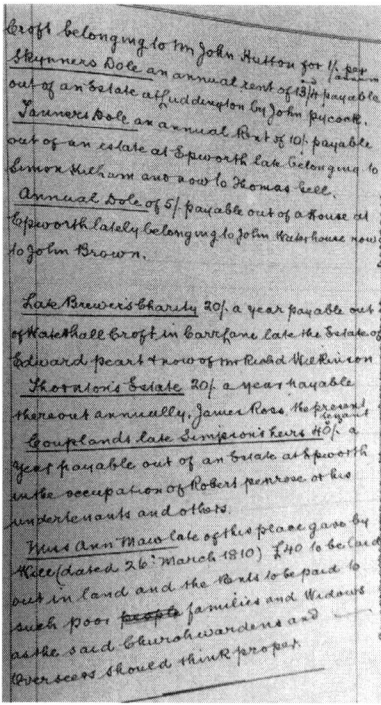

Page from the Epworth Charities book

from arable land in the fields, meadows and pasture in the parish. Rents and profits from Halifax Farm went to clothe the 'ancient poor' of the town every 11th day of November.

Another contributor was Thomas Walkwood, who gave five acres and 20 perches of Crowle land to the minister and churchwardens 'for the use of the poor forever' and to provide an education for the poorest children of the parish. In 1721, Richard Clarke set up a foundation for 32 scholars. It was enough to pay the master £32 a year plus an allowance for coal. This increased later to £48 for 48 scholars.

In Epworth, annual rents from Skynners Dole (from an estate at Luddington held by John Pycock); Tanners Dole (from an Epworth estate formerly belonging to Simon Kilham); an Annual Dole; Brewers' Charity from Waterhall Croft in Carr Lane; Thornton's

Estate; Coupland's Estate, and the estate of Miss Ann Maw were distributed to the poor widows and orphans on Christmas Day. In 1885 this amounted to the princely sum of £68.

Following the Poor Law Amendment Act of 1834, these overseers were replaced by a Board of Guardians comprising elected and ex officio members. This group of local ratepayers who administered the workhouse, dealt with financial affairs, staff, pursuing maintenance payments, the boarding out of children, and payments to paupers. The workhouse for Axholme residents was at Thorne. It was under the control of a Master who was responsible for its proper running and administration. He had to be 'a person of sufficient education, strength of will, and firmness of purpose' and to 'have due control over himself, and never exhibit or allow others to exhibit, violence of temper, or use profane or irritating language'.

Axholme paupers admitted into the workhouse were searched, cleansed, clothed and classified. They would listen to prayers before breakfast and after supper each day. There was work, and training for any of the inmates deemed capable undertaking the toil involved.

In the 1881 census the following Islonians found themselves in Thorne Workhouse:

(Name, Mar Age, Sex, Relation, Occupation, Handicap, Birthplace)
Benjamin BALDERSON, 11, M, Inmate, Scholar, Crowle

Frederick BALDERSON, 13, M, Inmate, Scholar, Crowle

Charles BASSONDALE, U, 50, M, Inmate, Agricultural Labourer, Belton

Matthew BLACKBURN W, 67, M, Inmate, Agricultural Labourer, Epworth

Jemima BROWN, 12, F, Inmate, Scholar, Belton

John BURCHBY, M, 75, M, Inmate, Joiner, No Occupation, Crowle

Ada BUTTERFIELD, 10, F, Inmate, Scholar, Wroot

Charles BUTTERFIELD, 2, M, Inmate, Scholar, Wroot

George W. BUTTERFIELD, 8, M, Inmate, Scholar, Wroot

Robert BUTTERFIELD, 6, M, Inmate, Scholar, Wroot

Sarah A. BUTTERFIELD, 4, F, Inmate, Scholar, Wroot

Elizabeth CLARKE, U, 81, F, Inmate, Housemaid Domestic Servant, Epworth

Alice COCKING, 13, F, Inmate, Scholar, Eastoft

Elizabeth COCKING, U, 36, F, Inmate, General Servant (Domestic), Eastoft

John H. COCKING, 13, M, Inmate, Scholar, Eastoft

Peter COCKRANE, M, 65, M, Inmate, Agricultural Labourer, Epworth

Elizabeth DUCKER, 12, F, Inmate, Scholar, Belton

Jesse DUCKER, 4, M, Inmate, Scholar, Belton

Teresa DUCKER, 7, F, Inmate, Scholar, Belton

Elizabeth FOWLER, U, 18, F, Inmate, Housemaid (Domestic Servant), Crowle

David FRETWELL, M, 78, M, Inmate, Farm Servant. No Occupation, Wroot

Fred HODGSON, 8, M, Inmate, Scholar, Crowle

Martha HODGSON, 4, F, Inmate, Scholar, Crowle

George HORSEFIELD, U, 54, M, Inmate, Pork Butcher, Garthorpe

George LOCKWOOD, 8, M, Inmate, Scholar, Amcotts

Solomon MAW, M, 72, M, Inmate, Shoemaker. No Occupation, Crowle

William J. MINTON, 10, M, Inmate, Scholar, Crowle

Charles NICHOLSON, 10, M, Inmate, Scholar, Epworth

Edith A. NICHOLSON, 15, F, Inmate, Scholar, Epworth

Margaret NICHOLSON, 12, F, Inmate, Scholar, Epworth

William NICHOLSON, 10, M, Inmate, Scholar, Epworth

Sarah A. ORFORD, U, 50, F, Inmate, Pedlar (Hawker), Epworth

Jonathan PICKHAUER, U, 42, M, Inmate, No Occupation, Lunatic, Crowle

Frank POPPLEWELL, 14, M, Inmate, Scholar, Althorpe

Mary A. POPPLEWELL, 16, F, Inmate, Scholar, Belton

Jabez PROUDLY, 12, M, Inmate, Scholar, Belton

Jane PROUDLY, W, 66, F, Inmate, No Occupation, Belton

Rose READ, 12, F, Inmate, Scholar, Epworth

Ada REVILL, 13, F, Inmate, Scholar, Crowle

Betsy RIGGLE, 15, F, Inmate, Scholar, Belton

Dinah RIMINGTON, U, 55, F, Inmate, No Occupation, Epworth

George SMITH, M, 85, M, Inmate, Brickmaker. No Occupation, Epworth

Mary SMITH, M, 74, F, Inmate, No Occupation, Althorpe

George STANIFORTH, M, 75, M, Inmate, Blacksmith. No Occupation, Crowle

Alice TAYLOR, 13, F, Inmate, Scholar, Epworth

Charles TAYLOR, 15, M, Inmate, Scholar, Epworth

Annie THORPE, 13, F, Inmate, Scholar, Belton

John WAITE, M, 17, M, Inmate, Agricultural Labourer, Epworth

Henry WARD, 16, M, Inmate, Scholar, Epworth

Sarah WATKIN, 14, F, Inmate, Scholar, Amcotts

William WATKIN, W, 70, M, Inmate, Farmer, Althorpe

Martha WATSON, W, 78, F, Inmate, No Occupation, Belton

Ellen WILDBORE, U, 48, F, Inmate, No Occupation, Althorpe

Elizabeth WILSON, W, 75, F, Inmate, No Occupation, Belton

Elizabeth WREFOLE, U, 48, F, Inmate, No Occupation, Blind, Eastoft

Esther WREFOLE, U, 64, F, Inmate, No Occupation, Lunatic, Belton

To avoid the poor house, some residents of Axholme opted for an acre of turbary land on which to set up a small holding. The map of the turbary shows how it was divided up to allow for the requisite acre.

'The school bobby'

In the 50s and 60s, the Attendance Officer for Axholme Schools, (or school 'bobby' as they were called by parents) was the redoubtable Mr. Polhill. These officers had been around since Victorian times but had been viewed widely by headteachers as useless. Typical responses by headteachers included the following: 'There are several children in the parish who ought to be in school, but do not attend anywhere. The Attendance Officer's attention was called to the matter, but nothing has been done. The general laxity in enforcing attendance is such that his notices are treated as so much waste paper!' Mr. Polhill was something of a different creature and became feared by pupils and parents alike. One of his first duties was to liaise with a large family who were squatting in a Nissen hut up Burnham Road, Owston Ferry. On several occasions his visits to pupil's homes saw him return without having contacted the family. On other occasions he records that, although no one answered his knock, it was quite obvious that someone was in. He developed a system whereby he would walk away from the house then spin around suddenly. He would often see a curtain twitching as he caught an occupant checking whether he was leaving!

Men of the soil

The 'hole diggers of Epworth' turned up at the Ellers' Tavern for their third annual 'excavation'. Challenged to the contest by a team of Irish navvies, there was disappointment when they failed to arrive. To provide some form of spectacle for those present, the men from the Tavern decided upon a competition among themselves. Mr. D. Gravel won the event and, in the process, collected 5s each from his four rivals. His time of 46 minutes for the six feet square, four feet deep hole, beat his previous best by six minutes. The 'Bells' reporting on the event summed up the view of many by stating; 'Somewhat nonsensically (in view of the fact that nobody else seems yet to have tried how fast they can excavate 144 cubic feet of soil) the Epworth performances have been elevated in some accounts to British Isles champion status.'

The last of the Mowbrays

Anne de Mowbray was born at Framlingham Castle, the only (surviving) child of John de Mowbray. The death of her father in 1476 left Anne a wealthy heiress. On 15th January 1478, aged 5, she married Richard Shrewsbury, 1st Duke of York, the 4-year-old younger son of Edward VI. She became the second most important female in Britain.

She died nearly two years before her husband disappeared in the Tower of London with his older brother, Edward (The princes in the Tower) and was buried in a lead coffin in the Chapel of St. Erasmus in Westminster Abbey. In 1502 when workmen demolished the chapel to make way for a Lady Chapel, they moved Anne's coffin to a vault under the Abbey of the Minoresses of St. Clare, Aldgate. The coffin was 'lost' for four hundred years. In December 1964, construction workers in Stepney accidentally dug into the vault and found Anne's casket. It was opened, and her remains were analysed by scientists. They noted the red hair that remained on her skull and the shroud that still encased her body. Her body was returned to its original resting place in Westminster Abbey.

Bridging the gap!

In December 2017, The Royal Engineers arrived on the disused airbase at Sandtoft to remove a bridge that spanned the 7m width of the Hatfield Water Drain. Named after its inventor, Charles Inglis, the bridge was a triangular construction that could be assembled swiftly but was strong enough to carry heavy military traffic. It was the first multi-use, component built bridging system taken into service by the Royal Engineers and was used extensively throughout both World Wars. The bridge at Sandtoft erected during the Second World War allowed staff to access storage areas of the airfield on the other side of the drain. Its construction involved a team of 12 men. It was a forerunner of the Bailey Bridge.

The project to remove the bridge involved a good deal of planning and engineering work (closely monitored by Highways England who own the bridge) as it had not been used since the end of WW2 and was in a delicate state. The Royal Engineers removed the 50-foot bridge from land owned by James Brooke with a specially constructed cradle bolted to the roadway of the structure and lifted by a 400-tonne crane. Parked on the M180

Removing the Inglis bridge at Sandtoft

motorway, which had to be closed, the crane reached over to the land and swung the bridge onto the back of a nearby lorry. After being renovated by the Royal Engineers Association at their army base in Nottingham, the bridge goes on permanent display at the Royal Engineers Museum in Gillingham.

Why take so much trouble over an old WW2 relic you might ask? The answer is simple – it is the only known surviving Mark 1 version of an Inglis Bridge in the world!

Henge and Barrow

Just off the road from Beltoft to West Butterwick, close to Clouds Lane Farm, are the remains of what is believed to be an Early Bronze Age, earth-banked henge, approximately 30m in diameter. Nothing remains above ground today, but it is classed as a Grade III Henge, having four gaps in the ring that would have served as entrances. Although there is no evidence that the henge was anything but some form of religious structure, close by there have been finds of flint and stone. This site has views to the south in particular with the hill at High Burnham dominating the near-distant skyline.

In his book, 'The History and Topography of the Isle of Axholme', William Brocklehurst Stonehouse mentions that 'until very lately, at High Melwood, in the parish of Owston, there were three oblong hillocks called the Giants' Graves, raised parallel to one another, and standing due east and west. They were most probably barrows' – early Saxon burial mounds. Stonehouse was not one given to 'flights of fancy' and backed up most of his work with hard, observable and, where possible, first-hand facts, so it seems reasonable to suppose that these barrows existed.

The two eras are separated by several thousand years, but it is tempting to speculate that the later one may have referenced the earlier structure in some way. Whatever, both stand as reminders that the Axholme landscape still holds undiscovered secrets – secrets that may one day throw extra light on the developing panorama of our historically eventful landscape.

A Crowle megalith

At St Oswald's Church, Crowle is a 10th century Saxon/Northumbrian shaft of a cross. The stone is over two metres high and has ornate carvings on three of its sides. At the bottom of one is a runic inscription (first discovered in 1868), which gives a clue as to its age – King Canute banned the carving of runic stones around the year 1000 A. D. so the cross must predate this. With this date secure, it makes the stone the oldest surviving carved relic in the area. On the front face of the stone, there appear to be two winged figures surrounded by a somewhat confusing circular motif. Below this are the images of three men; the two upper men face each other and seem to be interacting, perhaps in a dance. Below them, the third man seems to be riding on a horse. Celtic patterns and designs cover the rest of the shaft.

Several antiquarians who studied the carvings have given their opinions, but none have come up with a viable explanation as to what they represent. One idea is that they depict St. Paul and St. Anthony meeting in the desert and their journey to Egypt. Another interpretation sees the upper two figures as Noah entering and leaving the Arc. Beginning in the 10th century, many runic crosses like the one at St. Oswald's blended pagan images into stories from Christianity which strengthens the case for dating the cross.

The Crowle stone

From 1150, when the church was rebuilt by Norman masons, to 1919, the cross was hidden from view as it formed a lintel over the west door of the church. The cross now stands inside the church where it can be seen today.

Finally, a railway link

When the Joint Railway came to Axholme, it was lauded as a local engineering enterprise akin to the magnitude of Vermuyden's drainage scheme some 250 years previously. The project first mooted in 1833 took over sixty years to come to fruition. The first application to Parliament to build the Gainsborough, Epworth and Leeds, Wakefield and Pontefract Junction Railway came in 1845. This scheme reached the attention of George Hudson, 'The Railway King' and he proposed a line from Goole across Axholme, to be called the Isle of Axholme, Gainsborough and York and North Midland Junction Railway. It did not receive the assent of Parliament. Further plans over several years kept the scheme at the forefront of the public's thinking and the directors of the Great Northern, and Great Eastern Railways received numerous petitions signed by owners and occupiers of land, shopkeepers, merchants and others resident of Axholme. On each occasion when proposals for the railway came up for discussion, residents in Epworth crowded into the Temperance Hall with updates being relayed outside to those unable to find space inside.

In August 1898, the news came that the Isle would have its own rail link. Church bells across the Isle 'struck up a merry peal and rang at intervals until sunrise hour'. When complete, the line would run from Marshland Junction in the north to Haxey Junction and have a length of just over 17 miles. Apart from deep cuttings on either side of Epworth the rest of the line would be embanked with many culverts to take the route over dykes and drains. There was disappointment in Owston Ferry, however, when news came that the proposed rail link to the village, crossing the road close to the gasworks with a station close to Laming's blacksmith shop would not form part of the line.

The first sod was cut at Eastoft on 22nd September 1898 by the chairman, Mr William Halkon. On 20th July 1899, Miss Bletcher of Grove House, Thorne, using a silver spade provided for the event, turned the first turf at Epworth. The Goole to Crowle section opened for passenger and goods services on 10th August 1903. Just over a year later on 14th November 1904, the line from Crowle to Haxey Junction opened for goods traffic.

On Monday 2nd January 1905, a day the Epworth Bells called

Cutting the first sod at Epworth

'The Dawn of a New Era', the inhabitants of Axholme turned out in large numbers to witness the Official Opening of the whole line. As the 7.18 a.m. train from Goole entered Epworth station from Belton with 81 people already on board, 'hearty cheers' filled the air. None cheered louder than Mr. W. A. Ross of Belton who celebrated his good fortune when becoming the first person to buy a ticket.

However, regular complaints about the lack of suitable connections at Haxey Junction and competition bus services in the 1920s saw passenger numbers dwindle. For a time, the line operated a freight service, but on 1st February 1956, the Haxey to Epworth section closed. Following the Beeching Report, the line from Marshland Junction to Epworth closed on 5th April 1965.

Connecting to the wider world

In 1922 regular wireless broadcasts for entertainment began in the UK and the Epworth Bells reported that Mr. Harrison of Owston Ferry had been picking up an American station, W.Y.G. from Schenectady. It was his first attempt to access American radio stations, and he believed this constituted a record for a one valve receiver. He ventured to suggest that this 'has not been beaten in this neighbourhood'. His fifty-foot aerial enabled him to listen clearly to continental stations from places such as Madrid, Paris and Hamburg. Mr. Oughtibridge of Crowle, testing his 'Brownie' Crystal Wireless receiver, around the same time, succeeded in getting news from the Hull Wireless Station and a concert from London; both of which he 'heard distinctly'.

Power to the Isle
Consent was given for the building of Keadby Power Station in November 1947. The site opened on 1st April 1956 (officially on the 20th April), and it became one of three new stations constructed by the Yorkshire Division of The British Electricity Authority. In figures, the six 60,000kilowat turbo-alternators churned out 360,000kilowats of power. The station occupied an area of four and a half acres on a site of 181 acres. All coal supplies came by rail with sidings sufficient to hold 650 wagons. The station took water from the River Trent through three 72 inch inlets and returned it through another three of the same size. When in full production, the estimated quantity of the circulating water was 16,200,000 gallons per hour. The three iconic chimneys stood 325 feet above ground level and had an internal diameter of 19 feet at the top. Each chimney served one pair of boilers.

The station provided lockers and showers for workers, covered storage for cycles, a football and cricket pitch and recreation rooms. The plan was to provide 250 residences altogether, 150 of which would be on a site in Keadby village. The Education Authority proposed to build a new Infant and Junior School adjacent to the site and the development plan specified new shops and a community centre.

The site closed in 1984. In 1993 Scottish and Southern Electricity began plans to resurrect a power station on the site. This one would be one of the most efficient gas-fired power stations in Europe. Given the name Keadby2, the site also houses the largest onshore wind farm in England.

It's a secret!

It has been said that in the 19th century, Britain had a greater number and a wider variety of clubs and societies than anywhere else in the world. The Isle was no exception. In 1873 the Epworth Bells reported extensively on the activities of local friendly societies, primarily the Oddfellows and the Free Gardeners, and on the formation of a neighbourhood lodge for the Freemasons. Today there are four lodges of freemasons meeting at Crowle - the Isle of Axholme Lodge 1482, the Temple Belwood Lodge 8073, the Vermuyden Lodge 9482 and the Trent Valley Daylight Lodge 9748.

Belton had a Lodge of Druids, a fraternal order whose motto was 'Justice, Philanthropy and Brotherly Love'. The Lodge operated within the founding principles of the Order, that of looking after fellow members when they fell on hard times and 'doing good' in the community. Membership was restricted to men with each swearing an oath of secrecy. Like all clubs that adopted some degree of confidentiality, the Lodge attracted growing local suspicion. Belton's links with secretive societies began hundreds of years earlier with the grant of 'certain lands called the Cow Pasture, at Belwode,' by Roger de Mowbray, to a Preceptory of the Knight Templars which he founded at Balsall, Warwickshire about the year 1145. Members pledged to live a life of chastity, obedience and poverty.

Perhaps the most contentious society formed in the Isle was the Epworth Zetetic Society that began with an initial membership of 19. The aims of the society were to give its members a comprehensive insight into liberal arts, sciences and moral excellence on the firm basis of 'Right Reason'. They discussed subjects, such as, whether the loss of one's left arm was a greater misfortune than the loss of one's right leg; what choice one would make given the need to jettison a son, wife or mother from a sinking boat, and whether the ship was of greater benefit to the country than the plough or the loom. One could, perhaps, smile at the notion of grown men discussing such questions and persuading themselves they were helping to 'Establish Moral Excellence on the basis of Right Reason', but the essence of the meetings was to stimulate discussion and reasoned argument. To help spread knowledge, members hoped to form a lending library containing books on History, Geography, Theology, Poetry and Philosophy. The Zetetic Society in Epworth disbanded two years after its formation, but it paved the way for a worthier and longer serving organisation – the Mechanics' Institute.

Out of England …!

Of all the place names in the Isle, Wroot seems to be the one that has undergone the most changes. The earliest name on record was Wroe (or Wroth in 1157), and over the years it has morphed into Wroyt, Wrot, Wrotte and Wroote. In the early 1720s, Rev Samuel Wesley became Rector of Wroot. The present-day Rectory stands on the site of two former buildings, and it was to one of these earlier ones that Samuel and the family came when he officiated at services. Indeed, there were times when they all sought refuge here away from the trials and tribulations of their Epworth residence, even though it was a humbler dwelling full of damp and in a poor state of disrepair. The thatched parsonage smelled of damp and rotten wood. There was a pigsty at the back and rotting weed in the marsh beyond. It was here that Susanna kept poultry in a small yard and ran a simple dairy, both of which brought in a few extra pounds. Arthur Quiller-Couch wrote that for half a year 'the parsonage rose from the world of waters as a cornstack in a flood'. The dwelling consisted of a kitchen and two sitting rooms, one of which Samuel used as a library and a place to prepare sermons and write. With the family of six or seven daughters living in the Rectory, space was at a premium, so the girls would spend much of their time out of doors. Here they supplemented the knowledge of nature gained from books by experiencing it in the raw. Often, they would sit on the slight knoll and gaze across the reed strewn dykes and fens to Epworth – five miles away to the east. Of an evening, among the marsh vapours and the echoing sound of fowler's guns, long shafts of light traversed the fenland void, illuminating the honeyed stone tower of Epworth Church. During Samuel's tenure, the Rectory underwent repairs to window casements and the fireplace in the parlour and saw the addition of new larder. The one downside was that the family found the labourers carrying out the repairs 'surly and boorish'.

The present-day Church, dedicated to St. Pancras is not the Church at which the Wesley's officiated, having been built in 1879, but it does incorporate parts of the 14th century one. According to Stonehouse, the earlier one consisted of a nave and a chancel built from local boulder stones and set in mortar, 'of such hardness and durability, that it was found easier to break the stones than to separate them from the cement'. He goes on to state that these broken stones were transported to Epworth to help pave the town's streets.

Although the living was a meagre £50, in Samuel's poor financial state, it was not something he could easily turn down. After the Dutch settlers drained the fen, most of the water routes disappeared, and the village became quite possibly one of the most inaccessible areas in the country. For this, it acquired the dubious title of Wroot – 'Out of England.'

Samuel's journey to Wroot was hazardous in all seasons, but in early autumn, when only a gentle breeze stirred the sedge, he would often be plagued by midges. Across the land, clouds of these aquatic insects, which enter their winged state in the warm months, fill the skies over the Axholme wetlands. Locals refer to these as 'Men of Wroot'. When autumn mists cloaked the landscape, and winter rains turned the surface of the water to a boiling froth, many a time Samuel would arrive at his destination 'being lamed with having my breeches too full with water, partly with a downfall from a thunder shower, and partly from the wash over from the boat. I wish the rain had not reached us from this side of Lincoln, but we have it so continual that we have scarce one bank left, and I cannot possibly have one-quarter of oats in all the levels. We can neither go afoot nor on horseback to Epworth, but only by boat as far as Scawsit Bridge and then walk over the common'.

At the age of sixty-four, however, Samuel found the task of serving two parishes almost beyond him. He prevailed on John to help him by taking on the role of curate but believed him incapable of travelling between Wroot and Epworth 'without hazarding his health or life; whereas my hide is tough, and think no carrion can kill me. I walked sixteen miles yesterday, and this morning, I thank God I was not a penny worse'. Although veiled in Samuel's quaint humour, there can be no doubt he was beginning to feel the strain! A year later, John walked into a living as a parish curate when he took over the duties at Wroot. For the next two years, it would be he who made the journey 'out of England'. His wages, paid from his father's own pocket, could have been as little as £30 per year but as a member of the clergy, John was now regarded as a gentleman.

By common consent, John worked hard at Wroot, and developed a punishing schedule, studying in the morning and visiting his parishioners in the afternoon. It was in the village that

John Wesley at Wroot

he spent most of his time, and he seems to have felt at ease with the secluded lifestyle. On many occasions, John rode the three miles each way to and from Epworth, on others he walked. Records for this period of his life are sketchy, but it goes without saying that he was methodical, diligent and committed to the role. He was laying the foundations for his great ministry of the future, unswerving in his desire to become a straightforward and honest disciple of Christ. When the time came to look for a successor to his father's ministry, it was the people of Epworth and Wroot who lobbied for him to be selected. So committed were they to his methods and his spirit that twelve years later, when he found himself accused of 'seeking gain from all of his actions', he turned to them to rebut the charge. 'Ye of Epworth and Wroot, among whom I ministered for nearly three years,' he wrote, 'what gain did I seek among you? Or of whom did I take or covet anything?'

Diligent servant that he was, John still found time to swim on balmy mornings in the local waterways, play tennis, and shoot plovers in the low-lying ground between Wroot and Epworth. He loved family time, sitting by the fireside with convivial company, reading about philosophy, history, science, plays and poetry or reviewing the day's events. He worked in the rectory garden at Wroot, and there is some evidence that a part of one of the seats he made can still be seen today. His time at Wroot and Epworth revealed him to be an affable and welcoming man. He often attended the local fairs and spent a good deal of time dancing with his sisters. It was almost certainly through this that he met Kitty Hargreaves a clever, articulate young lady from Epworth. The pair enjoyed the allegorical poetry of Edmund Spenser, and they would go on to spend much of that summer together. Her visits to the Rectory became so frequent that Samuel ordered her away, believing it was she who was courting John. For his part, John appears rather smitten with Kitty, and it is possible there was a brief period of physical contact between the two. On one occasion, John resolved to 'never touch Kitty's hand again', but he must have relented as later on, he makes a commitment to 'never touch a woman's breasts again!'

It was during the 'Wroot period' that the headstrong, yet naive Hetty, went against her parents' wishes and eloped intending to marry a local lawyer called William Atkins who she met in the household where she was in service. She slept one night with her lover, convinced they would elope together and be married the next day, but he had no intention of committing to the union. A distressed Hetty, faced with no alternative, returned home to face her disapproving parents. Apart from Molly and John, the rest of the family showed little sympathy for Hetty. Even though John preached a passionate sermon on charity and forgiveness at Wroot, there would be no reconciliation. Indeed, in what looks like an attempt to remove his problem daughter from the family home, Samuel urged Hetty to marry the first man that offered such a union. So it was that she consented to marry William

Wright, a local plumber and glazier. It did little to re-establish her relationship with her father, however, who, from that day, regarded her misadventure with horror. It seems he only spoke to her 'with the utmost detestation'. In his eyes, she had failed to live up to expectations and her status in the local community as the Rector's daughter. Wright turned out to be something of a waster; a man given to drunken and debauched behaviour of a sort far removed from his accomplished yet emotionally fragile wife.

Hetty gave alms to the parish, altough the locals recognised they were small in value and offered in a somewhat condescending manner, they welcomed the generous acts. Hetty wrote of the inhabitants of Wroot to her sister Emilia:

Fortune has fixed thee in a place,
Debarred of wisdom, wit and grace
High births and virtue equally they scorn,
As asses dull, on dunghills born;
Impervious as the stones their heads are found;
Their rage and hatred steadfast as the ground
With these unpolished wights, thy youthful days
Guide slow and dull, and Nature's lamp decays;
Oh, what a lamp is hid 'midst such a sordid race!'

Susanna Wesley had a rather colourful description for the inhabitants of Wroot stating they were 'unshaven and unshorn and bastards upon dunghills born!'

After two years as a parish priest, John preached his farewell sermon in Epworth Church in the autumn of 1729. His time at Wroot would be his only experience of parochial work. On the first day of 1790, in the last full year of his life, John Wesley returned to Epworth to preach in the town where his life had nearly come to a premature end 80 years earlier. He bemoaned the fact he was 'now an old man, decayed from head to foot. My eyes are dim; my right hand shakes much; my mouth is hot and dry every morning; I have a lingering fever almost every day; my motion is weak and slow. However, blessed be God, I do not slack my labour; I can preach and write still'.

Anne Wesley was married from Wroot to John Lambert, a land surveyor, at Wroot, and the couple went on to enjoy a loving relationship.

Another Wesley connection is the Wroot youth, Johnny Whitelamb, a thin, gangly young fellow, whom the Wesleys rescued from Wroot Charity School to raise in the Epworth Rectory. He was well treated, educated, and sent to Oxford and eventually succeeded Samuel as Rector at Wroot. The family never imagined that their crippled daughter Mary would ever marry, but Mary fell in love with her beloved Johnny, and they spent just one blissfully happy year in the Wroot Rectory after Whitelamb was appointed Rector. Mary died in childbirth and was buried in Wroot Church, possibly with her infant. The somewhat crude headstone of Johnny Whitelamb can be seen in the church cemetery.

Finally, John Romley, who served as the Superintendent of Wroot Charity School, later became the Rector at St Andrew's Church in Epworth. He was the parson who refused to allow John Wesley to preach in Epworth Church, leading to the Methodist Leader preaching from his father's gravestone.

Susanna Wesley's 16 home rules

To describe Susanna Wesley as meticulous in the home-training of her children would be an understatement. Her ruling principle was that all displayed implicit obedience. She insisted upon conquering their will 'because this is the only strong and rational foundation of a religious education without which both precept and example will be ineffectual'. Neither profane language nor rude talk was allowed in the family circle, and all children were expected to treat the servants with respect. She set out the following rules, many of which would be frowned upon in today's more liberal society:

1. Eating between meals is not allowed.
2. Children to be in bed by 8 p.m.
3. Take your medicine without complaining.
4. Subdue a child's self-will
5. Teach a child to pray as soon as they can speak.
6. Require all to be still during Family Worship.
7. Give them nothing that they cry for, and only that when asked for politely.
8. To prevent lying, punish no fault which is first confessed and then repented.
9. Never allow a sinful act to go unpunished.
10. Never punish a child twice for a single offence.
11. Comment on and reward good behaviour.
12. Any attempt to please, even if poorly performed, should be commended.
13. Preserve property rights, even in smallest matters.
14. Strictly observe all promises.
15. Require no daughter to work before she can read well.
16. Teach children to fear the rod.

Finding your own way!

For those who feel the need to do their own research about Axholme, a good starting point is the Epworth Mechanics' Institute. The reference section contains many books that relate directly to the landscape and history of the area. As previously mentioned, copies of The Epworth Bells and The Crowle Advertiser provide fascinating insights into everyday life over the past 150 years.

Books that reference Axholme's past include:

'A Topographical Account of The Isle of Axholme' by William Peck (published 1815); 'The History and Topography of the Isle of Axholme' by William Brocklehurst Stonehouse (published 1839) and 'Read's History of the Isle of Axholme: its manors and parishes with biographical notices of eminent men' – though this covers much of the same ground as the previous two.

Readers may also be interested in the following books by Stephen Garner, 'Burnham: The story of an Axholme village' (published in 1994), 'A Topographical Study of the Wetlands of Axholme, with particular regard to Messic Mere and the Skiers before and after the Drainage' (published 1997) and The Historic Boundaries of Axholme' (published 2003).

Terry Fulton's book 'A Treasure Beneath Our Feet: The Fields of Belton In Axholme' (published 2011) gives a fascinating insight into the features of the open-field farming system in the village, while 'Belton in Axholme – A Landscape Survey', by Marjorie Miller (published 2001) gives a gazette-type overview of the village at the turn of the Millennium.

Those interested in life through the eyes of a conservationist and naturalist may find Eddie Exton's book 'When I was Born a Poacher' (published 1997) rewarding.

For an equally interesting overview, the books by Colin Ella; 'Around the Isle of Axholme: An alphabetical journey through the villages' (published 1993), 'Historic Epworth: Heart of the Isle of Axholme' (published 1994), and 'The Isle of Axholme in Old Photographs' (published 1999) demand attention.

'Easter at Epworth, The Story of a Pilgrimage' by H. L. Gee (published 1944) may be a book of interest to Methodists and residents of Epworth. 'Epworth and its Surroundings' published by Barnes and Breeze contains some interesting photographs of the town. In contrast 'Notes on Epworth Parish Life' by Dr. A. F. Messiter (published 1912) gives an insight into life in and around Epworth Parish in the eighteenth century.

Those wishing to know more about Haxey Hood will find much of interest in 'A Fool's Game – The Ancient Tradition of Haxey Hood' by Jeremy Cooper (published 1993). 'Temple Belwood – Its Past and Present' by J. G. Rees (published 1933) needs no explanation.

The Rivers of Axholme: With a History of the Navigable Rivers and Canals of the District by George Dunstan (first published 1909) includes a map of the Isle of Axholme from Walkeringham to Owston and from Wroot to Kelfield. It shows the lordships of Haxey, Misterton, Stockwith, Gunthorpe and Owston, the towns, the rivers, tributaries and bridges, the names of fields and woods, windmills, and the boundary between Lincolnshire and Nottinghamshire.

For those wishing to know more about the Mowbrays, there is 'The Mowbray Legacy' by Marilyn Roberts.

A book entitled 'Folklore from the Isle of Axholme – letters from C. K. Stafford of Gunthorpe, Owston Ferry, to Ethel H. Rudkin of Willoughton' (published by Old Chapel Lane Books, Burgh le Marsh) may bring amusement to some.

If historical fiction interests you then there are John Hamilton's 'MS in the Red Box' and 'Captain John Lister'. There is also the diffident and somewhat bizarre story entitled 'The Settlers at Home' by Harriet Martineau (published 1842). Intended for children the story seems to be based on little more than cursory reading of Stonehouse's book of 1839.

Finally, those who prefer to do their research online will find much to interest themselves on the Crowle Community Forum and at www.axholme.info.

Of course, it is all well and good reading about Axholme, but there is no better way to experience its marvels and curiosities than to be out in the highways and byways and, with permission, its fields and woodlands. Do not be fooled by Daniel Defoe's statement that there are 'no towns of note or anything to be called curious …' Believe me, there are!

APPENDIX

The Mowbray Deed in full

THIS INDENTURE between the thrice honoured Lord, Lord Sir John Mowbray Lord of the Isle of Axholme and of the Honor of Brember of the one Part Rawlyn of Brumham John Thetilthorpe, Thomas Melton, Jeoffrey Laundels, Vincent Bavant, John Gardner, John Cutwolf, Richard of Belwood and John at Hogh, his tenants of the Isle of Axholme, and all the tenants and resiants within the said Isle on the other part, witnesseth that all the said tenants and resiants have supplicated their said Lord Sir John Mowbray to have remedy against divers claims touching their rights and divers debates and grievances to them made by ministers of the said Lord Sir John Mowbray upon which supplication it is agreed that the said Sir John Lord aforesaid hath granted for him and for his Heirs to the said Rawlen, William, Roger, John, Thomas, Jeoffrey, Vincent, John, John, Richard & John, tenants aforesaid and to their heirs and to all having their Estate or Parcel of their Estate and to all the other tenants and resiants within the Isle of Axholme and to their heirs and to all that hereafter shall have their estate all the things underwritten. That is to say - that the said Sir John nor his heirs shall not approve any wastes, moors, woods, waters, nor make, or shall make any other manner of approvement of any part within the said Isle of Axholme; and that the said Rawlin, William, Roger, John, Thomas, Jeoffrey, Vincent, John, John Richard and John and their heirs, and those that shall have their estate, and all other tenants and resiants within the Isle of Axholme shall have their common which is appendant to their free tenement according to that which they have had and used time out of mind.

And also that the aforesaid Rawlyn, William, Roger, John, Thomas, Jeoffrey, Vincent, John, John, Richard and John and their heirs and all those which have their estate or a parcel of their estate, shall have, all other the tenants and resiants within the aforesaid Isle may dig in the moors and marshes, turfs, and roots found within the soil of the said moors and marshes. And that one pound containing one half acre be made at the cost of the said tenants and maintained hereafter by the said Lord and his heirs in Belton Car and one other in Haxey Car containing as much, and they be made in places for the most ease of the said tenants. And that no chase of beasts of commoners be made but once a year and that the said beasts be not otherwise driven but to the pound of the paster where they shall be taken and there the beasts of the said tenants to be delivered by the tenants aforesaid, or by their servants, and saving always to the said tenants and to their heirs and to their servants that they may take their beasts and receive them in the drift, or before the drift, So that the drift of beasts of strangers be not thereby disturbed.

And that in the severalities of the said Lord adjoining to the places in which they have common which is open and not inclosed no beast of the said tenants and commoners to be taken nor impounded but easily driven out and that the said tenants and resiants and their heirs and all those which have their estate or parcel of their estate shall have, may dig and take turf or other earth for the walls of their houses and for all other necessaries of the said houses and for to inclose the walls of their messuages or mansions and to dry flags in all the said wastes for to cover the ridges of their houses and walls and for bringing of trees to repair the River of Trent where cause of repairing is and to make them new.

And that the said Rawlyn, William, Roger, John Thomas, Jeoffrey, Vincent, John, Richard and John aforesaid and all other the tenants and resiants, their heirs and all those which shall have their estate or parcel of their estate be not for the future amaced or grieved for default of not appearing to ring their swine, and that they may put hemp to be rated in all the waters of the Isle (except the Skiers which are severed to the use of the said John Mowbray) and that the said Lord nor his heirs, nor his ministers, make no molestation nor grievances to the dogs of the forenamed tenants and resiants aforesaid, nor to their heirs nor to those which shall have their estate or parcel of their estate, and if they do, the tenant shall have their recovery at the common Law.

And that the aforesaid Rawlin, William, Roger, John, Thomas, Jeoffrey, Vincent, John, John, Richard and John, tenants aforesaid and all the other tenants and resiants their heirs and all those which hereafter shall have their estates or parcel of their estates, may fish through all the water and wastes of the said Isle without impediment of the ministers of the said Lord Sir John Mowbray, except the Skiers aforesaid.

And also that they may dig turf and all other manner of turf in all of the wastes aforesaid to carry and improve their Land at their pleasure, and that none of the tenants aforesaid or of their heirs or of those having their estate impeached of trespass without answer given in court and then by their peers to be fined and taxed if they be amerceable.

And the said John granteth that all the tenants and their heirs and all those which shall have their estate which are bound to inclose the woods of the Lord, may take them underwood to make them new hedges or to repair them, as much as shall be necessary, that is to say....in the places of the said woods of the said tenants, their heirs and those which shall have their estate without being Impeached or grieved by the ministers of the said John, granteth for him and all his heirs that all the things and articles aforesaid be of effect and force in the law as well to those which are generally named tenants, and their heirs, as those which shall have their estate or parcel of their estate, as those which are named by proper names, and their heirs, and those which shall have their estate or parcel of their estate.

And if in the articles aforesaid, there be any point which may have divers Interpretations or Intendment, that it shall be taken to best advantage of the names of the tenants aforesaid, and of their heirs, or of those which shall have their estates and not otherwise.

Given at our Manor at Epworth the first day of May in the year of the reign of Edward the Third after the Conquest Thirty-Three.

Printed in Poland
by Amazon Fulfillment
Poland Sp. z o.o., Wrocław